KILLER WOMEN

KILLER WOMEN

Crime Club Anthology #2
The Body

FOREWORD BY LAURA LIPPMAN
EDITED BY SUSAN OPIE

This edition first published by Killer Women Ltd 2017

www.killerwomen.org

Cover design by Books Covered
Formatting by Polgarus Studio
Cover image by Shutterstock

TABLE OF CONTENTS

FOREWORD
LAURA LIPPMAN

Do people really have love-hate relationships? I'm pretty good on keeping those two things separate. Yes, I get that indifference is the opposite of hate, that if someone screams, 'I hate you' and then throws something at your head, she might, in the next minute, say, 'But I love you, Mama' and put her sweaty tiny hand in yours. Hypothetically. So I've heard.

At any rate, 'girls' and 'women' have been having quite a moment in crime fiction and I think I hate it, except when I love it. The love part should be obvious, I hope. I hate it because it keeps being framed as a trend or a fad, which indicates that it's a temporary thing, not meant to last. The implication seems to be that proper crime fiction will return to its default setting, which tends to be male, white and heterosexual. Never mind that such a reading of crime history wipes out Agatha Christie, Dorothy L. Sayers and Ngaio Marsh, among others. Ignore the fact that it was women who rescued the PI sub-genre when it was –- you may insert your own really good 'deader than' joke here. Pay no attention to the fact that while Stieg Larsson's 'Girl' may have come first, it was Gillian Flynn's seething Amy who changed the playing field. Always at my back I hear, the market's over-correction drawing near. No one is more interested in fair play than a man who perceives the game no longer favours him.

The thing is – crime, as a genre, and fiction as a whole, are robust because of female readers. Ian McEwan once wrote in a *Guardian* essay that he tried to hand out thirty novels in a park near his London home. Women took them cheerfully, whereas men 'could not be persuaded'. He concluded: 'When women stop reading, the novel will be dead.' It seems reasonable to me that female-centric stories take up a good deal of bookstore and library real estate, if not always on shortlists for prizes. Yes, it's important to read about people who are not like us. But women readers deserve to see their lives reflected in the pages of the books they choose, to be affirmed that our experiences are universal, too.

Besides, this collection of stories, the second Killer Women anthology, reminds us how varied the female perspective can be, how limitless our concerns, fears, preoccupations – and rage. You will meet all sorts of women here, of every age and from every background.

Marriage, perhaps inevitably, is a preoccupation here. The collection starts with two wonderfully complementary stories – a youngish couple, where the wife fantasizes about attending her husband's funeral, and a long-married couple celebrating a milestone. The two tales have nothing in common and everything in common. You think all unhappy families are unhappy in their own way? It's probably even truer of unhappy marriages.

Stalking is another subject that warrants multiple takes. It's funny – unwanted attention is so ho-hum in a woman's life that the best-known Hollywood variations tend to centre on men – *Fatal Attraction, Swimfan* – but it's practically a coming-of-age ritual for women. So it's suitable to see variations on the topic here, including a female-on-female version in Julia Crouch's 'Beach Ready Body.' And then there's Laura Wilson's 'Sex Crime', which combines stalking with a very singular kind of betrayal and the all-too-topical gaslighting.

Social media shows up, too, although Amanda Jennings's 'Etta and the Body' is really about loneliness and the need for real connections, a concern that has always been with us. Our plugged-in world and the yearning to be seen can also be self-destructive, as illustrated in Sarah Hilary's 'Ten Things You'll Miss About Me'.

These Killer Women know a thing or two about men. (The prey has to know its predator as surely as the predator knows its prey. Possibly better.) Several of the men here are ambitious to a fault, with definite ideas about what they want in their partners – and dangerous misconceptions about what their partners want from them. There are bad partners galore, but also good men – or are they simply too good to be true? That's another question that women probably ponder more often than men do.

The one constant, I think, is wit. To be a woman in this world requires wryness and wariness in equal parts. It's fun to quote Kipling, but the statistics don't bear him out. We are not more deadly than the male. Still would you deprive us of seeing ourselves as protagonists, of imagining stories that transcend the crime novel cliché in which a pretty woman dies and a man feels bad? Writing a story in which an abusive man is pushed down the stairs won't change the world. And it won't begin to address the broader problems of racial injustice and inclusion, the latter of which the crime fiction world needs to address.

But in the moment, whether one is the writer or the reader, such vicarious acts can feel pretty damn good.

SMOKING KILLS

ERIN KELLY

'I can't believe you're cheating *again*,' said Olivia. She would not cry. If she cried, Jez would tell her she was being a typical overemotional bloody woman again, the line he used when he considered an argument closed, and this was far from over. The tears were on their way, but the muscle that held them back was getting stronger. 'I can't believe you *lied* to me.'

Jez's eyes went to the coffee table. Art books arranged in neat piles framed the thrown spoils of Olivia's snooping: a half-smoked pack of Marlboro Gold and a cheap Bic lighter. For Olivia these confirmed the warning signs. A dullness to the teeth he'd had bleached when he quit, the sudden appearance of mouthwash in the en suite.

Jez deflected the accusation. 'I can't believe you've gone through my pockets like some kind of jealous housewife. God, you're acting like I've slept with someone else! Could you get some proportion, here?'

He did this: belittled her feelings into submission. She

1

wasn't going to stand for it this time. 'Well, it *does* feel like an infidelity. We promised. We said we'd do this together, we'd support each other. You know what the experts say, you've read all the …' Jez cast his eyes up in a look that said *if you mention research one more time …* Olivia answered as if he'd spoken. 'It *does*, though! All the research says that couples who quit together have like ten times more chance of staying smoke-free than couples who don't support each other …' Her voice trailed off. She felt stupid for trusting him. After all, a husband who could lie to you about big things wouldn't think twice about having a sneaky fag in the back garden when he thought you weren't looking. Looking at him now, sneering down his long nose at her, she realised that he'd lost any respect he'd ever had for her.

'I never knew, before all this, what a *nag* you were,' he said. 'I was an idiot to think you were different. I'm astonished, really, that you kept the act up this long.'

He'd hit her rawest nerve: hadn't she always been the cool girl, the wife who let him do what he wanted? They had never disapproved of each other's lifestyles, never bought into all that suburban nonsense. Their relationship was never going to *age* like that. It was the thing – apart from the house in Crouch End full of limited edition prints and mid-century furniture, the twice-a-year holidays they had maxed their cards out to afford – that their friends envied about them. It was one thing to present that front to the rest of the world, but she'd had enough of colluding in the deception with Jez.

Olivia gave it one more go. 'If you loved me, you'd do

this with me,' she said. 'You'd try, you'd *help* me.'

'Don't project your weakness onto me, Olivia.' Another bullseye. Well – of *course* it was impossible to stay off cigarettes knowing they were in the house, being able to see the soft boxy outline in Jez's jacket pocket, close enough for her to reach without even leaving the sofa, but she had done three months smoke-free *twice*, while he had never, in all the time she'd known him, lasted longer than a fortnight. Quitting had become a touchstone for everything rotten in their marriage, its myriad lacks: children, money, sex. Now that the fug of a lifetime's habit was lifting, everything was exposed and the result was wreckage.

'Did you buy those out of your own money or from the joint account?' she asked, knowing this would make him storm out, wanting him to go, mistress of the passive-aggressive.

'You know what really gets me?' he said. She braced herself. 'Your hypocrisy. All those years you smoked like a chimney and now suddenly you're the health police? Your body is suddenly a temple?'

'It's not my body that's the problem, is it?'

She was hitting him below the belt, literally. She looked pointedly at Jez's crotch. Fewer sperm than most thirty-eight-year-old men, those that did make it a weird shape, low motility. Nothing wrong with *her* body, her body was willing and able, and while the doctors couldn't *prove* it was Jez's smoking, they all agreed it slashed their chances.

'I don't have to listen to this,' said Jez, and gathered up his cigarettes and lighter. The house shook as he slammed the back door. Olivia knew where he'd be going: to the little terrace at the far end of the garden, to chain-smoke under the patio heater. She couldn't bear to watch, so went into the kitchen at the front of the house. The sitting room, which looked onto the garden, had the prettier view, but at this time of year, Olivia loved looking out on the street. A gentle spring breeze shook the cherry trees, and blossom tumbled like a parody of confetti, feathering unsightly parked cars and wheelie bins in pink. Knowing Jez would be gone for at least ten minutes, Olivia slid her fingers along the top of the cooker hood and found her own secret stash of cigarettes, Silk Cut, the slick white-and-purple packaging of her student days now replaced by a picture of a diseased lung, which she had seen so often she didn't even notice any more. She lit the gas ring, held the filter lightly between her lips, bent to the violet flame and filled her lungs. Olivia's hatred for her husband was like a living thing in her chest, something only smoke could suffocate. With each drag, calm infused her, chased by guilt and frustration. Either they both committed to becoming non-smokers, or they both smoked. She could not live with a smoker and get healthy. Olivia dreamed of living alone: of clean air in this house, of a night's sleep, of a nose that didn't permanently twitch with suspicion. She would, she realised, even forgo motherhood for life without Jez.

Yet she was trapped. Jez's debts that were in both their names had seen to that.

She stopped after one cigarette, ground it out and flicked it across their tiny strip of a front garden and into the street, where it landed in the petals. She was confident Jez hadn't guessed she was cheating too. Jez's sense of smell was so dulled that he would not detect smoke on her breath until he quit. And anyway, he would have relished the chance to call her out on it.

Turning her back to the window, her eye was drawn to a picture on the fridge that had been pinned by a magnet in every kitchen they'd had, every kitchen in their procession of increasingly expensive houses over the last eighteen years. Olivia knew she should take it down for a million reasons but felt that would admit defeat.

It had been taken the day they met, or rather the morning after the night that a cigarette had brought them together. San Antonio Bay, Ibiza, 1999, sunrise at their backs. They were twenty, their youthful bodies tanned to gold and the white sticks in their hands mocking death rather than beckoning it. Which club had they just staggered out of? Pasha or Manumission, the end-of-season party at some superclub or other. Danny Rampling on the decks, absolute carnage on the dance floor, everyone necking anything they could get their hands on because the alternative was to chuck it in the sea or risk smuggling it back past customs. Olivia was taking a break by a giant fan, distraught to find that her twenty-pack of Silk Cut had slipped from her pocket, the cigarettes presumably crushed on the dance floor. Jez appeared like a nicotine angel, pressed a Marlboro Light to her lips and lit it for her with a silver Zippo. The next morning they'd watched the sun come up over the glittering horizon, Jez passing his last cigarette between them, talking about the inevitable comedown and how much they were dreading going home. When they'd found out they lived two streets apart in north London, they'd called it destiny. She had loved Jez's clothes, his records, his job, his friends. She had loved these things so much she hadn't spent enough time wondering whether she even liked Jez.

Now, in a tiny overpriced house in the same neighbourhood, she observed her husband through the sitting room window. He still looked good if you didn't get too close: long and lean, full head of black hair and a perfect beard. He stood with his back to her next to the chrome rocket of the patio heater, a design classic that *he* had bought with *her* money. As Olivia watched the thin plume of smoke curling up into nothing, her instinct was to pull the garden door closed and lock him out for the night.

Cigarettes, Olivia realised, had been a life-support machine for a dying marriage. The smoking ban, for example, had prolonged their early delusion of intimacy. Jez would tell their friends who never went out any more that you met the most interesting people, had some of the best conversations under a patio heater in the gastropub garden, kettled by the velvet rope on the pavement. You still got to talk to *young* people, teenagers sometimes, you weren't stuck in this bullshit Moebius strip conversation loop of property prices and catchment areas. When he held court like this at dinner parties and Olivia noticed the other couples' secret eye rolls, she thought: when he's smoking, at least he can't talk. In the last five years or so, Jez's early years of shoving powder up his nose had taken their toll and he'd developed an annoying nasal whistle. When he was smoking, he exhaled differently, through the mouth.

Olivia, maddened by the relentless tiny noise, would slide the pack his way even when she didn't want one.

Olivia and Jez were the last of their friends still to smoke. The others had stopped, two by two, in couples. They started running marathons, and you couldn't do both. Serious running gave you a new respect for your lungs; you really started to think about your health in a different way after thirty, you know? They had their kitchens Farrow-and-Balled and didn't want actual tobacco discolouring paint shades called things like Old Nicotine. And soon their friends had children. Even Olivia and Jez didn't want to smoke around kids, and anyway it was easier to stay away from babies, for all sorts of reasons. Once at a barbecue Jez joked that they couldn't afford to raise a child because of the rising price of cigarettes. It got a laugh, but Olivia couldn't look at him for days.

She could not remember the first time she had looked at the old-fashioned razor he pretended to shave with (in reality, he used disposable Gillettes) and imagined dragging it across his jugular. The day she found out that he had sunk her life savings – thirty grand she'd parked in his ISA – and borrowed against the house to fund a mate's doomed coffee shop, it was all she could do not to reach for the blade and paint the white tiles red. The person she was supposed to be able to trust above anyone else had stolen from her. That was when her fantasies about living alone really began. Yet here they still were, hating each other, killing themselves in smoky slow motion.

The following morning, Olivia was up and on the bus to work before Jez woke. Even eye contact would spark a confrontation she didn't have the energy for. She smoked five cigarettes at work that day, leaning against the dry riser inlet outside the office and indulging in her favourite fantasy: head-to-toe in black at Jez's funeral, maybe even a veil for a touch of mafia widow chic, sympathy radiating from family and friends and the life insurance payout sitting pretty in the bank.

That evening, they ate supper in separate rooms. Afterwards, Jez was restless, jumping up 'to get some fresh air' in the garden once an hour. Olivia came close to joining him, following him down to the terrace to show how low he had brought her. Instead, she had three drags of one cigarette in the kitchen with the window open and the extractor fan on, stopping before she was fully sated. She knew what it would look like if he caught her: double standards. But it wasn't hypocrisy when her smoking was all Jez's fault, was it? If he could keep his promise, then she would stick to hers, she knew she would. If he had *any* respect for her – well, it was too late to hope for that. The thing with the money had taught her what he really thought of her.

Olivia played with her phone for a while, then trawled Netflix for something new before flipping through the channels on terrestrial. She could have smoked half a dozen cigarettes.

It was dark by the time Jez came inside. He took the remote from Olivia's arm of the sofa without asking and channel-surfed until settling on a fly-on-the-wall documentary about the emergency services. The fire brigade had been called to a bedsit where a woman had come home drunk and tried to light her cigarette on an old-fashioned one-bar fire and her life had ended in a whoomf. The first thing Olivia thought was how terrifyingly close it was to her own secret habit. The second was how much it made her want a cigarette. Rather than give Jez the satisfaction of another argument, she went to bed, where she lay rigid with a Nicorette lozenge in her cheek, its sharp tar kick fizzing against her gum line a poor second best. Jez came up at midnight, a top-note toothpaste and mouthwash overlaying fresh smoke. When he brushed against her in bed – accidentally, it was months since he'd touched her with affection or desire – Olivia flinched reflexively. *This is what it feels like*, she thought, *when flesh crawls. If my flesh could, it would sprint from his touch.*

Jez noticed her pull away. 'Don't flatter yourself,' he said, and then, as a minty afterthought, 'Frigid bitch.'

At 4 a.m. Olivia was woken by the click of the back door. She pulled the duvet around her and looked out into the garden. Jez was in shadow, reduced to three sources of light: the pale blue oblong of his phone, the soft orange glow of the patio heater, the bobbing firefly point of his lit cigarette. His after-dark routine, she'd noticed, was always the same. He lit the cigarette first, then fired up the heater, then settled in for a scroll through Facebook. One of these days, if he wasn't careful, he would –

The idea was instant and whole, an ignition deep inside her, thrilling and terrible.

On Saturday evening there was a boxing match on television, a huge fight that didn't start until 10 p.m. but that Jez had been preparing for since 6 p.m. by draining one bottle after another of strong lager. The doner kebab on his lap stank out the whole house and had already made a grease stain on the sofa. The fight hadn't even started – it was still just the pundit preamble – but already he was leaning forwards, the green beer bottle in his fist, shouting over the commentary. He sensed her watching him.

'You won't like this, Olivia,' he said, without bothering to turn around. 'It's about real men.' He grunted at the screen. 'I bet *they* don't get this kind of shit at home.'

'Probably not. I can tell by looking at them they don't spend their Saturday nights getting pissed, eating kebabs and smoking.'

She thought he was ignoring her. Then suddenly, he turned around and threw an empty bottle of beer at her. She ducked and it smashed into the limited edition Warhol print, shattering the frame. Olivia left the room before he could do anything worse. She took a pin from the kitchen corkboard and dug it into her palm to stop herself from screaming.

When the fight proper began, Jez's attention was all on the television. That much booze, that much adrenaline: he wouldn't survive the commercial break without a cigarette. Olivia slid the bifold door closed. She stood for a few seconds, confused by the way the TV sounded louder outside than it did indoors, then realised that the pub a few doors down was screening the fight in their beer garden. The thought came to her: this would help her get her timing just right. She would not have long. The molecules in propane, she knew from the documentary, were tiny, and it leaked much faster than other gases. *I'm really going to do this*, she thought, feeling giddy and unreal, as though *she* were the drunk one.

The little terrace at the end of the garden was a mess, butts ground into the paving stones, broken soldiers that died where they fell. Olivia's heart beat so fast and strong it was almost painful as she opened the little door on the front of the heater. The gas cylinder was connected by a thick orange tube, locked in place by a silver seal. The manufacturers weren't taking any chances. Olivia drew the pin from her pocket and thought about how, once Jez was gone, she would be able to breathe for the first time in years. She rolled the pin on her palm.

The pub crowd roared. The fight was over. Olivia tensed, waiting for the music that would announce the commercial break. When it came, she hovered over the tube with the pin poised between her fingers and then, as though someone else were guiding her hand, jabbed the pin into the tube. At first the rubber resisted, but as she pressed down hard, it finally punctured. Seeing movement in the house, she dropped to her knees: the hiss was audible only if you knew to listen for it.

Jez didn't come straight out as she'd expected but disappeared for a minute, into the kitchen for some water maybe, or another beer. His silhouette emerged through the back door, no beer but lighter in one hand and cigarettes in the other.

Seeing his outline, the man-shape of him, his face

obscured, briefly made Jez human again. The reality of what she was doing hit Olivia. *I can't take a life*, she thought, *no matter how much I want him out of mine. I'll divorce him. I don't care about the money; I'll go and live in a bedsit in the middle of nowhere, start again. I can't let him make me a murderer.*

'What now?' he said in a drawl that told her he was never going to apologise for throwing the bottle at her. Still, she couldn't go ahead with it. Leave him, and he'd never be in a position to throw anything at her again.

'Don't light your cigarette,' she said.

'Christ, Olivia, it's like living in a George Orwell novel. When are you going to stop *policing* me? I'm sick of the sound of your voice. I'm sick of the sight of your face. And do you know what? You look really *old* when you frown.' He sounded weary, as if the effort of hating her was starting to bore him. She knew how he felt. 'What next? Want to go through my bank statements? Check my inbox? Cut my bollocks off? D'you know what? I bet they'd be firing on all cylinders for another woman. I could look at a fifteen-year-old and get her pregnant. My swimmers probably took one look at the inside of you and thought, no, thanks.'

'Forget it,' she said, turning her back on him. 'You do what you like.'

'I fucking will,' he said.

Olivia slammed the garden door then ran to the kitchen. She could not brace for the blast without a cigarette. In the kitchen, the smell of greasy lamb and raw onions was almost solid. Olivia replaced the pin in the corkboard and reached for her secret supply – a little to the left of where they usually were, or maybe her shaking hands had knocked them to the side? – and with the filter between her lips, bent to the hob and pressed the ignition.

Streetlamps threw pools of light on the crime scene. The foamy pink cherry tree outside the front of number 36 was stripped and charred, shards of glass at its base. The eucalyptus in the back garden was the same, razed to its blackened bones.

It looked almost as though lightning had struck twice.

The explosions had been clean and simultaneous. It had taken two fire engines no time to extinguish the flames. It took an hour, though, to bag up the bodies and another three to check that the property was safe and allow the neighbours back into their homes. It was almost daybreak.

In the silent kitchen, the fire inspector and the scene of crime officer crouched in front of the remains of the oven, soot making zebra costumes of their white forensic oversuits.

'I've never seen anything like it,' said Kate, pointing her camera at the twisted gas pipe and blinking into the flashbulb's pop. 'I mean, what are the odds of two separate appliances going off at the same time, in the same way?'

Dave reached under his face mask to scratch. 'If there's one thing I've learned in this job, it's that there's no such thing as coincidence. It'll be a while before we know what's what with the patio heater, but this is foul play.'

'Why, though?' said Kate. 'I mean, who'd … I just can't make sense of it.' She nodded to the papers she'd found in the sitting room and spread out on the coffee table. 'I've seen their bank statements. They were in the shit financially, so I reckon it was an insurance job gone wrong. Like, they meant to somehow take the whole *house* down?'

Dave's knees made a crunching sound as he stood up. 'I did wonder, but then you'd get the hell out of the house, wouldn't you? You wouldn't spark a fag in the middle of it.'

'Break-in, then? There's no sign. And it's too weird for vandalism. Too precise.' She bent to pick up a charred photograph of a glossy couple on a beach. 'God, that's them when they were young. What a crying shame.'

'Are we done indoors?' asked Dave.

Kate nodded, and they packed up and went into the garden to inspect the heater. A light wind chased a cigarette packet across the grass; the slogan on the side read *Smoking Kills.*

Happy Anniversary
Colette McBeth

'Fifty years, who would have thought it? And look at us now, Harry, you and me.'

Elsie raises a cup of tea in Harry's direction. The table is laid with porridge, strawberries, blueberries, two croissants. Although Harry never did like a croissant. Not fond of the French. 'And the crumbs,' he'd say. 'Look at the bloody mess they make.' He was always so precise, her Harry, everything just so. 'Appearances matter' was his constant refrain. She used to nod in agreement, but in truth, it's only now late in life that she's come around to his way of thinking.

Elsie spreads jam onto her croissant and lets the crumbs drift to the table. Lately, she's begun to revel in life's simple sensory pleasures; a walk in the park with the spring blossoms lacing the air, a cup of coffee in a hot steamy café, the pair of them sitting together on the sofa, holding hands. The act of being together after all these years.

She takes her first bite and smiles as the warm buttery

pastry melts in her mouth. 'Not tempted?' she says, wafting it under Harry's nose.

He shakes his head in short vigorous movements.

'You don't know what you're missing.

'Now,' she says, licking the crumbs from her lips. 'I've got a surprise for you. Can't let fifty years of marriage slip by without doing something special, can I? Look at this.' She pushes a brochure across the table. 'We start in Montenegro and sail to the Greek islands, Kefalonia, Mykonos, just the two of us. And don't try to stop me. It's all booked and paid for, barely made a dent in that savings account of yours. Margie went to Kefalonia last year and says it's wonderful, Harry, so beautiful.'

She flicks through the pages, pointing out the beaches and the blue, blue water that makes her want to shed her seventy-year-old body and dive in right now. This is what the holiday is about, unwinding time, rediscovering the girl who met Harry all those years ago at the dance. 'We'll have the most amazing holiday, I promise you.' She gives his hand a little squeeze and is pleased to note how his eyes brighten.

His eyes. Those eyes were her downfall. So bright she could see herself reflected in them, or at least a version of herself, one with added buff and shine. But it was his feet that caught her attention in the first place. Elsie was at the dance in Sydenham Town Hall with Danny Wright. Sweet dependable Danny. She was in love, sure of it, and they'd talked marriage and kids and, yes, she could see herself growing old with him. But the night in question was a peculiar one. Even before they reached the town hall, she sensed a kick in the air, a fractional change that had set everything off kilter. Elsie put it down to the sun, which had blazed white hot during the day and had coated the evening in a layer of heat, thick and viscous. Perhaps it was the heat too that had melted all Danny's words because any attempt at conversation met with a stilted stuttering response. So when 'Let's Twist Again' had come on, and Danny pulled Elsie to her feet, she resisted. 'It's your favourite,' he said. And it was, but Danny had a limited dancing repertoire, and for all she loved him, she knew that twisting was beyond his skill set. Two left feet. His mother claimed it had something to do with his bad eye, which was lazy and uninterested. Whatever it was, Elsie wasn't in the mood to make a spectacle of herself (or Danny for that matter).

Yet Danny insisted, practically pleaded, and because she knew he was doing it out of love, and because she sensed it was some kind of test, she relented.

It was five seconds before they crashed into another couple, and then it was like someone had set him out of time, a clock that skipped a second and couldn't get back into rhythm. *Why me?* she thought because Elsie loved to dance, to be spun around until the ground dizzied. *Trust me to choose someone with two left feet (and a lazy eye).* And once that thought had snuck up on her, she couldn't push it away. It turned her back hot with shame and her eyes to the ground, where all she could see were her shoes and Danny's shuffling to no particular beat.

There were other feet on the dance floor that night. Spinning, twisting, jiving ones that caught the light, diamonds studded to their toes. Feet that barely touched the ground, effortlessly leading another pair around the room, kicking and shimmying, as if the music were air itself on which to take flight. The feet made her pine for what she didn't have, producing an ache, a sickness within her.

She remembered thinking it was all too much, and so it was, because seconds later she was on the ground, pretending to be out cold, to have fainted, anything better than face the shame of falling on her face in the middle of the dance floor.

'Elsie, are you alright?' It was Danny's voice. But there was another one too, louder and closer. 'Let me help you,' it said. The smell of boot shine and cologne and pomade drifted towards her, an exotic, intoxicating combination. 'My fault,' he said. And now she had to open her eyes because his hand was taking hers. She saw his shoes, and the room reflected in their shine. Her gaze travelled up to his face full of concern and a smudge of mischief too, if she wasn't mistaken. But it was his eyes that captured her. Dancing eyes to match his dancing feet. And she knew, somehow, just like everyone had told her she would, all the fairy tales and love stories, the histories passed down from her grandmothers and mother through the generations, that there would be a moment of oomph, a bolt that hit her when she met the man of her dreams. It hadn't happened with Danny; that had been a slow steady seduction without any of the fireworks. This was different, and Elsie reached out her hand to take his and felt the jolt of her future forking off in a new direction.

They married eleven months later and she had insisted

he wear the same shoes he'd worn that night, and when they danced, their first, she looked down and saw the version of herself he gave her, full of shine and lustre. As close to Hollywood, she remembers thinking, as was possible to come by in Sydenham.

Fifty years. She'd often bumped into Danny on the high street with his wife, Rita, a plain stout woman. That could have been me, she'd think. She always said hello and asked after the girls, moving on quickly when the throb of all the unsaid words became too much.

She stares at her Harry now, with her sharp appraising eye. His are rheumy and bloodshot. He rests his hand on the table, just out of reach of the cup of tea, the porridge. Strong hands, they were. Not any more. No dancing left in his feet either, not for a long time.

She searches for the man she met that night at the dance and allows herself a laugh at her own expense. What a bloody fool she was! How she wishes she could talk to her younger self, tell her the shine and the spin and dancing feet don't matter a jot. They won't make your life a fairy tale, least not when the foot has stopped dancing and is kicking your stomach. Full force. Harry was never one for half measures.

She was never quite enough. Didn't measure up to his expectations (nor he hers, but that didn't seem to matter). Why didn't she do this? And why not that? And look at her hair, hadn't she brushed it? Appearances matter, he'd say. Every day she carried the shame of disappointing the man she loved. Even when the love had disappeared, a bruise too

19

many, she stayed. Where would she have gone? He would have taken the children. She had no money of her own. No fairy tale warned her about that.

Fifty years! That counts for something though she wishes it didn't. It tells the tale of her stupidity and her powerlessness and her fear.

'I'll get you back one day, Harry Lloyd,' she promised herself after every knock.

True, he had mellowed over the years, not quite as strong, as nimble. And she had taken to scoring little victories. Switching his clothes around, moving his shoes, all to make him believe he was standing on ever-shifting ground.

It was the toothbrush that did it in the end. She was hiding it in the airing cupboard when she sensed him behind her. He yanked her back, trying to position her for the incoming blow. *I'm too old for this now*, she thought and she did what she should have done a long time before. She pushed him back with the force of forty-nine years behind her. If only she'd known her own strength! *Look at him now, falling backwards, tumbling down the stairs. Haven't I been there a few times myself.*

Unlike Harry, she didn't offer her hand to pull him up. He was proper like that, a gentleman even in violence. 'Come on then, Elsie, up you get,' he'd say. 'No harm done.' Broken nose, bruises, a cracked rib, she could go on. But no harm done.

Elsie had done harm. His face told her as much when she reached the bottom of the stairs. A kinder woman would have called for help, but Elsie wasn't a kinder woman. She wasn't the woman Harry had married. He'd changed her and tricked her.

Stupid girl.

She stepped over his body in her slippers, careful not to disturb him. *Just walk out and don't look back.* But curiosity got the better of her, and she was glad it did because the sight of him lying helpless on the floor stirred something in her that she hadn't felt in a long, long time.

A bus pulled away as she reached the stop. She wasn't planning on going anywhere and it wasn't a particularly scenic spot on the roundabout next to the chicken cottage. But she was happy for the fried-food smell and happy for the traffic fumes and horns and beeps and impatience and the circling clouds. Elsie was happy. She was so happy she started to cry, sobs that carried the weight of the years, the hurt and the shame, and all the times she'd curled up tight so as to make herself disappear; they rolled out of her each one more powerful than the last.

'There'll be another one along soon. It's not worth upsetting yourself.' She turned, hadn't noticed anyone sitting at the bus stop through the mist of tears. It was his feet she saw first, two left ones shuffling towards her, and his hand outstretched, offering her a tissue. 'Now, Elsie, come on, pull yourself together,' he said with a smile that erased all the time between now and then.

'The Greek islands?' Danny said when she asked him. 'I've always wanted to go, but Rita didn't fancy it. Didn't like the Greeks for some reason I could never fathom.'

'We'll send you a postcard,' Elsie tells Harry. 'From every stop along the way. Maybe the nurses can read it to you; that'll be nice, now won't it?'

Katya the nurse comes in with Harry's medication. He needs round-the-clock care, but Elsie still comes to visit twice a week. Appearances matter.

'Happy anniversary,' Katya says, looking at the cards and flowers. 'Must be so hard for you.' She touches Elsie gently on the shoulders. 'You enjoy your holiday. You deserve it, doesn't she, Harry?'

Harry's eyes glisten with all his fury and the trapped insults he can no longer speak.

Elsie turns and leaves. She still has a bit of packing to do, after all.

BEACH READY BODY

JULIA CROUCH

Over in the east, beyond the two piers and the marina, a pink tinge creeps into the cold grey half-light.

Shepherd's warning.

Shona unloads her car and lugs the heavy equipment to the spot she has chosen on the lawns behind the beach huts. A newly qualified personal trainer, today she opens her first ever Beach Ready Body Bootcamp. She wants everything laid out and prepared well before the 6 a.m. start.

And here they come. The nine clients who have signed up for her six-week challenge. Most look gratifyingly unfit – soft around the edges, bodies covered in thick tracksuits. Two, however – arriving together on bikes – look as if their bodies are already pretty beach-ready underneath their Lycra.

'So. What are our reasons for being here?' she asks after the introductions.

Lose weight and tone up is the general consensus. The cyclists – Zoe and Cara – share this aim, which prompts a raising of eyebrows among the chubbier ones. Shona knows, however – both from general observation and her recent training – that whatever their shape or size, women are prey to self-hate, which, while generally depressing, is specifically good for business.

'Believe me,' she tells them, 'if you follow my programme, you *will* lose weight and tone up. But I'm here to give you far, far more than that. By the end of my Beach Ready Bootcamp, over and above how you feel about how your body *looks*, you will come to love and respect it for what it can *do*. You will be fitter, faster and stronger: the "you" standing here this morning will be amazed by the "you" that will be here in six weeks' time.'

Anticipation ripples through the group.

Yes, this is a pep talk, but it is truly what Shona believes. She is a woman on a mission to change the lives of her clients. Above everything else she is going to teach them – the burpees, the kettlebell swings, the boxing moves, the stretches – they will receive the greatest gift of all: self-respect. And, as she surveys the group as they stand listening to her, arms folded across their chests, nervous smiles on their early-morning, rolled-out-of-bed faces, she can see that this is, at the very root, why they are here. Something is lacking for them, and she will stop at nothing to provide it.

'It's not a bit of magic dust I can sprinkle over you. It's hard work: four mornings a week down here, two sessions at home, and for best results you have to follow my diet sheet – which isn't about counting calories, but just about eating good, simple food that you cook from scratch – easy recipes, which can quickly be adapted to feed the whole family. You don't have to be MasterChef!'

'Phew.' Pip, a mother of four in a sweatshirt with MUM emblazoned on the front laughs and smiles at the others. 'I burn baked beans!'

'There'll be no baked beans on this course,' Shona tells Pip, trying to keep the mood light but on-message.

Sal, a doughy woman of about thirty with almond-shaped, intensely blue eyes, puts up her hand. 'What about the challenge? Your leaflet says there's a challenge.'

'I was just coming to that,' Shona says. 'The challenge is that the biggest loser – in percentage terms – of both kilos and centimetres wins a year of free bootcamps with me.'

'Wow.' Sal smiles at the women around her.

'Is that fair?' Ruth, a secondary school teacher, asks. 'I mean, those two' – she points at Zoe and Cara – 'aren't going to lose as much as, say, me and Sal.'

'Course it's fair,' Sal says. 'Percentage, isn't it, Shona?'

'Indeed. It's all about the percentage.' Shona isn't actually quite sure if it is, strictly speaking, fair, so she claps her hands and changes the subject. 'Now, first we warm up, and then we do the initial fitness tests. Has everyone got their signed medical forms for me? And don't forget to upload your "before" pictures and stats onto the private Facebook page. Side, front and back, in underwear.'

'And no one else will see these photos?' Ruth asks.

'Don't worry. It's completely private, only shared in this particular group.'

The session is a great success. Pip can barely run five

metres, and certainly not the five hundred that Shona times for their fitness test run. Only Cara can hold a plank for more than ten seconds, and no one can do a full press-up. Shona looks forward to reaping enormous satisfaction from this, her newly minted, life-saving career.

At the end, Pip and Hannah – a new mum trying to lose her baby weight – race off to relieve their partners from childcare. Ruth leaves to 'don the armour' to face Year Nine. Orla, a sad-eyed Irish girl, dashes to her car to shower and change for her morning commute to London. The others stay and help Shona carry the equipment back to her car.

'Your fitness test was pretty impressive,' Shona tells Josie, a short woman who, when she peeled her tracksuit off, had revealed that her bulk was mostly meaty muscle.

'I used to be a sprinter,' Josie says as she helps Sal lug the Ikea bag full of boxing gear up the tarmac path to the car. 'Ran for the county. But that was years ago.'

'You've still got it. You were the fastest by nearly a minute.'

'Where did I come?' Sal asks as the three of them head back to the lawn to pick up the rest of the gear.

Shona stops and consults the phone app where she has recorded the morning's activity. 'Well, it's not really a competition, but you came in seventh.'

Sal frowns, a kettlebell in each hand. 'Big room for improvement,' she says.

'And that's what you'll see,' Josie tells her. It comes across, unfortunately, as a little patronising.

Shona is just putting her sack of yoga mats on the front

passenger seat when there is a thud and a yelp from the back of the car, where Sal and Josie are loading the kettlebells into the boot.

'Oh God, I'm so sorry,' Sal says.

'FUCKINGJESUSCHRIST!' Josie cries.

Shona rushes round to the back of the car. Josie is sitting on the pavement, nursing her foot. Sal hovers over her, wringing her hands.

'She dropped the kettlebell on my bloody foot,' Josie says through teeth gritted in pain.

'It was a complete accident,' Sal says. 'It just slipped out of my hand.'

'She swung it up and whacked it down on my bloody foot!'

'I was just getting a bit of momentum to get it in the boot.' Tears well in Sal's eyes. 'I'm really, really sorry …'

Thankful that she has taken out public liability insurance, Shona squats down beside Josie. 'Let me take a look,' she says.

With great care, she unlaces Josie's trainer and gently prises it off her foot.

'Oh my lord,' she says.

'I'm so, so sorry,' Sal says again.

'Sal, can you just run down there and get the skipping ropes, please? Josie, I'm going to help you into the car. We're going straight to A&E.'

'Josie has had to drop out,' Shona announces to the remaining eight participants the next morning. 'Due to an injury.' She looks over at Sal, who has not even asked how things went at the hospital.

'Is she OK?' Sue – a fifty-five-year-old woman fighting menopausal weight gain – asks.

'She's got two smashed metatarsals and had a crushed toenail removed,' Shona says.

Over the course of the five-hour stay in A&E, Josie had repeated her claim that Sal had dropped the kettlebell on purpose: 'She properly slammed it down on me.'

'But why on earth would she want to do that?' Shona said.

She was relieved when, in exchange for a full refund of the bootcamp fee – the doctor said she was to put no weight on her foot for eight weeks – Josie agreed not to pursue anything against Sal. The last thing Shona needs is the bad PR such an accident could generate for her just as she is starting out.

Word of mouth is everything in the fitness game.

Apart from losing Josie, the first week goes exceptionally well, with visible signs of improvement in all of the women. Shona starts the second week with a circuits race.

'Twenty reps at these eight different stations,' she tells them after their warm-up. 'First finisher gets a goji berry bliss ball – my own recipe, all raw and organic ingredients.'

Cyclist Zoe – whose initial fitness test had been almost as impressive as Josie's – comes in first, resplendent in leopard-print running tights that make her legs look amazing. She is closely followed by her friend and fellow cyclist Cara. Sal, amazingly, is third.

'Here, have a bliss ball too,' Shona says, offering them round after giving Zoe her prize.

the boot and I'll just nip back and get the bib bag?'

'Sure,' Sal says. 'Would you like to grab a coffee when we're done?'

'Oh, I'd love to, but I've got a ton of admin to do.'

'Suit yourself.' Sal turns to the dumbbells and Shona runs across the lawn for the bibs.

When she turns back to the car, she sees that the man from earlier has returned and has Sal by the arm. Sal is shouting at him, but Shona can't hear what she's saying over the clatter of the sea. She drops the bibs and pelts across the lawn towards them.

'Leave me alone,' Sal is yelling. 'Just go away and leave me!'

'I'm going to tell her,' the man says.

'You're not!' Sal bats at him with her free arm.

'What are you doing?' Shona says to him. 'Let go of her right now.' She sees his face and tries not to show her initial reaction, which is shock – the left side shines, purple and puckered with burn scars; half his nose is missing, as if it has melted away.

'Let her go.' Shona takes up a fighting stance. 'Or I have to warn you that I may have to hurt you.'

The man briefly pauses in his haranguing of Sal and takes in what has just been said. He sizes Shona up, which, as she is only five foot two, doesn't take all that long. Deciding she is bluffing, he starts to drag Sal away from the car, towards the beach huts.

But Shona isn't bluffing. In a neatly executed move, she has broken the man's contact with Sal, manoeuvring his arms up behind him. With a kick to the back of his knees, in seconds she has him gasping on the ground.

'Jump in the car!' she tells Sal.

'What about the bibs?'

'Sod the bibs. Let's get out of here.'

'What was that move you did?' Sal asks as Shona screeches her car away from the man on the pavement.

'I'm a level three certified Krav Maga instructor,' Shona says. 'Israeli military self-defence. It's how I got started on all this. But, Sal, who was that guy, and what did he want?'

Sal sits back and looks out of the window. 'Are you *sure* you don't have time for a coffee?'

'Peppermint tea, please,' Shona says to the barista.

'Make that two,' Sal says.

'He's my stalker,' she tells Shona as they take the bench seat in the window.

'Stalker?' Shona tries to banish her astonishment that someone like Sal might attract a stalker.

'It's an occupational hazard,' Sal says.

'What do you do?' Shona asks, edging almost imperceptibly away from Sal, who has sat down a little too close for her liking.

'I'm an actress. Theatre, mostly, before you ask me if you've seen me in anything.'

Again, Shona is surprised. Actors – certainly the few she has met – have a certain charm to them, a certain sense of knowing how they present themselves to others. Sal has none of this. In fact, her energy is so low it is almost a negative. Shona can feel it now. Sal is draining her.

She squashes her mint tea bag against the side of her cup.

'He's been on my case now for three years,' Sal says. 'I moved to get away from him, but it looks like he's found me, worst luck.'

'Can't you tell the police?'

'Oh, they're no use.' Sal waves a hand in the air. 'Bunch of wasters. They don't want to hear unless he harms me, and by then it'll be too late, won't it? Anyway, looks like I don't really have to worry, not with you on my side.'

Shona shivers and blows on her tea.

She drops Sal off outside her home, noticing the motley collection of doorbells at the front of the building and the varied, shabby curtains and blinds at each of the windows – one even has tinfoil behind the glass.

Sal stands and waves her off. Best, Shona thinks, to keep her at a distance. She had been warned about clients like this in her Group Dynamics module.

As usual, there are no spaces for her car in her own street, so she has to park on the main road, outside her local corner shop. She hesitates a couple of seconds, fighting the usual Pavlovian wine-buying urge. Bottle-a-night (at least) Shona belongs in the past, along with the Prada suits and the Jimmy Choos. She is a peppermint tea, Sweaty Betty and Saucony woman now. No chilled white wine for her. No, sirree.

And then she sees the Brighton *Argus* board on the pavement outside the shop, and a cold to equal the flintiest bottle of New Zealand Sauvignon Blanc shoots through her.

FITNESS GIRLS CYCLE TRAGEDY.

She runs into the shop, and avoiding the chilled wine section like the eyes of an ex-lover, she buys a copy of the paper.

Propelled by her pounding heart, she hurries back to her little terraced house – she downsized when she moved to Brighton – lets herself in, thumps her toned backside into a chair at the kitchen table and spreads the paper out in front of her.

She wishes she didn't have to read it, but there it is, in black and white, accompanied by a nasty colour photo of a pair of mangled but still-recognisable bikes lying on a hilly road, in a pool of red.

A woman cyclist has died and another is seriously injured after their bikes collided as they were heading down the notoriously steep Albion Hill on their way to an early morning fitness class. Emergency services were called to the scene shortly before 6 a.m. and, despite the efforts of paramedics, the first woman could not be saved. The other is in intensive care, where her condition is said to be serious.

Shona phones Zoe and Cara. Neither answer.

What is she running here? The doomed bootcamp? This is some kind of nightmare.

She picks up her purse, slams back out of the front door and runs to the newsagents, where she buys a bottle of wine, its green glass bottle rich with condensation.

'Did you see the news about those girls in that bike accident?' Sal asks early the next morning as she helps a bleary-eyed Shona lug the weights from car to lawns. 'Do you think it's Cara and Zoe?'

'I don't know.' Shona's head pounds with an acid, white-wine hangover.

'I wouldn't be surprised, though. Those bikes of theirs were in a shocking state. Wouldn't be surprised if the brakes failed, to be honest.'

'Can we not talk about it with the others?'

'Lips sealed.' Sal winks a blank eye at Shona. As if it's some kind of game.

But she's as good as her word. The session passes without mention, or sight, of Zoe or Cara.

Shona had planned the end-of-second-week session as a sort of celebration. She can barely face it, but she goes ahead with it for the sake of group morale. The morning finishes with a game of tail tag. Shona is the hunter and the others have coloured bibs stuffed into their waistbands, like tails. Working within a small area that she has defined by laying out the yoga mats, Shona has to grab the bibs. When your tail is taken, you drop out, and the winner is the last woman standing, who today is sweet, stressed and homesick Irish Orla.

'Oh, that's the best thing that's happened to me all week, so it is,' she says.

'Here,' Sal says, grabbing her rucksack and pulling out a Tupperware box. 'Aztec Bars. I found the recipe on the Internet. It's all raw and organic, sugar-free.'

'Lovely.' Shona turns to the others. 'This is what we can

all be doing. We know the diet rules, and there are millions of recipes out there that we can either use or adapt to fit them.'

Sal's shoulders twitch with pride. 'You have the special one for winning first.' She hands Orla a bar.

Orla tucks in. 'Mmmm. It's so sweet!'

'You're not having one yourself?' Shona asks Sal.

'Truth be told,' Sal says, 'I had one while I was cutting them up this morning. Couldn't resist it.'

Shona finishes her bar. She can taste that Sal is lying about the sugar. But she keeps quiet. It soothes her hangover-banged skull, lulls her into a mild stupor.

'Look at these guns!' She is roused by Sal flexing her biceps at the other women.

It's true. She's already showing some definition. For that to happen in two weeks is quite remarkable.

'I've taken up running,' she's saying to the others. 'Lunchtime. In the woods. Anyone want to join me?'

'There's that man again,' Hannah says, pointing to the figure lurking by the beach huts.

Sal turns and faces him and takes up the same Krav Maga fighting stance that Shona struck the night before. The man melts away; the others gasp and congratulate her.

'I've been watching a few YouTube videos,' Sal tells Shona when, yet again, she stays behind to help with the clear-up.

That evening Shona stops at the corner shop to buy another paper. The cyclists have been named. She buys another bottle of wine. What should she do? She hardly knew them, but she somehow feels responsible. Should she refund their fees? And if so, to whom?

She sits huddled in her duvet in her purple bedroom, drinking wine and shivering.

The weather is heading in a frosty direction for the forthcoming week.

The next day, with no early bootcamp to run, Shona props herself up in bed and works on the Beach Ready Body Facebook group. She takes a deep breath and removes Zoe, Cara and Josie. It is too painful to see those faces up there. Instead, she looks at the encouraging two-week measurements and photos that are coming in. Sue has certainly lost a bit of her menopause belly. Pip has shed five pounds; Ruth is half an inch down all over. Sal, however, is thirteen pounds lighter, and her thighs and the tops of her arms are three inches smaller. It would be unbelievable if it weren't for the photographic evidence.

Everyone except Orla has posted. But the deadline isn't until Sunday midnight, so Shona doesn't give it much thought.

At one on Sunday morning, a text message pings Shona awake.

'This is Orla's mother,' it says.

'She has asked me to let you know that she is currently in the Royal Sussex renal unit. The doctor says she has suffered mushroom poisoning. We will take her home as soon as she is well enough to travel. Please pray for her.'

'How do you manage it?'

The whole group –what remains of it – crowd round Sal.

It's Monday morning, and the air is so cold it burns Shona's lungs.

'I'm doing a bit more exercise than Shona's plan, and I've got these pills I found on the Internet,' Sal says, her jaw working as if she is chewing gum.

Shona – who didn't sleep a wink after the text message about Orla – can't face pulling her up on this. She just carries on setting up today's obstacle course.

Teacher Ruth speaks, however. 'That doesn't sound awfully safe. This is meant to be about health and fitness, not drugs.'

'Works for me,' Sal says.

Shona sneaks a look and sees her narrow her eyes behind Ruth's back.

'Where is everyone?' Sue asks.

'Orla's ill,' Shona says.

'And Hannah?' Sue says.

'We were supposed to meet for a run on Sunday up in Stanmer Woods,' Sal says. 'But she never turned up.'

Shona doesn't want to think where Hannah might be.

HAVE YOU SEEN HANNAH?

The *Argus* billboard stands on the pavement across the road from the coffee shop.

YOUNG MUM MISSING SINCE SUNDAY.

'You should go to the police and tell them about her not turning up for your run,' Shona says.

Somehow, Sal is with her on the coffee shop bench seat again, sipping peppermint tea and looking judgementally at Shona's own breakfast choice of cappuccino and bacon roll. She is sitting too close: her thigh rests firmly against Shona's leggings.

She shrugs, her large pale face hovering above her alarmingly thickened neck. 'Can't see what good it would do.'

'She posted her results on Saturday.' Shona opens up Hannah's photos and hands Sal her phone, hoping that it will cause some sort of emotion to cross her face.

Sal takes the phone and, much to Shona's relief, moves slightly away.

She scrolls through the pictures and her still, pale face shows nothing.

'This is outrageous, Shona,' Ruth shouts into the phone at lunchtime. 'I am the laughing stock of the school. Every single pupil has seen them. They're up on Twitter. One little brat has even strung them together into a ghastly YouTube video and set them to music.'

'I'm so sorry. I have no idea how it happened.'

'You changed the privacy settings. Every single photograph of me in my underwear can now be seen by every single person in the world.'

'I didn't!'

'I've a good mind to sue you under the Data Protection Act.'

'Look, I'm sure there's been some –'

But Ruth has hung up. Shona rushes to her laptop. With the exception of Sal's photos and results, every single Beach Ready Bootcamp Facebook group post has been made public. An angry direct message from menopausal Sue demands a refund.

Shona takes a couple of sleeping pills left over from her banking days and more or less passes out on the sofa.

The next morning, she is greeted at the lawns by a tall woman in a smart coat, who is accompanied by a man with a protuberant camera. The man steps in front of her and fires his flash right in her face.

'How do you feel about sharing the fat teacher photographs now?' the woman says, thrusting a data recorder under Shona's lips.

'What? Who are you?'

'Katie Vine, *Daily Post*. Do you really think fat shaming is the way to get results, Shona?'

'Please go away,' Shona says.

'Where's Hannah? And what about Cara and Zoe? Isn't this the doomed bootcamp?'

'If you don't go now, I will call the police.' Shona takes up her Krav Maga fighting stance.

Katie Vine raises her eyebrows. She and her photographer retreat to the sea wall, where they sit, arms folded, waiting. Shona stands by her car. When Pip draws up and parks behind her, she runs and taps on her passenger window.

'Don't get out. There's tabloid reporters over there,' Shona tells her.

'I have no intention of getting out. I've just come to tell you how disgusted I am with you for what you've done with our photos. I'm taking up with Joe Wicks online, I want my money back, and I'm going to tell everyone what a fraud you are.'

Pip revs the engine of her Mini and screeches away.

Shona puts her hand to her forehead.

'What a bitch,' a voice behind her says.

She whips round to see Sal standing right behind her.

'Leave it to me.' Sal nods over at the reporter and her henchman. 'I'm used to dealing with people like that.'

She hitches her rucksack onto her shoulder and strides across the lawns.

Shona rests her face on the roof of her car.

'It's her,' someone says.

She lifts her head to see a ruined male face rise from the other side of her car.

Instinctively, she takes up her fighting stance.

'Whoa.' The man holds his hands up. 'Believe me. Sal's your problem, not me.' He points to the scars on his face. 'I was her swimming coach. She stalked me for two years and did this when I tried to stop her. She did four years for it, and, now she's out, you're her new target.'

'Why didn't you tell me earlier?'

'She told me what she'd do to me.' He looks over Shona's shoulder and gasps.

Shona swings round to see Sal striding back towards her. Behind her, Katie Vine and her photographer are moving off in a hurry.

'But –' Shona turns back to the man, but he has disappeared.

'Shall we get started, then?' Sal says, dusting off her hands.

'I-I – What did you say to them?'

Sal grins and shows Shona the combat knife in her hand before returning it to her rucksack.

'I'm not feeling too good,' Shona says.

'But what about my session?' Sal says.

'Can we postpone? Would you like to do a double this evening, say?'

'You're on!' Sal flexes her biceps, which seem to have grown yet again.

'Meet you here at eight, then?'

'You go home and have a rest,' Sal tells Shona. 'In that lovely purple bedroom of yours.'

'What?'

Sal winks at her.

As far as Shona knows, Sal has never been in her house and has no way of knowing her bedroom colour scheme.

'We'll do sprints down to the sea and back, up the steps, five press-ups, twenty kettlebell swings and then repeat,' Shona tells Sal, who is dressed in leopard-print Lycra leggings just like poor Zoe's, with a matching vest top. Her unnaturally firmed white flesh glows in the darkness. She doesn't appear to feel the cold. The lawns behind them are already covered in frost; the sea thunders in front of them.

The beach, and the prom, are deserted.

'Get your timer ready, then,' Sal tells Shona. She barrels off down the steep pebble beach towards the waves, turns and powers back up, head down, feet slipping in the stones, arms pumping. She sprints past Shona, runs up the ten steps to the prom, then down again to return to the beach, where she drops to the ground and performs her press-ups. 'Only five, was it?' she says.

'Only five.'

Sal picks up the kettlebell and swings it. 'I think I'm the winner,' she says, beaming at Shona. 'We're going to have such fun together next year, you leading me through my fitness journey.'

'Sure,' Shona says, forcing a smile.

'Because I'm the winner, aren't I?'

'Three more circuits to go,' Shona says.

Sal runs back down the beach.

The sea crashes onto the stones.

The racket pounding her brain, Shona picks up the heaviest kettlebell in her set.

The Study

Tammy Cohen

'I don't want to.'

Oliver hadn't meant to say it quite so baldly. But he was too taken aback for niceties.

Professor David Taylor nodded as if he quite understood, exposing thick grey bristles that ended halfway down his neck.

'Nevertheless,' he said. 'The university's director of communications was quite insistent. It's a question of targets. Do you see? You're well short of your media target for this year.'

'How about I curate another exhibition in the lobby? The local paper went mad for the last one. Do you remember? They gave it at least half a page. Or I could contribute to another couple of academic journals.'

'It won't do, I'm afraid. The university needs to raise its media profile. Did you see all the publicity Reading got last week over that identical twins study? That's the kind of thing we need, and the director of comms thinks this is perfect.'

'But it's dumbing down. *Decoding the perfect woman*. It's just an excuse for the media to use close-ups of women's bodies.'

'Exactly.' Professor Taylor beamed, revealing long yellowing teeth. 'The director of comms is proposing that you use the results of a proper scientific study carried out here in laboratory conditions to build up an identikit of the perfect woman, with celebrities as reference points. Do you see? Angelina Jolie's face, Beyoncé's bottom.'

The professor pronounced the American singer's name with an exaggerated French accent.

Oliver made no attempt to hide his disdain. 'It's also sexist,' he complained. 'Why aren't we doing men as well?'

'In good time. If this is as big a success as the director of comms thinks it will be, we can do men as a follow-up study. She thinks it could even make a book. A proper mainstream Christmas-gift-type book from the university press with the university logo prominently on the cover. And it's not as if it's a million miles away from the work you've been doing on the biochemistry of sexual attraction.'

'That's not its actual –'

'And don't forget, Oliver, your contract comes up for renewal at the end of the year. This is the type of thing that might make all the difference. The modern system being what it is. Alas.'

On the way home, Oliver thought of all the arguments he should have used.

'You poor thing,' said Sylvie, laying a tentative hand on his arm. She'd cooked a Thai green curry, and the pungent aroma of fresh sweet basil in his nostrils calmed him, even though he could see from the jar on the kitchen worktop that she hadn't made it from scratch.

'He wants me to get a hundred male subjects to come into the lab and wire them up to the fMRI scanner to measure the activity in their cerebral cortex when confronted with different body types. Then we build up this bloody identikit of the perfect female body based on the results, and then science the hell out of it so we don't just come across as a bunch of scummy perverts.'

'Poor you,' she said again.

Oliver glanced sharply at his fiancée. Despite her words, she didn't sound terribly sympathetic. But maybe she was just tired. Come to think of it, she did look a little pale.

'Is everything okay at work? Phillips not on your case again about you reducing your hours?'

'No, honestly, everything's fine.'

Oliver worried that her smile appeared strained, but he decided not to press her. Sylvie's job in a pharmaceutical lab under the dictatorial command of Dr Thomas Phillips had long been a bone of contention between the two of them, and the last thing he wanted was another row. Not after the day he'd had.

The following day, with the help of two PhD students, Oliver began designing his study, albeit with spectacularly bad grace. It made sense to start at the head and work down, singling out different body parts and narrowing each one down to twenty recognisably different types, so the men in his sample could have a properly representative cross section to respond to when they came in. Then he supposed it would be down to him to explain it away in terms of neurotransmitters and hormones and genetic evolutionary science.

To think he'd studied for seven years, taking out all those loans, just to end up doing this.

'I feel like I'm in some kind of slasher movie,' he complained to Sylvie that evening. 'Chopping women up into little pieces. It's so … grubby.'

Sylvie had made fish pie, one of his favourites. They used to share the cooking, but now she'd gone part-time, it made sense for her to do the lion's share. He always washed up though. Fair's fair.

The first week of the study, they focused on faces. Oliver spent hours hunched over his computer, scrolling through the disembodied features of unknown women, trying to pick out various facial types – heart-shaped or round, slightly crooked or perfectly symmetrical, pointed chin or square.

Many of the women in the photographs were caked in make-up, so their lashes were thick and black like spider's legs and their lips glistened moist and red as an open wound.

When Oliver first met Sylvie while he was in the last year of his master's and she just about to graduate, she never left the house without make-up, but over the years he'd persuaded her that she was beautiful just how she was. It had taken some doing, mind. She'd clung to the claim that it was just a bit of harmless fun, but finally she'd come to see that she was using it as a kind of armour, painting herself into the kind of person male society expected her to be.

A photograph of Sylvie on his desk taken on a skiing holiday showed her smiling up into the camera, the sun reflecting off the snow highlighting her natural, scrubbed beauty. The smattering of freckles across her nose, the tiny lines around her eyes that she hated so much.

That day he left work early, eager to see her. But when he arrived home, she wasn't there. There'd been some sort of breakthrough in their research and Phillips had kept them all late. 'But I didn't mind staying,' Sylvie insisted, so soft she couldn't tell when she was being taken advantage of. They had a big row about it.

Breasts was the next week. Even though the women in the images were clothed – that was one battle at least that Professor Taylor hadn't won – Oliver still found it deeply distasteful. He scrolled through the images with the screen as far away from him as possible, his arms at full stretch, resenting being made to feel like a voyeur.

Even while he was compiling his twenty images, he could guess with a dispiriting degree of certainty which ones the male respondents were likely to respond to.

'Of course I can put forward explanations from a genetics standpoint – symbol of fecundity, abundance, blah, blah, blah – but I still find the predictability of it bloody depressing,' he said when they were having dinner with his brother, Josh, and his wife.

Sylvie was quiet that night, hardly saying a word.

'Couldn't you have tried to make an effort?' he asked on the way back.

'I'm just tired.'

Come to think of it, she did look washed out. She was working too hard. Dr Phillips had no business keeping her late. Oliver bet he didn't get his male researchers to do the same hours. The only answer was for her to go down to two days a week. They could manage on his salary.

'I'm only thinking of you,' he told her when she protested.

Week three was derrieres. One of the research students showed him a picture of a celebrity he'd never heard of, Kim something, with long black hair and a ridiculously exaggerated bottom. He drew the line at that. There were enough pressures on women without throwing in totally unrealistic body shapes. 'Might as well include Jessica Rabbit,' he joked, but the research student was from China and had no idea what he was talking about, so it fell a bit flat.

When he got home, Sylvie was talking to someone on the phone, sounding more animated than he'd heard her in ages, but she rang off as soon as he walked in.

'Just my mum,' she said when he asked who it was. But when he checked her call list while she was in the bathroom some time later, he found a number he didn't recognise.

Afterwards Sylvie refused to listen to his perfectly reasonable arguments about trust and transparency. She kept throwing in stuff about privacy and passwords as if *he* was the guilty party. *Of course* he knew her password. He'd watched her key it in enough times. And anyway, they were a couple. No secrets. It was one of the more worrying aspects of their relationship, that she turned on him whenever she knew she was in the wrong. He didn't like having to take her phone away, but if she acted like a child, what else did she expect? The world was a dark place. He had to know she was safe.

The next week saw him trawling through images of legs. Short and muscly, long and lean, rounded and dimple-thighed like a Rubens painting. Many of the legs in the pictures ended in feet that were squashed into high heels, which changed the posture of the wearer and gave an illusion of length.

Oliver smiled to himself when he remembered the shoes Sylvie used to wear when he first met her. Towering black platformed boots, stiletto sandals with narrow straps that snaked up her calves. The first date they'd gone on, she'd had to bring another pair of flat shoes in her bag to change into at the end of the night because the shoes she'd squeezed her poor feet into pinched her toes so much. How happy he'd been to free her from the tyranny of fashion that said women had to suffer to look a certain way. 'I love your feet,' he'd told her the first night they slept together, planting a kiss on first her right sole, then her left. 'I order you to be kinder to them.'

Now she only wore flats. He was proud of how he'd liberated her.

The final week of the study was when they brought in the male volunteers. Students mostly, or shift workers who were glad of the thirty-five pounds they were offering as a 'goodwill' gesture. The odd pensioner.

The men would be cracking jokes when they first came

in to cover their awkwardness, but once on their backs in the scanner with their heads secured in place by the machine's moulded casing, they were all business. Watching them lying there so intently while the little rectangular screen above their line of vision flashed images of hundreds of disembodied female anatomies made Oliver's skin crawl. These were husbands, fathers. There was even a former primary school teacher. Studying all these photographs of bottoms and boobs, as if it were perfectly normal.

The results were analysed. There were few surprises. He hadn't expected there to be.

'I don't know what I was hoping for,' he said to Sylvie over an indifferent pasta bake. He felt a twinge of annoyance. Now she was only working a couple of days a week, shouldn't she be trying a bit harder with the cooking? But he bit back his complaint. She was so temperamental these days. Since the phone incident, he'd been walking on eggshells. He went on: 'It makes me quite ashamed.'

She didn't reply, but there was something about the way she looked at him he didn't like.

Oliver gave his findings to Professor David Taylor, who in turn passed them on to the director of communications to turn into a press release. 'She's very excited about this,' Professor Taylor reported back.

Oliver's study was embargoed for a couple of weeks to garner maximum media interest. On the day the embargo was up, he was astonished to find it had been picked up by all the national newspapers, including the broadsheets, with a double-page spread in one of the tabloids. Oliver instantly forgot which tabloid it was – they all merged into one as far as he was concerned – but he was amused to see the paper had mocked up an identikit of its own, featuring different female celebrity body parts to the ones he'd come up with. He snorted to see Kim whatsername in there. So she did exist after all!

He was even asked to appear on *Breakfast Time* television, sandwiched on a sofa between a woman wearing so much foundation her skin had the texture of buttercream icing, and a man in a suit whose face looked familiar. 'The subject matter of the study wasn't my idea,' he told them, feeling it was important to make his position clear. He was nervous beforehand, while the technicians wired him up to a microphone that clipped onto his jumper, but once the cameras started rolling, he found he quite enjoyed it and was proud of the clear and relaxed way he was able to explain the scientific theories to back up his data. He even managed a joke.

'Does the perfect woman actually exist?' the man in the suit asked him, cocking his head to the side as if it were a serious question.

'She does, and her name is Sylvie, and we're engaged to be married,' said Oliver, and everyone laughed.

Back at the university, he felt like a conquering hero. His two research assistants gave him a standing ovation when he walked into the lab, and the director of communications called him personally to tell him he'd done a great job. 'I had no idea you were such a media asset,' she said.

Professor Taylor came down in person to see him and

hinted at a possible future promotion and gave him the rest of the day off.

Oliver was on a high. The awful report not only completed, but also a roaring success. His job safe. On the way home, he stopped off at the Tesco Express and bought a bottle of Sancerre from the top shelf where the most expensive wines were kept. Even though it was still only lunchtime, he felt he'd deserved it. He couldn't wait to find out what Sylvie thought of his performance.

As soon as he walked through the front door, he could tell something was different. That smell for a start. When was the last time Sylvie had worn perfume? She knew he loved her natural smell. And that was before he saw the suitcases at the bottom of the stairs.

'I wasn't expecting you back so soon,' said Sylvie, teetering precariously at the top of the stairs in a pair of vertiginous blue shoes.

Oliver hardly recognised her in all that gunge, her lovely brown eyes clogged up with mascara and some kind of shiny stuff on her lids that glittered every time she blinked, her lips sticky with red gloss.

She was leaving him, she said. Just like that. No warning. No chance for him to put his side of things. She threw out words. *Controlling. Suffocating.*

'I used to have ambitions, a career, friends, a life,' she told him. 'I used to be whole, not this broken person who gives in to whatever you want rather than risk a row.'

For a moment shock and hurt pride took over and he thought about letting her walk out. Let her find out what the world was really like. That would send her scurrying back soon enough. But the instinct to protect her was too deeply ingrained. It wasn't safe out there. The kind of men there were wandering the streets. The kind of minds they had. Hadn't his study proved that?

He mounted the stairs towards her just as she started her descent. In those stupid shoes. He hardly touched her. Only the gentlest of nudges as she tried to push past him. As soon as he saw her at the bottom, lying on the Victorian tiled hall floor, he knew it was bad. Legs all crooked. Face mushed in on one side. All the different parts of her wrong.

She looked better after he'd cleaned her up a bit. Washed off the blood and make-up. Changed her out of the tight-fitting dress she was wearing into comfortable clothes. Brushed her hair over the worst of her face.

He arranged her in a chair at the kitchen table and poured her a glass of wine.

Then he sat opposite her with his own glass and told her about his day. He knew it wasn't normal behaviour, guessed he was probably still in shock, yet as he talked and drank, he found himself growing more expansive, his anecdotes more entertaining until by the time the last of the wine was poured, he realised he couldn't remember a more pleasant evening.

He glanced across at Sylvie. She was so quiet and attentive, sitting there. And now it was getting dark you could hardly see the damage to her head.

'Perfect,' he said, raising his glass to her. 'Absolutely perfect.'

AN UNINVITED GUEST
RACHEL ABBOTT

Today hasn't been one of my better days – I've spent every minute longing for tomorrow and the peace that only a weekend can bring. I don't usually wish my life away – time is so precious when you work as hard as I do – but I'm never at my best after a late night. It was my sister Lizzy's birthday, an event that was guaranteed to be boisterous because Lizzy's a real party animal and she just says the word and the pub fills up. I've felt foul all day with a rolling queasiness, clammy skin and a head that seems as if it's not part of my body, and I'm just hoping I haven't screwed up the month-end accounts. I am royally pissed off about having a hangover because I'm the sensible sister – always have been, always will be. I've never understood why people seem to think getting out of their heads is fun, and I was on lime juice and soda by halfway through the night, so I don't deserve to feel this bad.

I groan as I turn my head too quickly. Lizzy isn't answering her phone, and at a guess she's spending the day recovering. Somehow she doesn't seem to mind the headache and the dull, sickly feeling that follows a bout of heavy drinking. Why would anyone *want* to feel like this? All I want to do now is get home, have a warm bath, a fat Coke and climb into my lovely cool bed.

It's a relief when I turn the car onto the rough track that leads to my cottage. My home is tiny, but perfect for me. I love it, particularly as it backs straight onto a park, so it's quiet and peaceful. If I leave my bedroom window open, I can just about hear the sound of the stream sloshing over stones after a heavy rainfall, and the wind rustling in the trees is a comforting sound just before sleep.

'Oh, *what*?' I mutter as the cottage comes into view. I must have left the light on when I left the house this morning. Not a big deal, but it just serves to remind me of how out of it I've been all day.

I'm vaguely annoyed to see that somebody has parked in the spot right outside my door. It's probably one of the neighbours, but they're usually a bit more considerate. Muttering curses that nobody but me can hear, I drive to the far end of the track and pull over onto the grassy bank. It's tipping down with rain, and of course I don't have an umbrella, so I jump out of the car and set off at a trot, trying to jump over puddles as I go while pulling my door key out of my bag at the same time. The perfect end to a perfect day is all I can think.

As I push my key into the lock, I can hear music. Don't tell me I left the radio on as well! I shove the door open, and I'm right. An old Adele song is playing – one of my favourites.

But that's not all. There's a smell of cooking – some aromatic spices – cumin, coriander and cinnamon, maybe. And another voice is singing along to the radio – a voice I don't recognise.

There's somebody in my house.

I swallow a hard lump that seems to have formed in my throat and feel tiny prickles across my shoulders. Who is it?

I've got my key clasped between my index and middle finger. Not much of a weapon, but it's all I've got. I leave the door open behind me, not sure if I should make a run for it now or find out who it is.

The decision is taken out of my hands.

'Is that you, Emma?' The singing has stopped, and two seconds later a face appears around the door frame. It's a man – early thirties, black hair, beard, glasses. He's smiling, looking pleased with himself. And he's holding a knife.

Like a fool, I say nothing but back up against the wall, my heart thumping. *Who is this?*

'Hi,' he says, waving the knife in the air. 'I thought I'd cook us both dinner tonight. My treat. I'm making Moroccan chicken and couscous. I hope that's okay.'

He walks past me towards the door, still brandishing the knife. I don't move.

'You're letting all the cold air in,' he says, and with a fake shiver he pushes it closed and dodges back into the kitchen, singing again.

I have never seen this man before in my life.

I want to run back out into the lane and ask somebody

for help, but I haven't had time to get to know most of the neighbours – only Josie next door and she's away for a week. If he's here to hurt me and this is all part of some elaborate game – a game for which I don't know the rules – I won't get more than twenty metres. The track outside is rough and the road up to the village is steep.

A terrible thought hits me. A girl just two streets away was murdered by an intruder a couple of months ago. It turned out the man had been stalking her for weeks, and although she had reported it, nobody else had ever seen him, so they didn't believe her. Has this man been stalking me?

I grab my phone from my pocket and press my index finger down hard. Too hard. It doesn't recognise me. I try again.

'*Come on!*' I whisper. 'Calm down, calm down,' I tell myself, trying again. My fingers are sticky with sweat and my phone doesn't want to respond.

I need to call Lizzy. She only lives five minutes away. Or the police, but how long would it take them to get here? By then, it could all be over – whatever *it* is.

'Are you coming, Emma? I've poured you some wine.'

The voice doesn't sound nervous or uncomfortable. It's as if he knows me. But I don't know him.

He comes out into the hall and sees me fumbling with my phone.

'Are you okay?' he asks. 'You're soaked through.'

He takes a couple of steps towards me and I back away. 'Let me help you off with your coat.'

Two hands, attached to arms that seem longer than they

should be, reach out towards me, and for a moment I feel dizzy. This is different to what's been ailing me all day. This is fear.

I lean against the wall and somehow he must see the confusion in my eyes.

'Sorry,' he said. 'Am I being too pushy? I thought you'd be pleased.'

The hall light is reflecting off his glasses and I can't see his eyes. I don't know what he's thinking.

'Who are you?' I want to shout. But he's standing too close. I've got nowhere to go and I'm scared I might trigger whatever it is that's driving him.

Maybe it's better if I play along with him until I can get my bloody phone to respond to me. Maybe he's some kind of psycho – but how does he know my name?

I push the phone back into my pocket. 'I'm just going to the bathroom,' I say, my voice barely more than a whisper.

'Here, let me help you off with your coat. I'll hang it up so it can drip.'

I don't want him to touch me, but as I turn round, he reaches out and grabs the collar of my coat. His hand touches my neck and I shiver.

'God, you're freezing,' he says, his voice sounding full of concern. 'I lit the woodburner when I came in, to make it nice for you. When you get back from the bathroom, you should sit yourself down in there and warm up before we eat.'

He manages to wrestle me out of my coat and he holds it as I turn back towards him and reverse up the hall to the bathroom. He's between me and the door, blocking my exit. The fact that I know I wouldn't get far doesn't diminish the impulse to escape.

For the first time, I wish this cottage had a bathroom upstairs, but it's right here – where he can see me go in and come out. And he has my phone – it's still in the pocket of my coat.

Who is he?

I try to calm myself in the bathroom. Surely he's not going to hurt me? If he was here to steal, he could have cleared the house of anything valuable before I got back. But he's cooking my dinner.

How did he get in?

I don't know – but I want him gone.

I stay in the bathroom for as long as is reasonable, trying and failing to get my thoughts together, to work out why he's in my kitchen. But there's not a single thought in my head that would explain any of this, so I open the bathroom door as quietly as I can.

'There you are,' he says. He's standing leaning against the wall by the kitchen, arms folded, as if he's been watching the bathroom door since I went in. 'I thought I'd make some spicy fried cauliflower too, if that sounds good. I raided your cupboard and found everything I'd forgotten to bring.'

I'm about to open my mouth when I get the next shock.

'I've put my stuff in the front bedroom. It seemed the sensible place because it looks as if you sleep in the back overlooking the park.' *He's been in my room.* 'Don't blame you.' He shoots me a glance. 'Of course, I could always join you in there?'

Why would he think that? I don't even know his bloody name!

This stranger is going to make me into a victim, a newspaper headline. Lizzy will give the police the one photo she has of me smiling. The fear rises to burn the back of my throat.

'Don't look so shocked. We can take our time.'

'Why are you here?' Finally, I've got the words out, but even to my ears they sound shaky and far from the confident, authoritative voice I had planned.

He laughs. 'Stop messing, Emma. You know perfectly well why I'm here. Come through to the kitchen, or go and sit yourself in front of the fire like I suggested. I don't mind either way. Or better still, just come here and let me give you a hug.'

He starts towards me with his arms outstretched. I don't want him to touch me, but he's still between me and the door. I turn for the stairs before he reaches me.

'Just going to get changed,' I say, taking the stairs two at a time. My phone remains downstairs where I can't get to it.

There's no lock on my bedroom door and I can't bring myself to take my clothes off to get changed with him only feet away. But I can't go down in the same clothes after what I just said. I walk over to the window. Perhaps there'll be someone in the park – I could call them and ask them to phone the police. But in this weather not even the dog walkers are out. The park is deserted, the stark outline of the leafless trees standing black against the dark grey clouds.

I'm pacing the room, forgetting for a moment that he might be able to hear my footsteps below, and it's when I stop moving that I hear the creak of the fourth tread on the stairs.

He's on his way up.

I can't move. I look around me, but the only thing I can see in my room that might do any damage is a bottle of perfume. I pick it up, thinking that I can spray the scent straight into his eyes. That's bound to hurt, isn't it?

'Emma, can I come in?' he says.

'No! I'm getting changed,' I yell, not knowing whether or not he will listen. I wish I'd dragged the chest of drawers across to block the door. I quickly try, but it's too heavy and he would hear me and still have time to burst in.

'Here I come, ready or not!'

I stare horrified at the door handle as it starts to turn. He's coming in!

'Only kidding,' he shouts with a laugh. 'I brought you up a glass of wine. You seem a bit stressed. I'll leave it on the table out here.'

I hear footsteps as if he's gone away, but I don't hear the creak of the fourth tread. He must still be out there, waiting.

I grab some jeans and a jumper and lean on the door, trying to ease off my work clothes and pull on something that is at least dry. I rush so much that I nearly fall over as I step into my jeans.

Finally, I crack the door open and poke my head round. He's not there. I don't know where he is – hiding in the other bedroom, maybe?

And then I hear the singing again. Somehow he's managed to get downstairs without making the stairs creak. Did he do that on purpose?

I creep quietly down the stairs, hoping he's hung my coat in the hall so I can retrieve my phone. It's there, hanging up, and I walk silently towards it and reach into the pocket. My phone's not there.

'Looking for this?' he asks, leaning round the door again, waving my phone in the air. He turns and walks back into the kitchen, which even I have to admit smells tempting. He plonks the phone down on the worktop.

'Food's ready – or will be in about two minutes. I just need to finish off the cauli. Hope you like it crispy.'

I can't take this any more.

'I don't know who you are, or why you're in my house. But can you just leave, please?' My voice is shaky and he's going to know that I'm afraid of him. I'm fairly certain that's not a good thing.

He bangs a pan down on the stove top and pours in some oil before turning round to look at me.

'You've been acting weird since you got home, Emma. I don't know what's going on in your head, but I'm not going anywhere. We'll have this out after we've eaten if you like, but I've gone to a lot of trouble to make this good for you, so I really would prefer it if you didn't piss me off and spoil it now.'

I can see he's mad, and that's dangerous.

'I'll just make a quick call,' I say, reaching for my phone.

He leans over and jerks it away from me. 'Not now. I guess you'll be wanting to phone Lizzy. She's called a couple of times while you were upstairs, but I rejected the calls.'

'Do you know Lizzy?' I ask, suddenly wondering if this is something that she's arranged and has forgotten to tell me.

'I know everything about you, surely you realise that? But I'm not having you ruining my dinner, and you're making me just a bit angry with your attitude.'

I still can't see his eyes. His glasses have misted up and I don't know how mad he is, but I know I'm not safe. I can't run for the door. He'd be on me in a shot.

'Shit!' he shouts, and this time his mouth is a thin line of displeasure. 'You've made me burn the fucking oil.'

He spins round, the pan of oil in his hand, and glares at me, and I know something bad is about to happen, something that's going to scar my life forever.

I don't know how long I've been sitting here. Five minutes? Twenty? An hour?

It feels like forever, and it feels like mere moments. But it's over. He's gone. I'm rid of him for good.

I sit down at the kitchen table and know I should be relieved, but I'm shaking. My phone rings and I see it's Lizzy. I reach out with trembling fingers. I need to tell her what's happened.

She doesn't wait for me to speak. Being Lizzy, she just launches into whatever is on her mind and at some stage she will remember to ask how I am.

She's going on about the night before – how brilliant it was and how she had felt crap all day, but it was all worth it for the fun.

'Bloody Jamie was spiking our drinks, you know. I bet you felt rubbish all day too – but being Miss Goody Two-Shoes, you no doubt went to work anyway. God knows what he was putting in them, but I can't remember much and you were worse than me!' She laughs delightedly at this comment.

'Jamie was spiking our drinks? Why?'

'Oh, he thought it was a hoot. You're always so bloody self-righteous, it was great to see you let your hair down.'

I don't know what to say to her. I want to tell her what's happened, but I can't get the words out. I'm about to say goodbye and hang up when she speaks again.

'Oh, I forgot to ask. Did Liam turn up?' Lizzy asks.

'Who?'

'Jesus, Emma, you must have been further gone than I realised.' She giggled. 'Your new lodger, idiot. He said you'd offered him your spare room, told him where to find your emergency key. He even paid the deposit there and then on his phone – took your bank details from the debit card you used to pay for a round. Don't you remember? *Really?* God, how embarrassing. He seemed smitten. Anyway, when he turns up, make sure you're nice to him. You really need to keep this one or you'll be on your own forever. See you soon. Kiss, kiss.'

She rings off again and I wait, still gazing at the silent phone. If I stare at that, I won't have to turn round and see what's behind me.

So that's what he was called. Liam.

He never told me his name and I still don't remember him from last night. Why would I offer a man I had only just met a room in my house? Surely I wouldn't have done that – even if I was drunk? Did I fancy him? But I'm the careful one – the sensible one. Even if, as Lizzy clearly hoped, I might have been attracted to him, I would surely have found out more about him before I asked him to move in? He thought he knew me, but I knew nothing about him. Had he been stalking me, or had I given him my life story last night?

Whatever his name, however we met, to me he was an intruder, an intruder with a temper.

When he picked up the pan of oil and swung round, swearing at me, furious that it was burnt and shouting that it was my fault, I was sure he was going to throw it at me. Maybe he was just turning to the sink after all. How was I to know? I *still* don't know.

The thought of the boiling oil hitting my face had triggered an act of self-preservation that has left me numb, cold, shivering in the warm room. Next to me on the worktop was the knife he had been wielding when I arrived home. I grabbed it and hurled it at him with all the strength I could muster. The tip of the blade hit him in the neck, blood quickly pooling around the wound. Both his hands jerked upwards, probably to pull the knife out. The boiling oil from the pan flew everywhere, bathing his bare feet, and he howled in agony.

As he hopped around, lifting one foot to try to ease the pain, screaming at his burning flesh, yelling that I was a mad bitch, his other foot shot out from under him, sliding on the greasy floorboards. His head crashed onto the corner of the worktop, and the sounds of pain that had filled the air just seconds before were instantly replaced with nothing more than the inane chatter of some DJ on the radio.

Liam's still here, staring at me. I'll never know why he was in my house – whether this could have been the beginning of something or the end of everything.

His glasses fell off when he fell. They must have skidded under the table as he crumpled to the floor. I can see his eyes now. They're a soft shade of brown with thick black lashes.

It feels as if he's looking at me, but I know he can't see me.

ARTICULATION

ELLY GRIFFITHS

It's the worst thing, being called in to a private construction. Usually, when bones are found, it's on a building site. The foreman informs the police and then they send a forensic archaeologist. They're always expecting a man. My name doesn't help either; they hear Robyn Parker and expect some hairy Indiana Jones type, not registering the all-important *y*. When they see me, five foot nothing and looking, in my high-viz jacket and wellingtons, like a sixth former on a field trip, there's a flood of witty banter, like the milky, brown water that sloshes around inside the cement mixer. 'Hallo, blondie.' 'Come over here and hold my trowel, darling.' I blush easily and know that my face is bright red as I trudge through the mud, falling over the apparently random piles of bricks that spring up all over these places, until I get to the hole where, amidst the rubble and builders' detritus, I see the telltale gleam of a human bone.

Because that's what a forensic archaeologist does. We

look at buried bodies and we can tell, by the way the soil lies on top of a corpse, whether they were deliberately laid in the earth. We look for clues; we read the landscape. Nettles, for example, only grow where there's human waste. So if you have nettles growing in your garden, you may have a body buried there. You think I'm joking, but I'm not. Any big city is built on top of bones: graveyards, plague pits, fever hospitals, charnel houses. Richard III was found under a car park because that's what urban car parks *are*. They're places where archaeologists know that something or someone is buried, so they can't build a house or an office block on top. What they do is slap some tarmac over the site and park cars on it.

And what often happens is that some young couple, dreaming of private ownership after years of renting, buys a plot of land. They start building their dream house and, after a bit of digging, they find bones. A forensic archaeologist comes in and holds everyone up, digging up the bones – oh so carefully, one by one – examining them, photographing them. Then they send samples off for carbon-14 testing, which could take weeks or even months. No wonder the fresh-faced young couple soon become choleric with anger. No wonder they swear at the archaeologist, weep at them and sometimes clumsily offer a bribe. Because this isn't the way the dream of home ownership is meant to go. It never happens on *Grand Designs* or any one of those myriad programmes where photogenic thirty-somethings build fantasies of chrome, glass and exposed brickwork. Kevin McCloud never has to stop work because some old shin bone is found in a drain. It's just not part of the plan.

And, after all that, the bones always turn out to be Victorian or earlier. Then, unless they are really archaeologically interesting, the building work goes on in an atmosphere of sullen resentment, and a brand new house is built on top of the skeleton and its fellows. Because if you've got one body, there are probably others. Sleep well, I often think as I drive past a year later, on top of that paupers' graveyard. The outcast dead, they're sometimes called. The bodies thrown into unmarked graves: the lepers, the paupers, the prostitutes. Unimportant then and now. But not forgotten by me.

But as soon as I got to number 14 Shelley Drive, it was different. The builder, Mark Wallace, was also the homeowner. He was doing everything himself: surveying, plans, construction work, the lot. But he wasn't a typical home improvement type. He was considerate, intelligent, even a little sad.

'It was our dream, me and my wife,' he told me that first day as we drank tea in a prefabricated hut surrounded by mud and abandoned machinery. 'We had a little bungalow here, but we always planned to knock it down and build our dream house. Took us ten years to raise enough money and ... well, here I am.'

I didn't need to ask about his wife. It was obvious she wasn't around any more. Mark had the look of a man on his own. Not that he seemed lonely or pathetic in any way. He was always smartly dressed, clean and well-shaven, smelling of expensive soap. But I knew that he slept in the hut; I'd seen the folded camp bed and the suitcase. I didn't know where he had showers and used the lemon-scented soap. He talked about staying with friends, but no one ever came to the site.

I started on the excavation that morning. The man driving the mechanical digger had spotted what looked like a human bone when he was churning up soil for the foundations. He had stopped work and informed the police. And the police had sent me. Climbing into the pit, I gently exposed the margins of the bone with a pointing trowel. It was a femur and I could see at once that another bone was attached.

'It's articulated,' I said.

'What does that mean?'

'Connected,' I said. 'It could mean that we've got a whole skeleton.'

I worked all day, exposing the bones but not moving them. It's important for an archaeologist to get a proper look at bones in situ. Position can be very important. A body lying from east to west could indicate a Christian burial, for example. Sometimes felons are buried face down, and there are even cases of mutilation after death to prevent evil spirits from escaping. It's a good idea, too, to let the bones dry out in the sunlight, as this can harden them. And it was a sunny day. After a few hours sweat was trickling down my back and I knew that my face was fuchsia red.

Mark brought me cold lemonade – he had a mini-fridge in the hut – and we sat on planks laid over the mud and talked.

'It must be an interesting job, being a forensic archaeologist,' he said.

'It is interesting,' I said. 'I like excavating bones. I like the order of it. I could never have taught; I'm not articulate enough. I get nervous talking to people. I never fancied working in a museum. So fieldwork was all there was, really.'

'You don't seem nervous now,' he said.

'One-to-one is different,' I said.

The skeleton was lying in a shallow grave. Although the topsoil had been disturbed by the digger, the layers lower down were intact. This meant that the body had, at some point, been buried deliberately. From the pelvis and the length of the bones, I deduced that the deceased was female. When I saw the skull, I was sure. Male skulls have prominent brow ridges and larger nuchal crests. This skull was small and smooth across the brow, the teeth small too, with a gap between the front two. When I told Mark about the brow ridges, he said, 'Does that mean we're all Neanderthals?'

'All Europeans have between one and four percent Neanderthal DNA,' I told him.

Mark went to the shop and bought us sandwiches for lunch. We ate them sitting on the planks, drinking water from bottles and talking about our lives. Mark was from Essex. He'd left school at sixteen and worked all round the world. He'd met his wife, Leah, while backpacking in Vietnam. 'She was into all that hippie scene,' he said with a smile, 'but it gets boring in the end and the music's terrible.' He played bass guitar, he told me, and had been in a group called Boromir's Horn. I told him about school and university, how my life had been crippled by shyness until I met Steven, who had been too self-absorbed to notice it.

In the afternoon, I excavated the bones. I lifted them out of the earth, one by one, and brushed them clean with a child's toothbrush. Then I marked each bone with a tiny number in indelible pencil and ticked them off my skeleton sheet. Mark watched me. By the time I had finished, it was nearly nine but still light, the air heavy with pollen and the sounds of the city in summer: children playing in gardens, cars hooting, the far-off siren call of an ice-cream van.

'You'll be late home,' said Mark.

'It doesn't matter,' I said and felt myself blushing, because I knew I'd given something away.

But Mark didn't say anything. He helped me put the bones into evidence bags, which I then packed, wedged around with newspaper, into a cardboard box. When he touched my hand, I felt a shiver cut through me, deep into the marrow of my bones.

Mark laughed when he saw that the box was from a butcher's.

'Very appropriate.'

'Actually I'm a vegetarian,' I said.

There was a silence. We were standing by my car, an old VW Golf. Mark's car, a new Audi, stood in the driveway. It didn't look like a car that belonged to a man who slept in a hut.

'So what happens now, Robyn?' said Mark. 'Will you be able to date the bones?'

'It's difficult,' I said. 'They don't look very old, but the soil is clay, which can have a preservative effect. I'll send some samples away for carbon-14 testing. That'll give us a better idea.'

'What's that?'

'Carbon-14 is present in the earth's atmosphere. Plants take it in, animals eat plants, we eat animals. So we all absorb carbon-14 until the day we die. By measuring the amount of carbon-14 left in a bone, we can estimate how old it is.'

'How accurate is it?'

'Plus or minus about a hundred years,' I said.

Mark laughed. 'I thought you'd say it would tell you exactly when a person was killed.'

'Nothing's that accurate,' I said. 'Carbon-14 testing can be skewed by lots of things – solar flares, sunspots, nuclear testing. Results can take up to six weeks.'

But somehow I knew that Mark would contact me the next day. He rang and suggested a meal in South London. It was warm enough to sit outside, one of those evenings when London feels like Paris or Rome. We ate delicious vegetarian food and drank white wine. He told me more about his wife. 'Leah was a wild child,' he said, 'Dyed hair, home-made tattoos. My parents disapproved of her, but I thought she was the most exciting person I'd ever met.'

I told him about my ex-fiancé, Steven. 'He wasn't exciting and my parents approved too much. He was an accountant, very sensible, very steady. They couldn't believe it when I broke off the engagement.'

'Why did you?'

'Because he bored me senseless,' I said.

That wasn't the only reason. It was also because, although I could envisage a future of regular mortgage payments and half-board holidays in Devon, I couldn't quite face up to a lifetime of faking orgasms. But, that evening, when Mark put his hand on my arm to steer me across Wandsworth High Street, I knew that wouldn't be our problem. He took me back to the hut and we made love on an old tarpaulin, the foxes singing in the background.

The carbon-14 results took almost two months, by which time Mark was living with me in my bedsit, just until our dream home was completed. I had done many other tests on the bones found in Shelley Drive. I had found, for example, a mark on the femur that could have been a sign of a periosteal infection. There are many causes of such infections, including bone disease or a homemade tattoo that has become septic. I didn't say anything to Mark. Hadn't he said, that first day, 'I thought you'd say it would tell you exactly when a person was killed.' When they were killed, not when they died. I knew even before I saw Leah's gap-toothed grin in her wedding photos. I knew that Leah wasn't in Marrakesh with her new lover. I knew that Mark was probably living with a woman, and using her lemon soap, when he wasn't in the shed. But I didn't articulate this knowledge. It was like the shiver that had run through me when he touched my hand. Lust and fear are layers that run very close together.

The test results, when they came, were inconclusive. The bones were anything from ten to a hundred years old. I didn't recommend referral to the coroner. Work started on the house again. Our double bedroom with its en-suite bathroom was full of light and the dappled reflections of trees. It was spring again by the time we moved in, the cherry blossom was in flower and Mark carried me over the threshold. It turns out that you can sleep quite happily over a burial ground. Ask anyone in London.

SEX CRIME

LAURA WILSON

Thank God he's in, and still awake – there's a light on in one of the upstairs windows. It's a Victorian terrace, steps up to the front door, three storeys. I ran all the way, past fried chicken shops, all-day breakfasts, hairdressers offering weaves and extensions, Turkish grocers, dodgy-looking electronics stores, Pak's Wig World – a half-mile blur of littered pavement and rolled-down shutters, broken up at intervals by the peeling sour-cream paint on the rough pubs on the corners: gentrification hasn't reached this part of North London yet. It wasn't easy running in ballet pumps, but they were the first things to hand and I had to get out. I'd have let him know I was coming, but I wanted to put as much distance between me and *it* as fast as I could. I did try once, as I was scrambling to leave the house, but his phone was switched off.

I couldn't think. The continuous loop of images in my head, synchronised with the pounding of my feet and the thumping in my chest, the feeling … the … the *all of it*. Still repeating, over and over, even though I've stopped running and I'm leaning against the portico, heart jackhammering, too out of breath to cry.

Where he lives is alongside the park – nicer than where I am, especially now, in the summer – and I'm pretty sure he must have the whole house because there's only one bell. He opens the door cautiously. He's dressed – black sweater and jeans, the first time I've seen him in anything except a suit – so he's obviously not *just* about to go to bed, anyway. Perhaps he's a night person.

He looks not so much surprised as utterly blank. It takes a second for him to compute – I'm usually here in daylight, by appointment – and then he says, 'Donna? What are you doing here?'

I open my mouth to speak – and then I burst into noisy, ugly tears. An expression I can't decipher flicks across his face and, for a desperate, terrible second, I think he's going to tell me to go home.

'I'm sorry,' I gasp, wiping my eyes and nose with the sleeve of my hoodie (grabbed from the bedroom floor with my trackie bottoms, both sweaty from the gym), 'I didn't know what else to do.'

'All right,' he says, and I don't know if he's telling me it's all right – that I'm going to be all right – or if he's just resigning himself to my turning up on his doorstep at 2 a.m. in full meltdown. He frowns and stares past me into the road, running his hand through his springy hair. 'Well, you'd better come in.'

When I close the door behind me, he says, 'Stay there for

a minute – I'll be right back,' and runs away up the stairs. I do some more wiping and try to pull myself together enough so that I can tell him what's just happened. Even out of business hours, the spacious hall is impersonal, no coats or shoes or umbrellas – nothing, in fact, except a console table (French vintage, cabriole legs, painted soft grey in keeping with the neutral decorating) with a vase of dried cream hydrangeas and a small plastic box full of his cards: *Christopher Poynter, Psychoanalytic Psychotherapist.*

Originally, I'd wanted to see a woman, but I had no idea of who, or how to find them, and Christopher was suggested by a friend. Marie said he'd really helped her after her mum died, so I thought, why not? She warned me he was gorgeous – which he sort of is, I suppose, and probably *would* be my type if I thought about him like that, which I don't – and told me I mustn't fall in love with him by transference, or whatever it's called, because a) it would mess up the therapeutic relationship and b) he's gay. He didn't tell Marie that, because therapists don't tell you about their personal life, but she met his partner once, here.

I went for one session with Christopher and felt comfortable talking to him, so I decided to carry on. His being gay definitely helps – I've told him stuff I'd never be able to talk about if he was straight. I've been coming for about six months now, and recently I've started to tell him things I've never told anyone else, ever. That was the reason that, after what happened – after I *realised* – I thought of him first.

I close my eyes and shake my head, trying to clear away the jumble and clamour so that I can organise my thoughts, but I'm all over the place. I half expect to hear voices upstairs, but there's nothing, so perhaps his partner's away and he's just gone up to collect his notepad and turn off the light. Actually, I don't know if Christopher's partner even lives here, but it's a pretty large house for just one person, so I should think he probably does.

By the time he comes back, I've got my breathing under control and feel calmer and, at least for the moment, safe. He unlocks the door of the therapy room. Apart from the hall and the small downstairs loo, it's the only bit of the house I've seen. The door to the room at the back, which I imagine is the kitchen, is kept closed. I have no idea what it, or the rest of the rooms, might be like – the hall and the therapy room, pleasant, inoffensive and designed to soothe, give nothing away.

Even in my distracted state, I can tell there's been a gear-shift while Christopher was upstairs. He's still in the black jeans and sweater, but he's crisper, more formal, professionally caring, with the suit worn metaphorically if not literally. No notebook, though.

He closes the door as I take my place in the patients' armchair. Beside me, within arm's reach, is a small table with a small bottle of mineral water, a glass, and a box of tissues. Even in the middle of the night, with the heavy curtains drawn, the room is ready for secrets and confessions.

'What's brought you here, Donna?'

I can't speak yet. My tongue feels swollen, a foreign object in my mouth. I reach for the water and pour too fast, splashing the little table, then drink the whole glass in two gulps. 'Sorry.'

'Take a deep breath and tell me what's happened.'

'Yes. Right. It's …' There's a spot on the taupe-coloured wall, about three-quarters of the way up, in the corner behind Christopher's chair. It's a stain of some sort, a couple of centimetres across. I always fix my eyes on it whenever there's something I'm finding hard to say, because it's easier not to look directly at him. 'The thing is …' The rest of the words come out in a rush. 'I think I might have been raped.'

The words crackle in the air between us for a long moment before he earths them with two syllables that plop into the space between us like pebbles thrown into a pond. 'OK.'

I gulp more water.

'What makes you think that? Were you out somewhere?'

I know what's in his mind. A bunch of women, all old enough to know better, lurching down the street, raucous. Losing sight of each other in a crowded bar. Drunken flirtations. Unattended drinks. Waking up in an alley with no memory and no underwear. 'It wasn't like that.'

'What was it like?' His voice is calm, gentle.

'It was … It's what I was talking about last week, what we do. I only realised afterwards, so I didn't … I couldn't … It seemed all right at the time – more than all right, actually – and now I … I …' I can't go on.

'OK,' he says again. 'Let's take it one step at a time. When you say "what we do", do you mean what you and Alex do?'

'Yes, only it wasn't –'

He puts a hand up, palm outwards like a policeman, to

stop me. 'Are you talking about your ... "game"?'

His tone is bland, carefully non-judgemental. I don't know, but rather suspect, that he sees what we do as something that therapists call 'acting out', a symptom of a destructive impulse, and not how I described it. I called it a game because it is, in a way, and because I couldn't think of another word. I think I may have used the word 'arrangement', too.

I haven't known Alex that long – about four months – and the stupid thing is, I can't now remember who suggested it, me or him. I don't even know how I feel about Alex, not at the moment, anyway. We met at a party and went home together – mine, because it was closer – and we chatted and drank some more and ended up in bed. We swapped numbers, but he didn't call or text, just appeared on my doorstep two days later at 11 p.m., and it's gone on from there. I suppose I don't really know that much about him, other than that both his parents are dead and he's an only child and works in IT. We've been out to restaurants a few times, and once to a film, but mostly it's just him coming round to my place, usually late at night. He lives right over the other side of London – somewhere near Epsom – but he works in the centre, so it's just easier, with travelling and stuff.

I know how that must have sounded to Christopher, even before I explained about the game, but I'm not in a very good place right now and haven't been for a while, hence our weekly meetings. About nine months ago, I came out of a relationship I'd been in since the beginning of college – so nearly twelve years – which ended badly, and I suppose I got a bit carried away making up for lost time. Tinder, which didn't even exist the last time I'd been single, made that easy, and what with having to sell our flat and move somewhere else that wasn't half as nice and just feeling … *adrift*, I suppose, my judgement hasn't always been brilliant. Plus, I'm scared of intimacy. I want it because I don't want to be alone, but I'm afraid of it because I never want to get that badly hurt again.

I know all this. I'm not an idiot.

The thing is, I trust Alex. Not with my emotions, because I don't trust anyone with them – except Christopher, and that's different. But I trust Alex enough to give him the key code for the front door of the block where I live, and, on certain prearranged nights, to leave the door to my flat on the latch when I turn out all the lights and go to bed. We've discussed it thoroughly – what is and isn't acceptable, how rough he can be, what he can use, safe words and all the rest – but basically, it's what Alex calls 'rape by request'.

I get a big thrill out of the pretend danger, and from my own daring, too, being the kind of person who does that sort of stuff, because it's one of the few things left that's taboo. I mean, nobody but a complete idiot would believe that women who have rape fantasies actually *want* to be raped, but it's still a dodgy area because it's not exactly feminist, is it? It's way more complicated than that, of course – but it makes me feel really hot, and Alex enjoys it, and it's super exciting, so it's OK.

Except it isn't. Not any more.

'Yes,' I say, and stare at the stain again. It seems larger than it did a moment ago. 'The game. We'd agreed on tonight, only Alex wasn't sure about the time – he was out of town for a work thing and didn't know when he'd be back – so I put out the lights at about eleven and I must have dropped off to sleep because the next thing I know he's in the room and on top of me. He's got his hand over my mouth and I can feel the blade of the knife against my throat. It's pitch dark, because I've got blackout blinds, and he's wearing a hood – that's part of it, like I told you, the fantasy thing, and not speaking – and he turns me over and ties my hands and I buck and twist and try to fight him off, only I can't, and I'm really wet and we come at practically the same time and it's the best yet.'

Christopher's forehead crenellates in a frown. 'So … what's upset you?'

'It wasn't Alex.'

The frown deepens. 'Go on.'

I look at the stain again. I'm sure it's bigger. 'I didn't realise until afterwards. It was different.'

Christopher frowns again and blinks. 'In what way?'

'Alex usually puts on the light and unties my hands, and I go and get us a drink or a cup of tea or something, and we have it in bed. But this time he didn't do either of those things, and when I asked him to, he still didn't, and he didn't say anything, either, so I switched on the bedside lamp. That must have taken at least a minute because I had to untie myself first – I was surprised how easy that was because Alex is pretty good at knots and I wouldn't usually be able to do it myself – and of course it was dark. I kept asking him to help, but he didn't, and he didn't speak. While I was fumbling around, I could hear him moving about, doing up his trousers or whatever, and when I finally got the light on, he was in the hall, on his way out. I could see him from the bedroom.'

'You said Alex "usually" puts on the light and unties you. Does he always do that? Does he ever just leave?'

'No, he stays the night. I only saw the guy from the back, and he still had the hood on, so I couldn't see his hair. He was similar to Alex, the height and build, and I thought maybe this was part of the game, something new he'd come up with – although we've always discussed everything in the past, so that would have been unusual … But I thought maybe he'd deliberately made the knots easy so I could untie myself and be ready for whatever was next, or … Well, I didn't know what to think, really. I looked at my phone and there was a text from Alex, sent about ten minutes earlier, to say that he was still stuck somewhere outside Maidstone because a woman had had a baby on the train, so he was going to go straight home. I thought the excuse seemed a bit unlikely, so I googled it, and it was completely true. It was on my Twitter feed, too, tweets from Alex and some of the other passengers with congratulations and jokes about the baby being issued with a penalty fare because it hadn't bought a ticket, and that sort of stuff. So yeah, I'm sure it wasn't Alex.'

'What happened then?'

'Well, he'd left, and I was just … I sat on the edge of the

bed. I don't know how long for – I must have been in shock, and I felt really confused, as well. I mean, I'd just had great sex and I'd experienced it as this, like, *fantasy* thing, except it wasn't that because it wasn't Alex, which means it wasn't fantasy, but actual rape by an actual stranger. So it was something completely wrong – and I enjoyed it! I mean, I thought I was in control, and I wasn't. *Anything* could have happened. I couldn't get my head round it. Still can't. It's just …' Blinking away tears, I reach for a tissue. 'It's … No, sorry, hang on.' I focus on the stain – which is definitely bigger, I'm not imagining it – and try to breathe slowly. Not crying and getting my brain into gear, even just to say what happened, feels like a gargantuan physical effort. 'I just managed to get to the bathroom in time to be sick. I went and locked the front door, and then I stood under the shower for ages. I had to get him off me. I know you're not meant to, but it's not like the police are going to do anything, so it doesn't matter.'

'You're not going to report it?'

'I can't, can I? They'd ask how the man got in and I'd have to explain that I left the door on the latch and went to bed, and they'd want to know why, and I'd have to tell them, and they'd roll their eyes at each other and start talking about contributory negligence. They'd say I asked for it. Literally. And if the details ever got out … Also, you know I told you about the creepy bloke who lives two floors up from me, who I thought was a bit stalky? I thought it might be him – I couldn't tell from the back, with not being able to see the hair colour, but he's about that shape and size, and he's probably in his early thirties, so the same as Alex. I thought he was odd but harmless – and maybe this is nothing to do with him – but he could have been spying on us and realised what Alex was doing. Perhaps he saw that my door was on the latch – it's a regular thing, so he might have noticed a pattern … And if he's on social media, he could have looked at Alex's Twitter account and realised he was stuck on a train in Kent. But I can't dob him in with no evidence – the police wouldn't be able to arrest him, and the guy's practically next door, so I see him nearly every day … I just don't know what to do. I can't face talking to Alex. I mean – and I know this is going to sound *mad* – it's too personal, too difficult. We never really talk about feelings, so I don't think it would help me – he's got his own agenda and it doesn't involve that level of commitment, so I don't think he could handle it. Besides, I just want someone to explain what happened, and he can't tell me, can he?'

I look at Christopher, but he's frowning into the fireplace. Surely he can make sense of it? He sighs and turns his head to look at me. 'We still don't really understand how the brain functions, Donna. What we experience isn't objective reality, but rather more like a story we are continually telling ourselves – that's as close to the truth as we can come. In fact, one might almost say that there is no objective reality. What you experienced, you experienced as role play, something very enjoyable, while it was happening. You didn't experience it as rape until after it was finished.'

'Yes, but I would have experienced it as rape if I'd known it wasn't Alex.'

'Of course, but the fact is that you enjoyed the experience at the time it was taking place. You were complicit – but that doesn't mean you weren't raped. It was, in fact, both fantasy and reality at one and the same time: you were role-playing, but your partner was doing it for real. Or, alternatively, if it was the man from upstairs and he knows about what you and Alex do and he likes you, he might have thought that he was – in the absence of Alex – performing an act of altruism by giving you the experience you desired.'

I goggle at him. I need some help here – I mean, I know Christopher's not going to wave a wand and make it all go away, but all the same … 'I can't believe you just said that. I know there are a lot of seriously delusional men out there, but surely none of them actually think that they'd be doing someone a favour by breaking into their house and raping them?'

'But, as you pointed out earlier, he didn't break in. He didn't have to.'

'No, but I left the door open for Alex, not for some random pervert.'

Christopher doesn't look at me, but past me, and I suddenly wonder if he's got a mark on the wall somewhere behind my head that he fixes on when things get difficult. When he speaks again, his tone is detached, as if this is an abstract intellectual problem that he's inviting a bunch of students to consider. 'All I'm saying, Donna, is that the truth depends on the observer's perspective. You've heard of Schrödinger's cat, I take it?'

I nod, but I'm not sure he notices.

'There's a theory about Schrödinger's cat called the "many worlds interpretation": when the box containing the cat is opened, the observer and the dead-and-alive cat split into two realities, which coexist. In one, the observer sees a live cat; in the other, a dead one. Now that you have – as it were – opened the box on your experience, you also have two coexisting realities: a desirable experience in which you were complicit, and an undesirable one in which you were not. Two experiences, two different outcomes – things which are not alternatives, and which happened simultaneously. Quantum physics, in fact, which –'

A sudden surge of pure fury bounces me out of my chair. 'In case you've forgotten, I'm not a hypothetical cat. I'm a real human being who's just had a horrible experience, and this is a complete waste of –'

The door opens.

A woman is standing there, about my age, wearing a floor-length cream satin nightdress. Spaghetti straps, lacy edging. Sexy. Her feet are bare, which is probably why neither of us heard her coming down the stairs, and she looks beautiful but so completely spaced out that I wonder if she's sleepwalking.

Christopher's sister, perhaps, or his partner's sister, or a friend.

'I'm sorry,' she says. 'I came down for a glass of water, and I heard noises.' Her voice is thick and vague.

'It's OK, Eva.' Christopher crosses the room, takes her gently by the elbow and turns her round. 'Come on.'

They go off towards the back of the house – I was

obviously right about it being the kitchen – and I wonder if I should just leave, because there doesn't seem to be any point in continuing with this. I pull back the curtain and see dawn light, grey and wan, creeping across the park. I may as well go home. I can call in sick, lock the door and stay in bed all day.

I'm about to leave when they come back down the passage, Eva carrying her glass of water. 'I'm sorry,' she says again.

As she turns to go back upstairs, Christopher reaches out a hand and strokes her hair. 'I shan't be long.'

Not his sister, or his partner's sister, or a friend. I look at the slender hand holding the glass and see a wedding ring.

Jolted, I take a step back and collide with the console table. Some of the cards spill out of the little box onto the floor. I bend down to pick them up. One of them has gone underneath the table, and I have to crouch to get it.

Christopher Poynter, Psychoanalytic Psychotherapist. He isn't who I thought he was, either. But he hasn't lied; I mean, he didn't tell me he was gay, Marie did. Whoever she saw here wasn't his partner, but somebody else – a brother or brother-in-law, perhaps, or another patient.

Eva pauses at the turn of the staircase and looks back for a moment before continuing upwards, out of sight. I can't read her expression. I think about the stain on the wall for a moment, whether it was actually getting bigger or if I'd imagined it. Then I think about all of the things I've told Christopher, about Alex and about me – now, as I reach for the stray card, I remember telling him that the combination for getting into the block is my birthday. He's got my address on file, and he knew – *because I told him* – that it's always Fridays when we play the game. I'd even laughed with him about Alex's silly Twitter handle. The only piece of information I hadn't given him, in fact, was about what me and Alex do afterwards.

Christopher is the only other person who knows about the game. It would have been easy enough for him to find Alex's Twitter account and see the tweets about the train being delayed. And he was still dressed when I arrived, and, judging from Eva's groggy demeanour, she'd taken – or been given – a sleeping pill.

I think of our emotional intimacy, and of how much I've laid myself open to him, never dreaming that he could have any investment in what I was saying apart from professional concern.

Now, he steps past me to the door of the therapy room, turns and looks.

His professional self might well have thought, as I'd suspected, that it was a symptom of something deeper, but his private self – compartmentalised, like the rooms in his house – had turned it into something else. Not my game, or our game, but *his* game. Or … all that stuff about quantum physics. *His experiment.* He probably called it Schrödinger's Pussy.

I feel sick.

He was waiting for me to come and tell him about it, looking forward to the details.

Not so soon, perhaps – hence the blank look when he

opened the door – but certainly in our next scheduled session.

I see it there, written on his face.

His eyes narrow. He knows I know.

I can't look at him any more. I glance down at the card in my hand, instead. *Christopher Poynter, Psychoanalytic Psychotherapist.* The elegant letters dance and blur on the heavy cream surface, and the last word seems to detach itself from the rest and split into three unequal parts, which jump out at me, one at a time, like an optical illusion.

I imagine the excuse he'd offer – he was accepting and affirming my sexual needs, or some such rubbish. I'd told him I'd had a shower and wasn't going to report it, hadn't I?

And I wasn't going to. I couldn't. If I did, he'd say that I was neurotic and had imagined the whole thing, and the police would believe him.

I scramble to my feet, yank the front door open and stumble down the steps. As I dash across the street and past the black railings of the locked park, I can hear him shouting my name. The second before I turn the corner to the main road, I look back and see him standing, braced against the door frame, his face white and pinched, as if leaning into a high wind.

ETTA AND THE BODY
AMANDA JENNINGS

If Etta Harris hadn't run out of Felix, things would have turned out differently.

Maybe if Geoff still lived with her, he'd have picked some up when he went for his four-pack of Carling and twenty Rothmans, but Geoff had left forty-three days earlier, so there was only her to remember the Felix.

That morning Gordon was pestering her, mewing and brushing around her ankles like a snake in a fancy fur coat.

'Oh, Gordon, love, give it a rest. I'm on my phone. You're not that hungry. Leave me be and I'll go in a bit.'

But still he went on. Mewing and snaking. She glanced down at him, noticing as she did some crushed cereal on the floor, tiny crumbs trodden into the wiry carpet. She had a flash of Geoff then, saw him leaning against the kitchen units, shovelling handfuls of Frosties straight from the packet into his mouth and scratching his nethers.

Gordon gave a sudden disgruntled shout and raised his paw to claw at the hem of her dressing gown.

'OK, OK,' she said with a weary sigh. 'I'm going.'

Etta checked her phone again, but the breakfast television presenter still hadn't replied, even though he'd asked people to tweet in.

'Some folk are so rude,' she muttered. 'I mean, why start a conversation then ignore those who reply?'

It happened all the time. No responses. No retweets. No little red hearts or happy blue thumbs. Some even blocked her. And for no reason at all. She hated that and made sure to write down their names in her Hello Kitty notebook, that way she knew to avoid them, a permanent reminder of the authors she'd never read, the actors she'd never watch, and the politicians she'd never vote for. She looked at her stats and tutted; still only eleven followers even though she followed over a thousand. Sometimes she didn't know why she bothered.

Etta dressed then grabbed her coat and left the flat, telling Gordon she wouldn't be long. It was early and Gosforth Road was quiet, most people not yet up and about. She smiled and breathed the air in. There was a clean spring crispness to it, the perfect morning, a bright blue sky, no clouds, birds singing merrily to each other from telephone wires and rooftops. She walked into the shop on the corner and immediately looked down to check the floor. She wrinkled her nose; it still hadn't been cleaned, the sheen of grime floating across it like crude oil on water. Environmental health would have a field day here, she thought. She walked quickly over to the cat food shelf, selected two sachets of salmon – Gordon's favourite – then took them over to the till, where she counted out the coins, mostly in coppers, and handed them to the man in the turban.

One thing was for sure, Etta certainly wasn't expecting to find a body on the way home.

She'd never even seen a dead body. Not a human one. Only flattened squirrels in the road, a dried-up mouse behind the fridge, and once, a while back, a dead dog. A spaniel, hit by a car and lying in a gutter with its back broken.

The body Etta found that morning was in the undergrowth by the canal. She'd taken the scenic route home, hoping to see the heron who occasionally fished there. But she found herself caught short, so after checking nobody was around, she nipped into the bushes, dropped her knickers and hitched up her skirt. It was when she crouched down that she saw it. She gasped and jumped to her feet, pulling her knickers up as she did. After a moment or two she stepped closer. The body was a girl. Unmoving. She could have been sleeping, but her eyes were open, staring upwards, glassy like two large marbles.

'Hello?' Etta said. But she knew there was no point. The girl couldn't hear any more.

The body was pressed up against some wire fencing. Her skin was grey. Lips deep purple. One hand stretched out towards Etta as if trying to touch her.

Etta's heart pounded. She reached for her phone, eyes fixed on the girl, and dialled 999.

'How long will they be?' she asked the rather brusque

lady who told her the police were on their way.

'It's showing seven minutes.'

Etta was about to put her phone back in her pocket, but hesitated.

'No,' she said, her voice loud against the deathly still. Then another hesitation. 'OK. But just one.'

She clicked the camera on and pointed it at the girl. She cropped the photograph to leave out her face so she couldn't be recognised, just her lower half, her jeans and the bottom edge of her T-shirt, ankles spattered with dirt and bits of leaf, one hand making it into the frame, the tips of her fingers showing chipped glitter polish and mud beneath the broken nails.

Etta opened Twitter.

youre not going to believe it but I found a REAL dead body

She attached the photo, then pressed the tweet button before she had time to change her mind.

Not long afterwards, Etta heard footsteps on the path, voices, and the crackle of radios, so she pushed out of the bushes and waved.

Etta took rather a shine to one of the policemen. He was young and handsome and listened to everything she said without drifting off once. He wrote down her words. All of them. Even the bit where she told him she'd bought Gordon salmon as a treat.

Nice blue eyes, she thought and smiled at him.

'Thank you, Miss Harris,' he said. His voice was soft and kind. 'You can go home now.'

'Etta,' she said. 'Please call me Etta. Are you sure you don't need anything else?'

'We have your address and mobile number. We'll be in touch if we need to talk more.'

Etta glanced back at the bush that concealed the girl. Men and women now crowded around. Yellow tape was going up. Serious faces talking in serious tones. She wondered then about the people who loved the girl, who missed her, who didn't yet know her skin had turned grey.

'Do you know who she is?' Etta asked.

'I can't answer that.'

He looks sad, Etta thought.

'Would you like a lift home?' the policeman asked. 'You must be quite shaken.'

Etta was about to say no, she was fine, but then he smiled and his eyes seemed to twinkle. 'Well,' she said. 'I *am* a bit shaken.'

She did her best to hide her disappointment when it turned out it wasn't him driving her home. Instead it was a policewoman who didn't have much in the way of conversation or, Etta decided after a few minutes, personality. The woman just stared silently ahead, thumbs drumming rhythmically against the steering wheel as if tapping out a message in Morse code. Etta studied the back of her head. Grey hair. Freshly washed. A thinning patch at the centre. Etta noticed a wedding ring, so even though she didn't care for the balding, she had to endure a sharp stab of envy.

Etta tore her eyes away from the woman's head and

reached for her phone. When she opened Twitter, she nearly died of shock. 689 likes. 457 retweets. 113 mentions. 6 new followers. Etta couldn't believe it. She rubbed her eyes and looked again.

It was real.

She glanced through the messages. So many people wanting to talk to her. Her hand trembled as she scrolled.

> @anniep345 oh my god that's insane!!! who is it?
>
> @sonofdragons I've always wanted to find a body. Was there blood?!
>
> @robocopper why are you taking a photo of that you sick fuck

Etta blocked this last one and reminded herself to write his name in her book when she got back to the flat.

And then …

> @LauraReadingTimes Hi, I'd love to talk to you about this! Can you DM me with your phone number. Lx

Etta's heart thumped like a herd of bolting elephants. Laura Bourne. A journalist. With 6789 followers! Etta gripped her phone to her chest and smiled. The car pulled up outside the flat.

'If you start to experience any symptoms of PTSD, you can call this number,' said the balding policewoman flatly.

Etta glanced down at the card she held out but shook her head. 'I'll be fine, thanks.'

Gordon was under her feet as soon as she walked into her flat. She tore open a sachet of cat food and tipped it on to his plate, which was dirty with dried and crusted food from the day before. She caught his hesitation. 'I've no time to get a clean one out, Gordon. If you're that hungry, you won't care.'

hi laura, can't dm you. You dont follow me.

Etta waited. Stared at her phone. More retweets. More likes. More mentions.

Then Laura's profile picture flashed up.

Laura Bourne followed you.

Etta could hardly breathe with the excitement.

hi laura its etta. about the body I found.

Hi Etta (what a lovely name!!) I'd love to talk! What's your number? Or we could meet for a coffee? I assume you live nearby? Our offices are on Portsmouth Road but I can meet anywhere in Reading.

Meet for a coffee? Etta took a couple of deep breaths to calm herself. She'd never met anybody for coffee. Not even Geoff, who only drank beer. Her finger trembled as she typed.

coffee sounds good. i'm at gosforth road but can meet anywhere. when?

Are you free this afternoon?

Etta beamed. Gordon jumped up on to her lap and she pressed her lips against his fur and kissed him as she leant forward, eyes fixed on her phone. She left about the amount of time she assumed it would take for somebody to check for prior afternoon engagements.

ive just checked my diary and im free so we

can meet today.

Great! Do you know The Green House by John
Lewis? They do fab cake!

Etta knew it. Posh. Grey and white colour scheme. Hessian chairs, jam jars with flowers on every table, a menu filled with what Geoff would call 'organic crap'.

yes. what time?

2pm? Have you spoken to any other
journalists?

Etta shook her head as she typed.

no

Wonderful! Please don't. I'd LOVE a Reading
Times scoop! x

Laura had signed off with a kiss. Etta couldn't wait to meet her.

The retweets and likes and mentions were racking up, which was exciting, even though there were more bad comments coming in now.

@samantha123 Let the poor girl rest in peace.

@bilsterking let the police do their job you
stupid bitch

Blocked and written in the notebook.

Etta spent the next few hours replying, blocking – and writing in her notebook – and grinning. At one o'clock, she went to the bathroom, dragged a brush through her hair, and changed her sweater, which was stained from her dinner a few nights before.

Etta was nervous walking into the café, and when she finally plucked up the nerve, she was glad she'd changed her top. The Green House was full, mainly women, well-dressed with perfect make-up and shouty gold jewellery decorating their slender necks and wrists.

A young woman with shoulder-length brown hair that shone like a polished conker sat on her own and looked at Etta with a quizzical look on her face. Etta stared at her and the woman smiled. Then she raised a hand in greeting. 'Etta?' she mouthed with a questioning expression.

Etta felt the rush of heat spread over her skin and swore silently. Her rosacea would have flared with the blushing and she knew her face was now patchy puce.

She sat opposite Laura, eyeing the pad of lined paper and pen that rested on the table between them. Laura was drinking a glass of fizzy water with a slice of lime in it. She was slim, wore a small diamond engagement ring and a nice gold watch, a cream shirt, grey trousers and ballet-type shoes in a smart beige. She had brown eyes, which sparkled, and when she talked to Etta, she looked right at her. If Etta could have chosen a best friend, it would have been someone just like Laura.

'You've had quite a morning,' Laura said with a gentle smile.

Etta nodded, tummy fizzling with nerves.

'Would you like a drink?'

Etta managed to ask for a white coffee. When Laura asked if she was hungry, she said yes and ordered a slice of lemon drizzle.

Laura told Etta to tell her everything from the very beginning. As Etta spoke, Laura wrote down her words in a series of unintelligible squiggles.

'Shorthand.' Laura smiled when Etta asked.

'And did you know it was Emily Crowley when you saw her?'

Etta stared at her. 'Emily who?'

'The girl who was abducted from Fosters Park when she was walking her dog a few weeks ago. They found the dog, strangled, in a skip, but Emily never showed up.'

Etta shook her head. 'I didn't know it was her.'

'And why did you tweet her picture?'

Etta started at the sudden note of hostility in Laura's voice. The growls of the online trolls echoed in her head.

What kind of person takes a photo?

Why did you tweet it?

Poor girl. You should have left her be.

Etta looked down at her cake. She took a mouthful. As soon as she did, she wondered whether she should have used the fork that came with it.

Then Laura touched her hand. Etta looked up in surprise. Laura smiled. 'Don't worry,' she said, her tone now honeyed. 'I'd have tweeted it too.'

'I didn't have anybody else to tell,' said Etta after a moment or two.

'Will you show me where you found her? I'd like to take your picture there.'

'My picture?'

'To go with the article. People like to see who they're reading about.'

Etta's hand touched the ends of her hair. 'But I didn't put any make-up on.'

Laura smiled. 'You look beautiful, Etta. Natural. People don't want to see everybody done up to the nines.'

Laura told Etta to stand in front of the bush and look sad.

'This isn't the actual bush,' Etta said, but Laura wasn't listening. She was fiddling with the lens on her expensive-looking camera.

'It's near enough,' she said when Etta repeated herself. 'We can't get any closer because of the cordon.'

Etta glanced back down the towpath and saw the white tent and the tape and the policemen standing guard, arms crossed, faces grim, eyes fixed ahead.

'Done,' Laura said a moment or two later.

'When will it be in the papers?'

Laura did a double take. 'Huh?'

Etta gestured at the camera. 'The picture and what we chatted about.'

'It'll be online in an hour or two.'

'Wow,' said Etta. 'That's quick.'

'Miracle of modern technology,' Laura said with a laugh.

Etta was about to ask her if she liked being a journalist, but Laura had turned away before the words came out.

Etta checked Twitter on her walk home. The retweets had gone mad. Nearly four thousand. Her stomach clenched with the thrill of it. She imagined her profile picture popping up in hundreds of thousands of feeds, people reading her words, taking an interest in what she had to say. She read a few mentions but stopped quickly; there was blocking to do and she didn't have her notebook with her.

When she got home, she closed the front door behind her and sat on the sofa to relive what had happened to her. It had been a remarkable day, going viral on Twitter, new followers, people wanting to talk to her, Laura buying her a slice of lemon drizzle and taking her picture as if she were Kate Moss or Angelina Jolie. Thinking about it gave her a buzz in her stomach.

At just after 4 p.m. an article flashed up in Laura's feed.

Local Woman Discovers Emily Crowley's Battered Body

Etta squealed, which sent Gordon scooting off the sofa. There she was, arms crossed, face serious, her words captioned beneath it: *Well, you just don't expect to find a body before breakfast.*

Etta was surprised to see Geoff's name flash up on her phone an hour or so later. Etta closed her blocking book. She was pleased to have the distraction. She'd had to write so many names down her hand had grown stiff. Since Laura's article, the trolls were coming out in bucketloads. A couple even had the audacity to suggest she was Emily's killer.

Etta hadn't spoken to Geoff since he left. They'd had a row. He'd been drinking so it wasn't really his fault. He found it difficult to keep his temper in check when he was drunk and, as he was always pointing out, she knew that so shouldn't have provoked him.

'Alright?' he said when she picked up the call.

'Yes,' she said. 'You?'

'I saw you on the telly.'

'You mean the computer.'

'No, you stupid cow. I mean the telly. The news. Channel 5.'

She jumped off the sofa and turned the television on, but it was only the weather.

'They repeat it at 6 p.m.,' he said. 'Anyway. I'm just checking you're in, because I'm coming round.'

'Oh,' she said. 'OK. How long –' But he'd put the phone down.

She sat back on the sofa and smiled. She felt wonderful. Warm. Glowing. The attention was like a heat lamp. For the first time in months, maybe even years, Etta didn't feel alone.

She sent a message to Laura.

> *im glad we got to meet each other. thank you for the coffee and cake. if you want to get together again let me know xx*

She stared at her phone, but no message came back.

The Channel 5 news came on again at six. The segment on Emily was the first item. Etta watched with bated breath. A few minutes in, clear as day, there she was. The telly had used Laura's photograph and the newsreader was talking about the Reading woman who'd found her body.

Etta was a star. On the television! She felt drunk on the emotions that flooded her. When Geoff knocked on the door, she bounced up and ran to open it. He stood there scratching the side of his face, clothes dishevelled, hair mussed up.

He walked in and went straight to the fridge. Reached in

for the packet of sliced cheddar. Took a slice. She swallowed back a hit of resentment.

Don't take my cheese, she wanted to say.

'Lend us some money, Ets.' As he spoke, small pieces of cheese flew from his mouth.

'What?'

'The money you got from the telly and newspaper.'

She lowered her head and noticed Gordon eating a tiny bit of the cheese off the carpet.

'Two hundred should do it. I owe Fat Jimmy.'

'I wasn't paid,' she said without looking up.

'Don't lie to me.'

'I'm not lying.'

Geoff laughed then, a mean, nasty laugh, and she realised he was already a few drinks down. 'You stupid bitch. Christ alive! You found that girl in the bush, took the photo, then gave it to them for *free*? Ha! Jesus, I knew you were thick, but that's fucking classic. Classic fucking Etta.'

'I liked her,' Etta said quietly. 'She bought me cake. At The Green House.'

Geoff's mouth twisted into a nasty sneer. 'Cake?'

She nodded. 'Lemon drizzle.'

'Well, that's all right, then. Cake is perfect for a fat cow. If you're a fat cow, cake is way better than cold, hard cash, isn't it?' He laughed and took another slice of cheese. The last one. He chucked the empty packet on the floor. Then he looked around the place. 'Fuck, Etta, you've not done any cleaning since I left, have you? You dirty bitch.'

Etta bit back tears and wondered if there was a message

from Laura on her phone.

'You know,' Geoff said then, 'since I'm here, we might as well have a jump.'

Etta looked up and saw he was undoing his fly. She touched her fingers to the scar above her eye and remembered his fist coming towards her the last time she'd told him she didn't feel like it. She nodded and went to him. Pulled her knickers down and bent over the arm of the sofa.

As soon as Geoff had pulled up his trousers, he started walking towards the door. 'If you get any more dickheads wanting to interview you, make sure you ask for money, yeah?'

Gordon mewed at his feet. Geoff looked down. His eyes narrowed spitefully, and before Etta could tell Gordon to run, Geoff pulled his leg back and kicked him. His foot made full contact and Gordon screeched as he hit the wall. Then he shot out through the cat flap.

'Bag of fleas,' Geoff muttered as he walked out of the flat and slammed the door behind him.

Etta called for him again and again, but Gordon never did come back.

Over the next few days, the retweets and likes began to peter out. By day three they'd stopped altogether.

She messaged Laura a couple of times each day, but Etta assumed she must be busy because she didn't manage to reply.

Soon the news was filled with the image of the man who'd killed Emily. He looked clean, wore a football shirt and jeans, and had close-cropped blond hair. He was the man who painted lines on the playing fields at Emily's school.

'Makes sense,' Etta said to her empty flat. 'They say she liked doing sports.'

She'd tweeted a couple of things, hoping her new followers might talk to her. But none did, apart from a couple of people who asked if she had any more photos of Emily. When she said she didn't, they unfollowed her.

She messaged Laura one last time.

A few minutes later there was a beep. A notification. She grabbed for her phone so desperately she nearly dropped it.

Hi Etta, I hope you don't mind, but I tend to keep my private and professional lives separate. Sadly I won't be able to meet up with you again. Please could you not message me any more? I hope you understand I can't cross boundaries, and going out for a meal with you would muddy the line between my job and my social life. Obviously, though, you can always contact me with stories you think might be of local interest. Many thanks and goodbye.

Etta lay on the sofa and pulled her knees into her chest. The quiet was so heavy it hurt her ears. She didn't move until the evening. She missed Gordon. She thought about Geoff and his foot and the noise her cat made as he'd hit the wall. She thought about all the people tweeting her. Her face on the television. In the paper. Those thousands of retweets racking up like pennies from a jackpot.

She was so lonely she couldn't think straight. She couldn't live like this. She would die of emptiness. It didn't matter what it took, she didn't want to be lonely for another moment.

Etta reached for her phone and texted Geoff.

I fancy a jump. Can I come over?

She waited, staring at the phone.

Then a ping.

Yes. I'm in. but I dont have long

That's ok, thought Etta. *I don't need long.*

She put her coat on and walked out of the flat with grim resolve.

'I'm lonely,' she said when Geoff answered his door.

'I don't give a fuck.'

'I know.'

Half an hour later, after she'd washed the blood from her hands, bleached the knife, and laid it back in the drawer, she got out her phone.

hi laura, youre not going to believe this but ive only gone and found another body …

TEN THINGS YOU'LL MISS ABOUT ME

SARAH HILARY

10. My name

My toenails, painted Blue Candy, show up a shade brighter than my skin. Fresh blisters from my new shoes and all the tender pink places I attacked with an electric pedi roller that trapped the dead cells like shavings from an eraser, the kind we used in school to rub out our mistakes. I have nice feet, considering the work I do. Not even the toe tag can spoil them. I'm Chris, by the way. Not J. Doe, which is what they've put on the toe tag because no one has found my bag yet and they don't know what to call me. They will find the bag, eventually. And they will find the phone, I made certain they would find the phone. The toe tag tickled when they first tied it into place, but I'm used to it now. It's just the name that's wrong. I'm Chris, but you can call me Chrissie.

9. My mask

Two of them rolled me in here and laid me down in this drawer, whose cold metal bites the backs of my legs like teeth. My lovely clothes are gone. They weren't expensive, but still, I saved up for them, so I am sorry about that. Purple satin, slippery under my hands, swaying with the music. I still have my sequins, stars at the edges of my eyes, winking at you. Pink and gold, aquamarine. Everyone loves sequins, and it was like wearing a mask, which made me feel brave. I needed to feel brave tonight. My shoes are in a bag, but it is not the bag I bought to go with the clothes. They haven't found that bag, but they will. The bag and the phone. Before this cold metal drawer, it was the trolley, dashing. Out through the double doors and up the corridor where the lights fly past like arrows, each one brighter and brighter than the last, the further back we travel. Everything speeding up until the first doors slam open like both barrels from a shotgun.

8. My breath

It's all happening behind me, somewhere past the crown of my head where my hair is matted thick and sticky. I can smell meat and it makes me think of the space programme because that's the last thing I remember reading, the last piece of news before my night unravelled. Space, I read, smells of seared meat and sweet metal barbecues. I tried to talk to Joe about space, but he wasn't interested. No one is ever very interested in what I have to say.

Someone is counting, 'One hundred and ten, ninety-six over seventy …' Counting me backwards, into my night. Before this moment where I have three cracked ribs, two cracked by the paramedic with the freckles, fighting to get me breathing again. I read the freckles on his nose, each small constellation standing out against the pale slick of his sweat. Like a mug of Horlicks, his freckles. Counting under his breath, thumping my chest with his hands, trying to make me breathe, breathe, breathe.

7. My fall

Dawn is coming, creeping in long low stripes across the car park, nosing under the wheels and bonnets, snuffling until it finds me. Here. Round the back of the old Rex, the one that's a Sofa Workshop now. By the bins, litter blowing at my feet, chip-paper leg-warmers. Stars in the puddles like glitter, like sequins, winking up at me. Passers-by, the last of the night's partygoers, do not see me bundled by the bins. No one does. I have always been very good at not being seen. I hear them trip past me, laughing, arms linked to stay upright, shoes spiking at the road, their laughter like lacquer, like armour. My loneliness makes no dent. No one sees the drunk or lonely fallen at the side of the road. You step around, away. The whole city sways aside to avoid seeing someone who is no longer a part of its body. Homeless, hopeless, helpless. The city sheds us like a skin and moves on.

One of my sequins has worked loose, scratching at my eye like a feather. A tiny sharp sensation, but it holds me here, pinning me to the tarmac like a needle through a moth. I think, *At least now I will be seen and found, and so will he. At least now I will count for something.*

Take me back before the puddles, further into the night, before the chip papers and the dawn nudging at my knees. Unfold me. Lift me to my feet and make me tall again, my full height, small height, my hands holding my guts like a baby, red. Hold me here, just for a moment. Because this is it, right here and now. The city shuddering as it sheds its skin, holds its breath, swerves aside. My knees buckle, but I'm on my feet, not fallen, not yet. Listen –

6. My time

Listen – to the sudden silence scooping out the night, throwing it away. It is that hour when the whole city is suspended, hanging off the last notes from the closing doors, departing parties, bottles rattling into bins. A long, long moment that ripples out across the city, smoothing every jagged surface, every spire and shard like a hot breath drawn across tall grass, bending everything it meets. My moment. Mine. Now take me back. Before the silence, before the blade. He has my sequins under his fingernails, each one a separate sharp light, flashing. My phone is tucked under the counter at the bar, blinking with his image. 'Joe,' it blinks. 'Joe. Joe. Joe.'

5. *My catch*

Noise, building in blocks as I step backwards, further and further away from the bins, from the tarmac's hard kiss and the stars waiting for me in the guttering puddles, where light dies like candles going out. My feet snag at the street. One of my shoes is off, I've staggered a long way. Surprising how far you can go when you're bleeding that badly. The knife makes a wet sound coming out, a dry sound going in. I swear I see the bones inside Joe's hands. He is not that big, but he is strong and wiry, made of muscle. His face is an axe against the streetlight. I think it is rings – that he is wearing rings and that is what makes his fist so bright, like his eyes, which are the first things I notice about him all the long way across that crowded bar. But it's not rings. It's a knife. I missed the knife, but it did not miss me. I make myself remember that this is what I wanted – to catch him. I have caught him now. I have made a difference, and just for one night I have lived, soared. I saw his eyes shining across the bar, searching. I took a photo, force of habit. I lifted my phone and clicked, catching him.

4. *My night*

I can see a green tree now, daubed on the wall of the bar. I imagine what the place will look like when it's all rainforest – and my armpits sweat. I'm dancing, dancing, dancing. Bodies all around me, smelling of honey and salt and Lynx Africa, throb-throb-throbbing with life and the music that has crawled under our skin, making us one. A sea of bodies moving together like a tide, I am riding the wave, cresting it in purple satin and sequins. I have never been *here* before, part of it all. I am drunk with participation. The bar is built of bottles, winking at me. Somehow I have worked my way into the city's blood, tricked it into carrying me, an ugly duckling on a sea of swans, deep inside its savage, sweating, beautiful-wicked heart. I am found, and lost.

3. My choice

'Murals,' he says. 'They wanted the place to look like a rainforest. Helped the apes feel at home.'

I don't believe him: 'I don't believe you.'

He says, 'Yes. They kept the apes down here in cages. You can still smell them sometimes.'

I shake my head. I am drunk, drinking vodka and red, the glass filling slowly the further back I slip into the night, my last night. Here is Joe, coming towards me for the first time. He doesn't know about the photo or my phone tucked under the counter because I panicked in that split second. Call it force of habit, call it gut instinct, but I saw two Joes, the one who smiled and the one who didn't.

Smiling Joe stands next to me and says, 'You know, this place used to be an ape house.' He picks up a corkscrew from the counter, sharing a joke with the bartender to catch him off guard. Joe is good, all slick moves and cold blue eyes that burn like stars. I watch as he moves close to the wall behind the bar and scores the metal tip of the corkscrew across its paint, uncovering the first leaf trembling on the branch of a tree whose roots must fall right through this floor into the basement beneath. Apes in cages, kept in cages, expected to believe in the murals, to imagine they were in a rainforest not under the floor of a building in North London, where they couldn't make money out of blue movies, so they decided to try monkeys instead. Joe enjoys telling me the story and I encourage him, making all the right noises. It excites him.

I think, *I will never catch him, not like this. He's too clever and too cautious. He has all the moves.* There is only one way I can catch him and that's if I go with him outside like the others did, believing in the murals, stepping into his cage. It is my choice. I choose to make it. But not before I lose the phone under the counter. The phone with his picture on it, and mine.

2. My promise

'Hand.' They stamp my hand at the door with the name of the place in red ink. *Scala*. Too much neon in the bar turns everyone's skin inside out, like an X-ray. I blink and feel the prickle of sequins on my cheeks, the shush of satin at my legs. The music is a wall punched full of holes where the light pours silver and turquoise, soaking my skin, drenching my fingers so that I have to hold my hands in front of my face just to see them shining, shining. A smell like turning earth and ear drops, waxy. Underneath, the punchier scent of his skin. I fancy him the first second I see him. I know him, that's how it feels. My body knows him: a hot pain in my stomach; cold biting at my back like teeth. I take a photo, a secret photo, because I'm so sure. I'm so sure I see two Joes. The lights are winking in the windows, sharing my joke. I can taste laughter on my tongue like sherbet sweets, syllabub, martinis. All the things I've ever wanted to be a part of, but never am. I'm going to be free, that's what I think, that's what I want. This is it. My night. I am going to soar.

1. My calling

I am going to dance and get drunk and forget for a second everything I have ever thought or heard or said about myself. This is the first night or it's the last night, and it's going to be fierce. It is going to be a fierce, full night. Maybe tomorrow I will go into work, put on my uniform, smooth my hair to the shape of my skull, live with the comments and digs, the sniggers and shoves. I will fill in paperwork and take phone calls from frightened people and angry people and people who find life so bewildering they might do anything, anything at all. I have seen young men in prayer caps beaten bloody on the street.

At work they poke fun at me for the photos I'm always taking, tucking away the city's secrets on my phone. When you live to one side of the city, you really see it. I've always lived to one side, of everything. So if you're scared or lonely or frightened, I will listen and make notes, file reports. I will make tea and give you a hug if that's what you need. I'll let you shout and swear at me, throw things at me – without turning away or running away. When I am needed, I will go into the broken places, the dangerous places, and I will deal with whatever is there because that is my job and, yes, it's punishing and painful and most days I wish I could take off, just take off into the city's open spaces – the fountains and flowerbeds and fields – but I won't, because I signed up for this. For broken bottles and blades, abuse and grief. The loneliest job in the world.

You can tell me your worst fears, your secrets and suspicions and your ghosts. Tell me about a man named Joe who scares you, who gets away with murder because no one knows his face. Let me do battle with your monsters. Let me live your life, just for a night. No one's ever interested in what I've seen or heard. I am not on a fast track and never will be. I look wrong and I sound wrong, too clumsy, too different. There is only one way I can make a difference. I have thought about it, night after night. Once upon a time, I wanted to fit in. Now I want to stick out, stick up for the people no one cares enough about. The dancing girls, the ones he takes. Bright and beautiful, I can never be one of them. But I can fight for them, if it kills me. And tonight, I *can* be one of them. Just for one night.

I'm Chris, by the way, but you can call me Chrissie.

Tick List

Louise Millar

At first Monica thinks it is the light from the grubby hospital window that's making her husband's nose look like a pig's.

He waves weakly from his recovery bed as she enters the ward.

'Aw. How did it go?' She makes a baby face and wiggles his foot under the blanket. *'Little soldier.'*

'Went well, I think?' James checks with the doctor.

The doctor, reading a chart by his bed, nods. 'Yes. There was more damage than we expected to the septum. But breathing should improve now.'

'Great,' Monica says, not caring about breathing, only about the pig's nose sitting on her husband's face. 'How does it feel?'

'Bit sore,' he replies.

'Aw …' She points to the inflated nostrils. 'And when will that go down?'

The doctor peers over his glasses. 'What?'

'The swelling?'

'There's no swelling. The work was internal.' He points to the bridge of his own nose.

'But –' She winks at James. *Leave this with me.* '– it does look a little different round the nostrils. You did say the operation wouldn't affect the shape of the nose.'

The doctor puts down the chart. 'Well, as we removed the damage inside, the nose naturally lifted and returned to its original shape. You would pay good money in a private hospital for that work.' He winks at James, and James smiles.

Monica grins hard to stop herself being sick.

It will be OK, she tells herself as she drives James home later.

That's what a marriage is about. For better, for worse.

But James's nose is the worst thing she's ever seen.

That evening, when he goes to brush his teeth and wash his face, gingerly avoiding his nose, she rests her chin on his shoulder. At least his height hasn't changed, she tells herself. James is the *perfect height.*

It was the first thing about him that ticked a box on her list when he walked into the bar on their first date.

Six inches taller than me, so we're in proportion in bare feet, but still two inches taller when I wear heels.

His nose was the second.

Bigger than mine, with a sexy boxer, macho look (e.g., Marlon Brando, Jason Statham).

Not too big, with a handsome little squashed bump

halfway down, caused, he told her on their second date, by an elbow in the nose when he was eighteen, playing in goal. A *sexy nose.*

His dark (*tick*) hair might have been more 'Colin-Farrell-wavy' than 'Poldark-tresses', and his salary £9k less than her bottom line, but you can't wait forever for the perfect man, can you?

She's not an idiot.

Monica nuzzles into James's shoulder, forcing herself to look at the pig's snout in the bathroom mirror.

'So what do *you* think? Around here?' She points to the nostrils. 'Is it just me, or is it a little different?'

James shrugs. 'Don't know. Maybe a little.'

His grey eyes – *kind eyes (tick)* – meet hers in the mirror. 'What's up?' he asks.

'Nothing. Just checking you're happy with the operation.'

He sniffs gently, trying out his new nose. 'Tell you what. I'm looking forward to breathing properly again. No more snoring.'

She smiles. The snoring never bothered her. *No snoring* was never on her tick list. It's not like she's a perfectionist, for God's sake.

If anything, the nostrils are even more alarming this close up. Yawning caverns that tunnel into his face, nasal hair on full show.

'I might sleep in the spare room,' she says, pretending to yawn. 'In case I bash into your nose. OK with you?'

James spits out toothpaste. 'Course.'

She kisses his shoulder. At least she won't turn over and see that monstrosity in the night.

When James is asleep, she finds his old photo albums in the sitting room cupboard and pores over them. Until the age of twelve, he had the small nose most kids have. After eighteen, it has the sports injury bash. Between, it's difficult to tell. Most of his early teen photos are taken from a distance, on a sports field or camping trip, and the pig's nose isn't obvious.

No. That doctor is lying.

He's messed up the operation and given James a pig's nose, and now he thinks he's going to get away with it.

When Monica wakes, she prays that it's all been a nightmare, and that when she goes to make James breakfast, his old nose will be back. But when he appears, looking a little sorry for himself, swallowing painkillers, it's worse. The nostrils flare out of his face, with space up each one for a twopence piece. He looks like a character from *The League of Gentlemen*. His eyes appear smaller too, as if the pig nose is pushing them upwards.

'Aw. How is it?' she asks, cooling his coffee, following doctor's orders to avoid hot drinks for a while.

'Bit sore, but he said it would be for a few days.'

'Hmm. You know, I'm not sure it looks right,' she says. 'I know he said it wasn't swollen, but I think it is.'

'Monica, it's fine.' He sits at the kitchen table and downloads a newspaper on his iPad. His hand lifts to his brow as he reads, hiding his nose from her.

'Good. Well, as long as you *feel* OK?'

'Yup. All fine.'

All day Saturday, she leaves the room on false pretences, repeatedly, just so she can enter again and check his face, hoping each new angle, new perspective, will reveal that the nose is starting to return to normal.

But it doesn't. It grows. By Sunday, it's turned into a long snout. And worse, his other facial features seem to be receding behind it, disappearing from view, his naturally tan skin (*tick*) turning pale pink.

She pretends to watch television, glancing over every few minutes.

James looks up from his book. 'What?'

'Darling, please don't get cross with me.' She points to her own nose. 'It's just looking a little more swollen. Maybe see the GP tomorrow. Just to put our minds at rest?'

'No. I've got a follow-up in a week with the surgeon. I'll wait till then.' He turns, so he's watching the television side-on. 'Can you stop staring?'

'Oh God. Am I? Sorry!' She leaps up and goes over to hug his arm. 'Sorry, sorry, sorry. I'm just worried. About you.'

He rubs her arm back. 'You don't need to. I'm fine. I just caught a breath up my left nostril. Felt great.'

'Brilliant!'

They watch a programme where twenty beautiful strangers have ten seconds to decide who to pair off with before heading to tiny desert islands on their own for a month. Two of the men do pretty well on her own tick list. Tanned, gym-honed, curly dark hair, white teeth, the perfect height. And both have perfect sexy, bashed-up noses.

In the reflection of the television, Monica sees James's forehead pushing back up into his hair, his mouth vanishing under the fold of the snout.

James has arranged a week off work to recover from the septum operation, so when Monday comes, it's a bloody relief for Monica to go to work and leave him and his pig nose behind. Perhaps by the time she goes home at 6 p.m., the swelling will have reduced. Yet the nose won't stop growing. By Wednesday, it is set in a thick, long snout, and his ears have shrunk into the sides of his head.

At work, Monica sits with her clients as they list what they're looking for in the perfect house in her area. *Good schools, good location, garage, three bedrooms* – and, of course, *the wow factor.*

James had the *wow factor*, she muses, shoving particulars at them of houses that are way out of their price bracket, and on busy roads with no garages, in the hope they'll compromise when they get desperate.

He was the first man to tick sixteen 'priority points' in her tick list.

Perfect height
University degree
Professional job
Good-looking (8/10–10/10)

124

Gym
Curly dark hair (full head)
Good social circle of friends
Kind eyes
Sexy mouth
White teeth
Nice car (sports or SUV)
Own house
Good dress sense
Not divorced
Sexy nose, bigger than mine
Not hairy …

It's not like she's the only one doing it. Oh, she's seen first dates sneak away from her in a bar when they've spotted her from a distance, realising she's a little older, younger, rounder, thinner, flatter, shorter, blonder, taller than they were expecting. It's a dog-eat-dog world out there. You have to compete.

'Monica? Got a minute?' her boss Sonya calls.

Monica realises her new clients are staring at her across the desk. She excuses herself and follows Sonya into her office.

'You OK?' her boss asks. 'You seem a little off. You just told the clients to fuck off when they asked you if you had a two-bed under three hundred thousand pounds.'

'Did I? Sorry. No, to be honest. I'm not feeling great. It's all been a bit of a worry. James and his nose operation.'

125

'Aw. Poor you.' Sonya grabs her coat. 'Come on – let's go for a coffee and a chat. Can't have my top sales agent under the weather.'

'It's his nose. I can't stand it.' Monica puts down her coffee in the café. It's a relief to tell Sonya. Sonya isn't one of Monica's friends. Not to be mean, she wouldn't exactly fit into her circle. Ten years and twenty pounds over the limit.

'Oh, how awful for you,' Sonya says. 'How upsetting.'

Monica sniffs and tells Sonya the whole story. How the doctor promised that the operation to fix James's deviated septum, which reduced his breathing after a sports injury, wouldn't change the shape of his nose, but it did, and now it looks like a pig's snout, and if he even comes near her with it, she's going to scream, and she can't let any of her friends see him ever again, because it will be the most embarrassing thing that's ever happened to her.

'And he doesn't even care,' she adds, tearful. 'He's just happy he can breathe through his nose again. He doesn't realise that when he goes back to work, everyone's going to laugh at him – on the bus, in the street, everywhere. And then they're going to laugh at m–' She stops. 'I just want his nose like it was. It was perfect. A *sexy boxer's* nose.'

Sonya's plump, soft hand touches Monica's. 'Do you want me to come over, see what I think? We can pretend to James it's a work thing.'

Monica wipes away tears, grateful. 'Would you?'

Sonya has met James on the few occasions he's popped in, on Monica's request, to pick her up from work, which she always enjoys because of the way the other women in the estate agency look at him. So Sonya knows what James's nose looked like before. And if she does laugh at it and tell everyone at work, Monica can easily hand in her notice. She is the top sales agent, after all. There are five other estate agencies within a mile who would snap her up. And Sonya really isn't in a position to laugh at anyone, with her husband. A man with *hair on the back of his hands.*

It's Saturday morning when Sonya 'pops by' to bring Monica some 'work'. Monica pretends to be on the phone and asks James to answer the door.

'Hiya, James!' she hears Sonya say. 'I'm just dropping this off for Monica. Won't stop.'

He snorts in reply.

The door closes, and he hands her the envelope, snout snuffling as he returns to the kitchen.

As arranged, Monica sneaks out five minutes later to 'fetch milk' and finds Sonya parked in her car on the corner.

'Tell me the truth,' she demands, climbing into the passenger seat. 'Don't try to protect my feelings.'

Sonya pats her arm. 'Monica, I can't tell the difference. His nose looks slightly straighter here' – she points to her own nostril area – 'but really, if you hadn't told me, I wouldn't have noticed a thing. He looks completely normal. As handsome as ever!'

Monica stares. 'Sonya, I know what he looks like. I need people to stop lying to me.'

Sonya frowns. 'Maybe you should go see the GP?'

Monica bursts into tears again. 'I've tried, so many times this week. But he won't go. He says he's going to wait and see the surgeon on Monday.'

Sonya blinks. 'No, sweetie, I mean y–' but Monica is already halfway out of the car, crying.

On Monday, she takes a sick day and waits for James to return from his follow-up hospital appointment. She offers to come, but he's adamant he wants to go alone.

'What did he say?' she asks the second he walks in the door.

James's snout wiggles. 'Says the stitches and packing will come out soon by themselves, and the breathing will keep improving.' Or she thinks that is what he says. *Snort, snort, snort*, it sounds like.

'That's all he said?'

'Yup. He's pleased. It's healing fine. Hey, talking of which. Why don't you come back to bed tonight? The pain's better.' He rubs her back with his trotter. 'I've missed you.'

'Course,' she says. 'Tell you what, I'll make us a coffee and we can chill out in bed and watch a film now.' She makes him a nice cooled-down coffee in the kitchen, with six crushed-up pills in it, then takes it up while he finds something on Netflix.

Then she waits for the pills to work and for James to fall fast asleep, his little snout snuffling away; then she goes out to the shed.

Poor James. He's such a sweetheart. That was one of the sub-points on her tick list. No. 23. *Bit of a sweetheart.* But sometimes people who are sweethearts are not the best at spotting when other people rip them off, do them over and lie to them.

It's OK, though, because she's got his back. She's his wife, for better or for worse.

So, if that stupid, lying doctor is not going to sort out his own mess, she'll have to do it for him.

Monica picks up a hammer and heads upstairs.

BABY KILLER
KATE MEDINA

I look down at my new baby sister. She isn't what I expected at all. She doesn't look anything like those cute, laughing babies on the front of the nappy packet. For a start, I didn't think that she'd be purple. I thought she'd be pink – baby pink. That's why it's called baby pink, isn't it? Because babies are supposed to be a pretty, pastel baby-pink colour. Or girl babies are, at least. Her clothes are baby pink, but she is a disgusting, furious purple colour like a beetroot. I hate beetroot and I hate her. She's wrinkled as well, like the old lady next door. I used to like the old lady next door, still do, kind of, but she won't talk to me or give me treats any more, even though *I* did nothing wrong.

About a month ago some workmen came and dug up the road outside our house. They made such a racket all day that my mum went out and told them to, 'Shut the fuck up.' My sister sounds just like that mega-enormous drill they were using to gouge holes out of the tarmac.

Remembering that the man operating the drill wore big

130

yellow headphones over his ears, I jam my hands over mine, but I can still hear my sister screaming. Dropping a hand from one ear, I lower it over the gaping wet hole of her mouth and press. Her reaction is much like the time I punched Billy Lyons in the face for bullying me. He'd been doing it for months and thought I'd never have the guts to fight back, because he's so much bigger and nastier than I am, but I finally lost it and snapped. He shut up in an instant, his disgusting little black rat eyes saucer-wide with shock.

For that first second, when my hand plugs my sister's gaping gob, she does the same. Her eyes take over her whole face, they're so big and starey, and she falls silent instantly like I found the secret emergency off switch. Perhaps I did. Then I feel a vacuum suck on my palm as she draws in a breath and starts to scream all over again. I can feel the warm wetness of her breath on my skin, a damp tickle of steam. A bit like the time I held my hand over the spout of the kettle when it was boiling, but not like that time at all either. I got burnt then. My hand was blistered for days after.

I'm not going to get burnt now. She is.

There is a pillow next to her in the cot, propped up in the corner like it's on display in the window of some posh shop. Baby pink. Another thing that is baby pink. The pillow is in the shape of a heart. Brian, her dad, my stepdad, bought it for her. She's his first child and he's obsessed with her. Weird to be so obsessed by something so repulsive. No one buys me pillows in the shape of hearts. No one buys me anything in the shape of hearts or any other shape for that matter. I know that this is because they don't love me any more. I'm not sure that my mother ever loved me. I'm not sure that she has ever loved anyone apart from herself. She loves herself fit to bursting. Brian though, is different. Even though he is not my father, he's nice. Nice, and nice to me.

Unpeeling my hand from her mouth, I reach for the little heart pillow. It's made from a really soft, fluffy material and it tickles my cheek as I hold it to my face. The scent is warm and milky. It's a nice smell. The only nice thing about her. I slide the pillow from my cheek to my mouth and kiss it, leaving a wet circle of saliva right in the middle of the heart. I look at the circle of saliva and I look at the wet, dark circle that is my screaming sister's mouth. Half-sister, actually. We're not proper sisters or anything.

I step forward so that the bars of the cot are pressing against my chest and I bend right over, far as I can, so that I am looming over her, like some cartoon horror film shadow. Unlike me, she hasn't yet seen any horror films, so she doesn't shy away or jam her hands over her eyes or cower, or any of the other reactions anyone with sense would have to a scary shape looming over them.

Clutching the heart pillow in both hands, I lower it towards her puce face. Even though it's the second time I block that screaming gob hole of hers, her eyes become as saucer-wide as the first time, bigger even, perhaps. I press and she goes even purpler than before as she gasps for breath. The pillow is so big – or maybe it's because she's so small – that, unlike my hand, it covers her nose as well as her mouth, and those hideous, brain-rattling road-drill screams have dried up.

Good, I think.

Peace and quiet at last, I think.

Just me on my own again, I think.

I lean farther, and I'm leaning so far that I'm right on my tippy-toes and all my weight is resting on my hands on that pillow, on her disgusting beetroot, purple face that's looking a more bluey-purple than purpley-purple now.

A noise behind me, suddenly. I rear back from the cot and spin around, my hands jammed behind my back, my best 'Wasn't me, Miss' expression on my face. It's the face I adopt often at school and I'm right good at it now. I've had enough practice.

But my mum isn't fooled for a millisecond. She's known me for ten years, after all. It's a long time to know someone.

'What the fuck were you doing?' she asks me.

'Nothin',' I say.

And it's true. I wasn't really doing anything. Or at least, I didn't *do* anything. The purple thing is screaming again, so she's fine. I was thinking evil thoughts, but they were satisfying too, and if I hadn't been interrupted, perhaps I would have done evil too, because then Brian would focus on me again and not on her, and Mum would just carry on focusing on herself like she always does, and we'd all rub along fine, like we did before. I was thinking, but not doing, so I'm not lying. Not real, big black lies anyways.

'What have you got there?' she asks.

'Nothin',' I say again, and then I realise my mistake. I'm clutching the heart-shaped pillow behind my back. I should have tossed it in the cot when she came in, but I was so caught in the act that I didn't think.

'Show me your hands.'

I do that trick of showing her one hand and then the other, swapping the pillow between them behind my back, but it doesn't wash with her for a second.

'Both hands NOW!' she bellows.

Both my hands fly from behind my back and I hold the heart-shaped pillow out to her.

But she doesn't take it.

An odd little smile has spread across her face. There's something in her eyes too, as if a light has just gone on in her brain.

'You put it back,' she says. 'You took it, so you put it back.'

The pillow has a few of my hairs on, I notice, but I'm shaking so hard that I don't pick them off. I'm sure that a few of my hairs won't hurt the baby. Won't choke her or nothing. I prop the pillow back in the corner of the cot, like it's back in the window of that posh shop again, soiled goods though, with that wet ring of my saliva and my hairs.

Mum wrenches my sister's box-bedroom door open with one hand and the other arm flies straight out, one finger pointing ahead.

'Bed.'

It's only one word, but it cuts through to the soft bit right in the middle of me that she, only she, can always find. I try to hide it, lock it away, squish it, burn it to death, cut it into a squillion little pieces, but she still knows exactly where to find it. Always. I scrabble for the door, ducking under the blur of her hand that still catches me horribly hard on the bottom.

As I lie in bed, I hear them fighting downstairs. They seem to fight all the time now, or at least my mum screams and Brian just listens. Listens and cowers. He's nice, but he's not strong. Like my dad. He was nice too, but not strong either. So Mum just tramples all over them, like she trampled all over the flowers in the old lady next door's garden. She did it at night though, so no one saw. She's clever like that is my mum. I felt sorry for the woman. She's old and I think that old people should be respected. When Mum and I first moved in with Brian, she used to give me things. Flowers from her garden, drinks and cakes, and once she gave me a couple of pounds for sweets.

She doesn't do any of that any more. She doesn't even look at me. I'm tarred with the same brush. The mum brush. I knocked on her door once, a few weeks ago, to tell her that I miss our chats, but she wouldn't even open the door. I knew she was in because I saw the tips of her fingers poking through the nets that cover her window. I ducked down and shouted through the letterbox that I was sorry.

'Sorry for everything,' I said.

Sorry for Mum – I meant.

She mustn't have any money either, like us, or she wouldn't live here.

She wouldn't listen to me, though. Wouldn't listen to my shouted apology. No one listens to me.

I know all the swear words. Shit, bloody, fuck, bastard, wanker. I even know the C-word. C U Next Tuesday. That one makes me laugh. But when my mother shouts it against Brian, she doesn't say C U Next Tuesday, she just uses the capital letters all strung together in one word. I don't really want to write it down here, because it's offensive and I hate to be offensive. It's my mum's fault. She used to scream at my father like that too. I'm not sure why men get sucked into marrying her, though she's always told me that men are stupid and pointless, so maybe that's why.

Jonie was supposed to be a Band-Aid baby. That's what Brian called her. He said it in that exasperated voice he uses virtually all the time now. 'Band-Aid baby.'

The scream wakes me up. It must wake up half the street. I peek out of my curtains and see doors opening across the road, neighbours emerging blinking-eyed out of the darkness of their hallways into the summer dawn, in their dressing gowns and slippers.

'What the fuck did you do?' I hear Mum screaming at me even before my bedroom door flies open. Brian is behind her, pale and shock-faced. I hold Pooh, my teddy bear, in front of me, as if he will protect me from the rabid fury that is my mother. '*What the fuck did you do?*'

I'm crying too now. I didn't do anything. I don't know what she's talking about, but at the same time I do.

'Has something happened to Jonie?' I mumble.

'You know,' she screams. She snatches Pooh from my hands and pulls at his arms.

Tears are streaming down my face and I'm shaking my head. 'Please no, Mum.'

I hear ripping. One of Pooh's arms tears from his body.

Mum flings it onto the floor and stamps on it, like she stamped on those flowers. She rips Pooh's other arm off too and throws it at me. It lands on my duvet, a little brown, severed limb.

I've had Pooh since the day I was born. He isn't a Pooh Bear, not a proper one. We couldn't afford a proper branded Pooh, but I called him Pooh anyway, because I wanted one so much.

'Tracy, stop,' Brian manages.

But she ignores him. She always ignores him.

'You fucking little bitch,' she screams at me. Her teeth clamp around one of Pooh's ears, her hands around his throat, and she rears her head back, a look of crazy madness in her eyes. Pooh's ear separates from his head. She spits it onto the floor.

I hear sirens.

'She's dead. My baby is dead,' she yells, right into my face. 'You … you suffocated her with her baby heart pillow.'

I'm sobbing. Brian is sobbing. Mum is screaming. Screaming and sobbing.

'No, Mum, no,' I sob. 'I didn't do anything.'

Why won't she listen? Why won't anyone listen?

She's not purple any more. She's blue now. Grey-blue. It's a prettier colour than the purple, and the fact that she's not screaming any more makes me smile. I'm still smiling when the police come into her bedroom. They look at me.

Mum is sobbing. Brian is just white like someone stuck him on a hot wash.

'She murdered my baby.'

No, I didn't. It wasn't me.

I'm trapped in a circle of adult faces. They're all staring at me. I think that maybe I see sympathy on the face of the young policewoman, but then I realise that's not true. It's hatred. Just a little less bald than the others.

'She killed the old lady next door's cat,' I hear Mum say. 'I should have done something then, called you. But –'

I try to spin around, but they're holding me tightly by the upper arms, and though I kick and struggle, I can't get away. I'm crying now, shaking and crying, trying to make them all understand.

It's not true. Mum killed the cat. I saw her do it. A couple of weeks after she trampled the old lady's plants. The cat kept digging up Mum's valerian plant. She grows it 'cause she says it helps with her anxiety. She doesn't have anxiety though. It's the rest of us that have anxiety living with her. I was watching from my bedroom window and I saw her swinging the cat against the back wall of the house. The sound was a clunk, clunk, clunk, until there wasn't a clunk any more, just a wet slapping sound. She shoved the cat's body in a bin bag and dumped it in the old lady's bin.

When she came back in, she was laughing. 'Can't swing a fucking cat in that backyard, Brian.'

'It's all we can afford, love,' he said, glancing up from the footie. He hadn't got the point at all.

But I had, because I saw.

They keep calling me baby killer. But I'm not. I didn't do it. Why won't they listen to me?

I think my mother would have killed me too, when I was

a baby, if she'd have been able to get away with it, but there was no one to blame it on then. They talk to me like it's my fault, but not my fault. Like I was too young to help myself. I am too young to help myself, but not in the way they think.

I see her looking across the courtroom at me, that same odd little smile on her face.

She likes her freedom. She's got it now. For the moment at least.

But I won't forget. I won't forget Pooh.

EYE ON THE PRIZE
MEL MCGRATH

If Julian didn't get the job, Emma would leave him. In a moment of panic, he'd told his wife the job was in the bag, knowing that, after last month's awkward confrontation with Leathwaite, his chances of being recommended for the chair in ophthalmology lay somewhere between slim and zero. Sooner or later he would have to fess up, and Emma would leave, and Julian couldn't allow that to happen. There was nothing for it but to beg, bribe or threaten Leathwaite into changing his mind. Since Leathwaite was no longer speaking to him, Julian's only chance was to crash his boss's retirement party and get the 'great man' on his own.

Now they were here, in the drawing room in Leathwaite's immaculate Georgian townhouse, surrounded by Leathwaite's astonishing collection of antique ophthalmoscopes, with glasses of champagne in their hands, admiring the view over the Thames to St Paul's and making polite chat about Leathwaite's retirement. Julian had dreaded this moment. Still, he had no choice. Desperate means and all that. His hope was that, once bathed in the admiration and affection of his colleagues and a good deal of champagne, Leathwaite might be in a mood to look more favourably on him or, if not that, then be open to some mutually acceptable financial arrangement.

Hoping to drum up some courage, Julian held out his champagne flute to a passing waiter and, as he tapped the rim for a refill, chugged the contents down in one and handed the empty glass back to the waiter. He noticed Emma giving him one of her looks.

'Darling, is that wise? You don't want to get into one of your *states*. Not here.' Naturally Julian hadn't told his wife about his plan. So far as Emma was concerned, her husband *was* the new chair of ophthalmology, but the news was being kept under wraps until the official announcement after the Appointments Committee meeting.

It was the demon drink that had got Julian into this mess. The half bottle of Bell's he'd downed to settle his nerves before last week's complex corneal transplant. He'd fixed dozens of cataracts while being three sheets to the wind in the last few months and, despite the greater complexity of the transplant, he was convinced he could have made a perfectly decent job of it. If only the patient had been anyone other than the sheikh of some godforsaken desert rathole, Leathwaite wouldn't have blinked an eye.

Emma was prodding him with her elbow and nodding to the other side of the room, where Leathwaite was deep in conversation with a young man in a slick suit. 'Why don't you go and talk to the great man? I don't think he's seen us.' Being 'seen' was very important to Emma.

'He looks terribly busy,' Julian said, by which he meant Leathwaite didn't appear drunk enough yet.

Beside him, Emma tutted. 'Don't be silly, darling, of course he's busy. It's his retirement party. Now off you go.' In the two years he'd been with her, Julian had never quite succeeded in saying no to Emma, a consequence, he supposed, of marrying someone so much younger and more beautiful than he had a right to deserve.

'Come with?' he said, in a tone he instantly regretted. Emma hated it when Julian openly supplicated himself to her. She had some kind of knight-in-shining-armour complex which, in the early days of their romance, Julian had indulged to such a degree that it had now become a dead weight he felt obliged to drag around. His role as Emma's husband was to appear manly and in control whilst acceding to her every whim. Honestly, it was exhausting.

Emma shook her head. 'You two need to talk *business*.'

Julian had learned the hard way that, for all her studied girlishness, Emma was implacable when she wanted to be. He pressed his lips to summon his courage, took a deep breath and turned on his heel. What was the worst that could happen? If Leathwaite wasn't receptive, he'd say hello and go in for the kill later in the evening. It might even be to Julian's advantage to bring up the topic of Leathwaite's successor whilst there was someone else present. The 'great man' might find it embarrassing to dismiss Julian's entreaties or to bring up his drinking in the company of another. Spinning on his heels, Julian strode over to his boss and did his best to smile. The young man who had been talking to

Leathwaite stepped back slightly to allow Julian into the conversation.

'What a wonderful optic collection. It must have taken you years.'

Leathwaite's eyes narrowed just a little. Turning to the young man, he said, 'Do you two know each other?'

'I don't think so,' said the young man, holding out an expensively manicured hand. 'Sam Evans.'

'My literary agent,' Leathwaite said. 'Sam, this is Julian Settle.'

'*Dr* Settle. I work with the professor,' Julian said, extending a hand, which Evans shook without making eye contact.

'Sam has just sold my memoir, *Eye on the Prize*,' Leathwaite cut in. He was tipsy but not yet altogether drunk. 'Ten underbidders, wasn't it?'

'Eleven, I believe,' Evans said.

Leathwaite heaved a humblebragging shrug as if to say 'who knew?' then smiled in such a self-satisfied manner it made Julian want to deck him. 'So it looks like I'll be spending the first six months of my retirement glued to my desk.' He nodded to a heavy mahogany librarian's desk in the bay window.

Julian's eyes tracked over and landed on Emma, who was now standing next to a young man. They were laughing and Emma was flicking her honey-toned hair.

As Leathwaite droned on about his illustrious career – the fact that he counted famous artists and royalty among his patients, his pioneering work in the favelas of São Paulo – a small hard bead shot up Julian's back and bloomed into a spasm at his shoulder. Remembering what was at stake and bracing himself, he said to Leathwaite, 'I was wondering if we might have a word?'

Leathwaite craned forward and gazed at Julian as if he had just asked something unfathomable. Beside him, Evans sensed an awkwardness in the air and seemed keen to leave the two men to it, but Leathwaite stayed him.

'What do you think of the view? Magnificent, isn't it?' he said to Evans.

Julian looked over at Emma again, now taking a glass of champagne from the young man.

'Amazing,' Evans said nervously.

Leathwaite smiled and, fixing his gaze on Julian, said, 'Oh, you've spotted Rodrigo. I brought him over from São Paulo. He's staying with me for a week or two, working on his English. *Very* charming young man.'

'What an incredible life you've had, Stephen,' Evans said, trying to steer the conversation back onto safer ground.

'If we could have that word?' Julian said, this time more insistently. 'It's about the board.'

Leathwaite beckoned to a waiter and pointed to Evans's now empty glass but did not offer Julian a drink. It was humiliating, this very obvious snub, especially in front of a young man like Evans. Somewhere in Julian's chest anger began to buzz, like a mad bee.

'We must launch the book here next year,' Evans went on.

'Oh, that would be rather rubbing it in, wouldn't it?' Julian said. His hostility was a dark comet on an unstoppable trajectory. He knew he needed to calm down but couldn't figure out how to do it.

'It would?' said Evans, a little uncertainly.

'Well, I should think so. They say the eyes are a window to the soul. It's a bit of a cliché but, like most clichés, it has a grain of truth about it. A few months from now the windows to Stephen's soul will be all but opaque. Isn't that right, Stephen? The view will be rather lost on you.'

Evans stiffened. Leathwaite evidently hadn't told the younger man. Leathwaite had kept the news from his colleagues too. Everyone assumed the great man was retiring because he was of an age and had other things to do. But Julian had spotted the telltale squint, the slight blundering of his boss's hand as he reached for his coffee in the morning. Choroideremia, he guessed, a rare genetic condition mostly affecting men. Untreatable and progressive. Oh yes, Julian had guessed Professor Sir Stephen Leathwaite's secret. The great ophthalmologist was rapidly going blind.

The sides of Leathwaite's lips turned upwards for a second; then his jaw tensed and a steeliness came onto his face.

'I think you've had one too many glasses of champagne, Julian. Perhaps it's time to go home, though it's going to be rather hard to wrest your wife away from Rodrigo, isn't it?' He gave a slow smile. 'Now, if you'll forgive me, I must see to my guests.' And with that he turned and walked away.

Evans followed Leathwaite, leaving Julian alone. Despite the tremble in his legs, the feeling of being unsolid, of having somehow dissolved, Julian made it back to the bay window and, reaching out a hand, slid his arm around his wife's waist. In the time he'd been away, Emma had evidently been knocking back the champagne. He could feel a familiar unsteadiness.

'My wife and I were just leaving,' he said, addressing himself to the young man.

Emma stepped away from his arm. 'Don't be silly, darling, we only just got here. Rodrigo was promising to teach me the samba later.'

There was a momentary unravelling, as if a tiny stitch had come undone in the social fabric, before, with his hand outstretched, Rodrigo said, 'Dr Settle, I'm so pleased to meet you. Emma has told me you're Stephen's replacement. Congratulations.' The young man was tightly muscled and wearing a figure-hugging T-shirt emblazoned with a palm tree logo. He spoke in unexpectedly fluent English, with only the slightest burr on the S. It occurred to Julian that he might be Leathwaite's lover but the older man wasn't comfortable about introducing him as such. The professor had been divorced some years, and so far as Julian could recall, there had never been any mention of girlfriends. Yes, he felt sure this must be it.

'Thank you,' he said, relaxing.

'I was telling Rodrigo he should come for supper while he's here.'

A sharp spike blazed across Julian's brain. A little flare going off. He no longer felt threatened by Rodrigo, but there were limits. He wasn't prepared to encourage Emma's flirtations with other men, even those that were clearly going nowhere. 'We live far out, in the sticks, really. I'm sure Rodrigo wouldn't …'

'That is, if we can drag him away from this view,' Emma said, choosing to ignore her husband.

'London is beautiful,' Rodrigo said. 'So much people coming and going. There is a woman on the fourteenth floor of that office building next to the bridge, every morning she takes a picture of her daughter from her bag and puts it on her desk. It's touching. I watch her, sometimes I wave, but she doesn't see me.' Rodrigo pointed to one of the new towers jutting like jagged teeth from the skyscape about twenty metres away. From where they were standing in Leathwaite's drawing room, it would be impossible to pick out anything as detailed as a photograph.

'Oh, a spot of Latin magic realism, how charming,' said Julian, pretending to be amused. 'Still, it's a nice thought.'

Rodrigo looked puzzled. 'Every day she is with the picture. The girl looks just like her. There, in that office above the blue light. The one with the movie poster on the wall. *In Your Eyes*.'

'God, I loved that film,' Emma said, in a tone of thinly disguised resentment, turned to Julian and added, 'You wouldn't come, remember, so I went with Steph.'

Julian oriented his sight to the blue light and peered upward. He could feel his focus narrowing, his interest in the young man moving into sharper view.

'What else can you see?'

Rodrigo shrugged. 'A cleaner at the back of the room. But she is not working, she is eating a packet of potato chips.'

Julian peered again then opened his eyes wide and finally made a pinhole with the index finger and thumb of his right hand. It was impossible that Rodrigo could see that far and in such detail. There was a possibility Rodrigo was lying, of course, but Julian thought not. He could see a slight shading, a blur of something moving in the room. A tick started up in his chest. He'd almost forgotten about Leathwaite now. Scanning the room, he spotted among the optical antiques an old telescopic magnifier of the kind that used to assist patients with low vision. He went over and picked it up, brought it back to the bay window and, using the blue light to fix on, gazed through the lens. He could just see a human figure, or at least, he guessed it was a human figure, but as to the details, nothing. He felt a fluttering in his throat. If what Rodrigo was saying was true, at a rough estimate the man had 20/3 vision, about the same as the average hawk.

'Have you always been able to see like this?' he said.

Rodrigo shrugged. 'I guess it got like this after the accident.'

'Accident?'

'Car crash. I hurt my head a little bit, not much.'

A hollow thump landed in Julian's gut. In his peripheral vision, he could see Leathwaite showing a group of guests one of his antique ophthalmoscopes. Turning back to the young man, he gazed steadily at his eyes. The sockets were of average size for a man of his build and age, the crease pattern and fat deposition around the upper eyelid typical of someone of Caucasian origin. The pupils were large, but not unusually so given the low lighting, the sclera normal so far as it was possible to determine, the cornea bright and hydrated but unremarkable, and the irises brown and somewhat lipochromic, with a small and distinct darkened coloboma in the right iris, but nothing that would account for the man's remarkable vision. In all his years as an ophthalmologist, Julian had only ever seen, at best, 20/10 vision. All the research so far suggested that 20/8 was the limit of the human eye. The man standing before them was a biological impossibility, a miracle.

'Does Stephen know about the office, I mean, about what you can see?' Was it possible that, with his own sight failing, Leathwaite hadn't yet spotted his guest's extraordinary vision?

Rodrigo shrugged. 'I don't think so. He's never mentioned it. Why, should I tell him?'

'Absolutely not,' Julian said hastily; then, so as not to spook his new acquaintance, he went on, 'I mean your eyesight is very good, so you hardly need a doctor, do you? As Emma said before, we'd love to have you over. Any time. Next week perhaps?'

Rodrigo said that would be nice and they swapped phone numbers; then Julian took his wife by the elbow and eased her from the drawing room and out into the street.

In an Uber on the way home, Emma said, 'Why were you so keen to leave? Did it go OK with Leathwaite?'

'Yes, just not the right time or place to discuss the handover. There didn't seem any point in staying.'

'Rodrigo's fun, isn't he?'

'You certainly seemed to be enjoying him,' Julian said.

Emma huffed and rolled her eyes. 'Don't be so silly. Anyway, *you* invited him over, if you remember.'

Julian spent most of Sunday thinking about his new discovery. He had a good feeling about it. A man with the natural vision of a raptor. An actual living human hawkeye. Screw Leathwaite. Screw the crappy departmental chair. This had Nobel Prize potential. His fingers trembled as he tapped in the digits. The line clicked then rang almost immediately to voicemail. Julian felt himself slump. He had hoped to speak to the man directly. Leaving his address, he suggested Rodrigo come round the following evening.

By Monday afternoon, with his call still unreturned, Julian rang again and, trying not to sound irritated, left a cheery message to say that he and Emma were hoping to see him later, but in case he couldn't make it, they were free any evening that week or indeed at the weekend and were looking forward to seeing him. When Monday evening came and went without a response, Julian even considered asking Leathwaite to convey the message to his lodger, then decided against it. Instead, on Tuesday morning, he sent Rodrigo a text, and at lunchtime he received a reply from the younger man apologizing for not getting back sooner and saying he would call later.

All evening Julian sat clutching his phone. Finally, at around 9.30, he asked Emma to call Rodrigo. They were in the living room after supper, drinking as usual.

'Do I have to?' Emma said, in her cups.

'Really? You two seemed to get on so well,' Julian said. He'd decided not to tell Emma his real reason for wanting to be in touch.

Emma yawned and stretched. 'I s'pose, but who cares? I thought he was a bit creepy actually. A bit starey.'

'What about the samba?' Julian said, noting the edge of panic in his voice and trying to calm himself. 'Wouldn't that give you something fun to do in the day when I'm at work?'

Emma rolled her eyes. 'Oh, all right, then,' she said, holding out a hand for Julian to fetch her phone.

But Rodrigo didn't answer her that night or the following day. Julian was beginning to feel genuinely worried. In his excitement at meeting the human hawkeye, he hadn't slept more than a couple of hours since Leathwaite's party and had caught himself drinking more than usual. Even Emma, who didn't normally notice such things, said she thought he seemed on edge and asked whether he was anxious about taking on Leathwaite's role.

'Yes,' he said, 'that's it.'

'Think of all that money,' Emma said.

Julian was not generally a cynic when it came to his wife, but it was hard not to pick up the subtext of this remark. In the days since encountering Rodrigo, he'd allowed himself to map out a fantastical future filled with gongs and prizes and the admiration both of his peers and of a constant flow of lovely young women, and he was determined not to let his Hawkeye – as he'd come to think of Rodrigo – slip through his grasp.

A week and a half went by without any further contact from Rodrigo, during which Julian thought he might be going mad. On Thursday morning he decided to take action. He had breakfast and kissed Emma goodbye as usual, but instead of taking his habitual route into work, he got on the tube to Waterloo and made his way along the South Bank to Leathwaite's townhouse, swigging the half bottle of Bell's he'd bought at a corner shop as he walked, and by the time he rang the doorbell, he was full of righteous anger at Leathwaite, at Rodrigo, even at Emma.

There was a long wait followed by a shuffling sound before a voice – Leathwaite's – said, 'Howell, is that you?'

The name set Julian aback. Howell Sumner had been a contemporary of Leathwaite's in the ophthalmology department but had gone off and built himself a trailblazing career in new surgical techniques at Harvard. Evidently, he'd returned.

Julian mumbled to get Leathwaite to open the door.

'One minute,' Leathwaite said.

A chain clanked, followed by a series of bolts. A bit over the top, Julian thought, though, if *he* owned a house like this – what was it worth, ten, fifteen million? – and all those antiques … when he thought about it, Julian was surprised there wasn't a camera too. Then again, his boss was rather old-school.

At last the door opened and Leathwaite's face appeared. He was wearing a pair of dark wraparound glasses and it took him a moment to see that it was Julian not Howell at the door, by which time Julian had stepped into the hallway.

'You've got a damn nerve,' Leathwaite said when he realized who it was. 'Please leave.'

'I've come to see Rodrigo.'

Leathwaite started then frowned. 'What on earth is your business with *him*?'

'As you said, it's my business.'

'Well, he's not here,' Leathwaite said, one hand on the door, the other making a sweeping motion as if to waft Julian back out onto the street.

'I'll wait.'

Leathwaite had turned his back to the door and was facing Julian. His jaw was tight, but Julian could not see behind the glasses to the expression in his eyes. 'Rodrigo's gone. He won't be returning. Now please leave before I call the police.'

'No,' said Julian, backing farther from the door until he found himself beside the staircase. He sounded petulant and silly, he knew, but he'd already written the script. He needed Rodrigo. Was nothing without him. 'Not until you give me his contact details in …' He stopped, his tongue a dead snake. At the top of the stairs where they gave onto the first-floor landing, he could see a T-shirt emblazoned with a palm tree slung over the bannister. In an instant he was at the top of the stairs. He heard Leathwaite following behind him, panting and shouting. There were three doors, two leading into what looked like bedrooms, and one giving onto the drawing room. Julian darted from one to the other, but there was no sign of Rodrigo.

He was in the drawing room now, surrounded by Leathwaite's collection of early ophthalmoscopes and surgical paraphernalia, the bay window dominated by the dome of St Paul's. Spots of light danced before his eyes like fireflies and his head felt as if it might erupt. He spun on his heels, only to find Leathwaite in the doorway, blocking his exit.

'For chrissakes, calm down, man, you're making a fool of yourself. Rodrigo left one or two bits and pieces behind, but I assure you he's gone.'

A terrible thought arose in Julian's mind. Leathwaite had found out, he knew about Hawkeye, perhaps Rodrigo had relayed the conversation at the party, and now Leathwaite was keeping the human hawk for himself.

Julian felt himself lurch forward and, as if he were being propelled by an unknown force, he reached for the telescopic magnifier he had first seen at Leathwaite's retirement party. Grasping it in his right hand, he was dimly aware of its cold weight bearing down rhythmically on his left palm. He could see Leathwaite hesitate, not knowing how to respond. The professor was older and weaker and most likely able to see only the outline of Julian's body and the telescope in his hand. For an instant Julian thought he was about to surrender when a loud roaring sound burst from Leathwaite's mouth and he began to come at Julian with his arms punching the air. Julian waited till he was close enough then grabbed him around the waist and tried to pull him down. There was a struggle for a moment. Leathwaite was powerful despite his age, but Julian managed to sling an arm around his opponent's neck and, twisting it, sent Leathwaite tumbling. The old man's glasses scooted across the parquet floor.

Leathwaite lay on his side, panting and groaning, his forehead resting on the floor. Julian stood over him, telescope in hand. Leathwaite turned his head to look at his enemy.

'You're drunk,' Leathwaite said. 'Go away before you do something you'll regret.'

'Yes,' Julian said. He was buzzing now from the heady mix of adrenaline and whisky. 'Yes, I am. I am drunk. To be accurate, I am bloody drunk and bloody murderous, so don't push me, don't make me.'

Julian had been watching Leathwaite's hands, but his gaze now fell on the old man's face. It was then he saw beneath the wrinkled lids of Leathwaite's eyes, shining brown irises, somewhat lipochromic and in the right iris a small, distinct and unmistakable darkened coloboma.

The old man raised himself up onto one elbow and looked directly at Julian through those tremendous, miraculous, human hawkeyes. This time Leathwaite's secret really *was* out though Julian already knew he would never be able to divulge it.

'As I said, Rodrigo left a couple of things behind.' Leathwaite's voice was calm now and the faintest smile played around his lips. 'So do go ahead, Julian, if you're feeling so murderous. Murder me.'

NANA

HELEN SMITH

She called out in the darkness, but there was no answer. How long before the body in the chair next to her began to decompose? How long before whatever had got him, got her?

Help would come, she had to believe that. It might not be official help from the government. But there must be others who had survived due to their cunning, or because of some quirk of nature, protected by their genes. They would team up, form an alliance to use the skills they had. Some would have medical knowledge, others would be good at hunting. What would her role be? She'd need to claim something for herself – something interesting – before she was assigned to a brothel, tasked with repopulating the world. She could be an investigator, a detective. Looking for clues, piecing things together. What had she wanted to be when she was younger? Now was a chance to reinvent herself.

She called out again in the darkness, but still no one answered.

She was in better shape than the man in the chair, but that wasn't much to celebrate. Her legs ached. Her mouth was dry. Her brain was fuzzy. She had a blanket over her knees, and under that she was holding a knife in case she should need it for her defence – against whom, she wasn't quite sure yet – but her hands were trembling and the grip on the knife was weak.

She tried to get her thoughts in order. If she could come up with the right questions, then she could try to find the right answers. So what were the questions?

First, was there an antidote? No! *First*, she needed to know what ailed her. Then she needed to know if there was an antidote. Then she needed to know if she was the only survivor.

She drew up her knees slightly, under the blanket. Every bone ached. Her stomach hurt. She couldn't seem to get warm, and yet her bones and her kidneys burned, as if someone had set fire to her from the inside. Whatever it was, this thing had taken hold of her and was consuming her. She had no idea how long it might be before the end would come. She had no idea if it would begin to hurt so much that she would welcome death – if she would start begging to trade places with her friend in the next chair.

Was help on its way? That was another question.

Had others been here with her? Had they formed a search party and gone out looking for food and medicine? Or had they abandoned her, vulnerable and alone and in pain, to be picked off by enemy soldiers, or marauding gangs of thieves? Was this what society had become? A place where sick women were left behind to be raped and murdered, while the stronger ones went out in the world to find a better situation for themselves?

No, she had to believe that help would come.

She was very thirsty now. There was a sour, chemical taste in her mouth. Around her, the smell of decay. She needed to pee, but she was afraid of getting up in the darkness ... afraid of what she might see out there. Were there others, like the man in the chair? If she was the only survivor, would she be expected to bury the bodies? That would be the decent thing to do, especially if they were contagious.

She sniffed and wondered if the smell of decay was getting stronger. Urine, blood, faeces, the smell of something rotten. The smell of death. She would make a pile of the bodies, hauling them into the centre of the room here and setting fire to them, before heading outside to find help. Then if she was too weak to go anywhere, or in too much pain, she could lie down on top of it and end it all with them.

Which would she prefer? Death by fire or death by drowning? Drowning would be better, but where was the nearest lake or river? She didn't fancy flushing her head down the toilet and trying to do away with herself that way. And now she wished she hadn't brought to mind flushing toilets, because she still needed to pee.

She could set fire to the bodies, sit back down in this chair and close her eyes and die from smoke inhalation. But then there would be no evidence, no chance of finding what had happened to them. Perhaps she should take on the role of guardian to the dead, preserving the scene of the crime, preserving the flesh of the victims.

What else was she fit for, really, in her condition? What *was* her condition? She let go of the knife and felt carefully up and down her body for tender spots, pressing gently, rhythmically, with the flat of her hand, then touching her clothes with the tips of her fingers, testing for warmth and damp.

The female body was a leaky ship at the best of times, oozing blood or milk or other secretions, depending on the circumstances. But there was no sign of any of that today. There were no wounds or sores. She was falling apart slowly, disintegrating from the inside, the victim of some kind of disease or poisoning.

Which would be worse? Plague or chemical warfare? That was another question. She didn't have time for an answer because there was a sound outside. An intruder? Or maybe help was finally coming. What if it was the wrong kind of help – a task force sent to despatch all the diseased people for the common good? She kept quiet, not wanting to give anything away until she was sure.

The door opened slowly. A figure stood in the doorway, feeling for the light switch. She had a few moments to assess the threat. He had a masculine stance, short hair. Youngish, fit. No uniform, so he wasn't a soldier. But even if she weren't so sick, he would easily win against her in a fight.

She needed to find that knife. She crept her fingers forward under the blanket, along her right thigh, trying to keep the rest of herself immobile. Where *was* it? She probed methodically down the side of the cushion. *Where's my knife?* She didn't want to draw attention to herself but she felt so vulnerable and afraid, she thought she might cry.

The light went on, flooding the room, giving more clues to her surroundings. It was an awful place. Ugly carpets, ugly chairs. She wondered if it was a sanatorium. Perhaps she'd been sent here when she'd first started showing signs of sickness. She couldn't imagine coming here willingly, though if there was food in the kitchen, and lights and water were working, she might have been drawn here by those, hoping to take refuge temporarily. One thing she knew: she didn't want to stay.

The new arrival wasn't carrying a weapon – or none that she could see. No weapon, no medical paraphernalia. He might be an ordinary member of the public, frightened and on the run. Could she trust him?

Eyes half-closed, sitting as still as she could, she played dead. If he was dangerous and he thought he'd found *two* bodies in here, he might move on.

She watched as he went over to the man in the chair, leaning in and listening, or smelling. Close enough to touch, but not touching. Perhaps he was afraid of contagion. If she decided to trust him, she mustn't let him know how sick she was. Ordinarily, it would be selfish to keep her symptoms concealed. But these weren't ordinary circumstances. Besides, if she was in quarantine, he was the one who had broken it.

He was moving towards her now. She watched him through the fringe of her eyelashes, trying not to feel agitated. She took shallow breaths so her chest moved imperceptibly. She willed her eyelids to keep from flickering.

He crept closer. The hairs stood up on her arms, her heart beat faster, and she reacted in spite of herself. She knew that if you rehearse something in your mind, it makes it easier to do it in real life. She rehearsed her next move now, rearing up, plunging the knife up and under his ribs, into his heart. In rehearsal she was a fighter, agile and strong. But she hadn't been able to find the knife. It was down the side of the seat cushion somewhere. Her spirit was willing. But her body was weak and it had let her down. Trembling, uncoordinated, without a weapon, she shrank from him, frightened.

She opened her eyes wide and stared at him, trying to convey defiance rather than piteousness. He was shocked, and then he was sorry, she could see that. He took a step away from her. 'I thought you were cold. I was going to pull the blanket up.'

She trembled at the mention of the cold. She still needed to pee. She was thirsty. And her friend was dead and she needed to find out who – or what – had killed him. Her hierarchy of needs was in that order and she wasn't going to feel embarrassed about it.

He took a step closer again. When confronting a potential attacker, you have to talk to them. It humanizes you. It makes it more difficult for them to harm you. She didn't know what day it was, or where she was, or how long she had left to live, but she had this fragment of memory, a woman's guide to self-preservation.

She nodded over at the body in the chair. 'Somebody's husband or brother or son.'

'Yes,' he agreed.

She still didn't know if she could trust him, but he didn't seem to be about to harm her. He could have done by now, if that's what he wanted. Perhaps her humanizing tactic was working.

If she chose her next words carefully, she could find out what he knew, without betraying how little she knew herself. If confusion was a symptom, she didn't want to let on how she was feeling. She wanted to show that she was resourceful, that she could be useful on the outside, if he would only help her get outside.

'We should put him in the fridge,' she said. 'Until the others come.'

He seemed surprised at that, as if he wasn't used to women having good ideas.

She laid it out for him, in case he hadn't understood. 'The cold will preserve the evidence. They might want to take tissue samples.'

'They?' He looked baffled.

'Rescuers. The government.'

He was quiet for a moment. He had bad news and he was wondering how to break it to her. She could see it on his face. When he spoke, his voice was soft, his eyes full of pain. 'Do you know the name of the Prime Minister?'

She didn't … So that was it! With no leader, the country would be in chaos. Help was not on its way. There was no one in a bunker, making plans to rebuild the country. There were no soldiers driving around, handing out medicine to the old and the sick. She'd known it all along, really.

He looked ready to give up. But she was not. She would inspire him with her bravery and determination. 'We will find an antidote. Our friend in the chair may be dead, but it's not too late for us.'

That look on his face. Something close to pity. He put a weird, fake smile on his face. 'He's not *dead*. He's only sleeping.'

What was it about men that made them want to protect women? Life was about making choices. Even now, staring death in the face, she wanted to make choices. She wanted to find an antidote. She wanted to *live*. How could she find out how to live if young men went about saying that dead people were only sleeping?

'It's not just about you and me,' she explained. 'If we can find out what happened to him, we might be able to help the others.'

He was irritated now. 'What others? There are no others.'

Were they really the only survivors? She'd known it was possible, but hearing him say it upset her. In her mind, she was strong, a fighter. But here was her body letting her down again. She couldn't stop the tears.

'Oh,' he said. 'Hey, I'm sorry. I'm sorry. I don't know what to say to you to make it better.' He went quiet for a moment, thinking about it. 'You know what? He *is* dead.'

She nodded. She had control of herself now. He looked relieved.

She faced him calmly. 'And the others? There must be others.'

He misunderstood. She wanted survivors. He thought she wanted dead bodies. 'There are others – loads of them, piled up outside, decomposing.'

'Oh yes. That makes me feel *a lot* better.'

He stared at her, to see if she was serious. But of course she was joking. What else can you do in that type of situation but try to make a joke of it?

He was a kind boy, with a kind face. She couldn't think of anyone else she'd rather have by her side in the aftermath of a global catastrophe. When she had recovered, the two of them would team up and go outside and save the world. If the cities had crumbled, they would rebuild them. If there were no hospitals, they would work together to create an antidote. There *must* be other survivors out there, with specialist skills and knowledge. They would find them. She just needed to rest here for a few minutes, and then they could be off.

'What's your name?' she asked.

He looked upset then. His face crumpled a little. She realized he might be in pain. If the body in the chair was at stage three, and she was stage two, he could be at stage one. Whatever symptoms he had, he would be trying to hide them, just as she had. He might not even know his name.

'Why don't you sit down?' she said kindly. His legs were probably hurting.

But he shook his head, squidging his mouth up, which made his face look sad. 'Robert,' he said. 'My name's Robert.'

'Well, Robert, it's you and me against the world.'

Her tongue was thick in her mouth where she was thirsty, and she found it difficult to get the words out. But he understood perfectly. He grinned at her.

Just smiling can help take the pain away. That much she remembered. She grinned back and already she felt better.

He perked up when he saw that her mood had improved. He was solicitous, suddenly. 'I should have brought you a water. You want a drink of water? Or a nice cup of tea?'

So British! Even in a crisis, there was this belief that a nice cup of tea could solve anything. Plague, chemical warfare, zombie apocalypse. Whatever they were facing, they would face it together with a nice cup of tea.

'I *would* like a cup of tea.' The pressure on her bladder was almost unbearable now. But she was finally reassured that he wasn't going to club her to death if he saw how ill she was – not if he was suffering from the same condition. She could risk the walk to the bathroom. 'I'll just go and freshen up, first.'

He reached out to take her arm.

'I can manage,' she said primly. But as she stood, her legs buckled under her.

He gripped hold of her under her arm and walked with her. As they drew level with the body in the chair, Robert swiped the walking stick that was hooked over the back of it, and offered it to her.

There was a loud snort, then the corpse shifted slightly and collapsed back on itself.

'Whoa!' said Robert. 'Watch out. I think he's reanimating.'

'You don't think he's a *zombie*, Robert?'

She had heard that air escapes from the body after a person dies, and the sound can be alarming. But this seemed more like ordinary snoring …

He didn't say *I told you so*. 'Maybe he wasn't dead in the first place?'

True. In which case the snoring and the sudden movement were reassuring. If the man in the chair was now at stage four – the recovery stage – then it was only a matter of time before she reached it, too. In a few hours, she would be feeling better. She felt as if she could skip across the room. In her mind, she turned cartwheels.

'You've cheered up!' said Robert.

'Looking forward to getting to the bathroom,' she joked. Though there was a part of her that wondered if she would make it in time. She shouldn't have left it so long. She really was desperate.

'Nothing as satisfying as a good, long pee,' Robert agreed. 'Apart from a nice cup of tea, and a hot bath. And a cigarette.'

'You shouldn't smoke,' she grumbled. 'It's bad for you. I need you in good health for when we get out of here.'

'You and me against the world!'

'Exactly. You know what's *good* about this situation? We can reinvent ourselves. We can be anything we want to be. We can be heroes.' She would have liked to stop still when making this declaration, for a more impressive effect, but she had to keep shuffling forward, because she needed to reach the bathroom with great urgency. The journey across the room seemed almost heroic. Pain in the feet, the hips, the bladder.

Robert opened the door for her and manoeuvred her through it. How could she have thought he was here to hurt her? There was so much good in him.

'You're my hero,' she told him.

He kissed the top of her head. 'You're my hero, too, Nana.'

HOW WAS THAT FAIR?

LOUISE VOSS

In the four nights since John was offered his unsolicited mission in the park toilets, he had dreamed about the body so many times that now he dreaded closing his eyes. The nightmare always started with him driving towards his victim, foot to the floor, eyes squeezed shut as his target loomed up in the middle of the road. Then the moment of impact, and the body spun up into the air.

Each time the nightmare recurred, John's subconscious embellished the appearance of the spinning body: one night it turned from a shimmer of sequins into a dead fox, snuffed-out roadkill; the next night, a ballerina, the body pirouetting in a pink tutu and blocked pointe shoes.

John always woke sweating and scratching, the flakes of psoriasis an embodiment of his fear, drifting down onto the stale blue polyester sheets. There was no way he was doing this, he thought. It was insane! He'd never get away with it. He would just hand in the money and forget about it.

But then – what had he got to lose? If he didn't do it,

he'd never see his kids. If he couldn't afford a better place to live soon, Ashleigh had flatly said they wouldn't be allowed to visit him any more. And she was the one who wanted a divorce! How was that fair?

He was sure she'd been seeing someone else before she finally gave him his marching orders – the number of times she'd gone out on some flimsy pretext and not come back till the early hours, stinking of booze and a particularly noxious aftershave – although she always denied it. He'd told her, over and over, he would battle her to the death for custody of the twins.

Bitter thoughts swirled round and round in his head like water flushing down a toilet: all night in his dreams, all day in the van; trudging in and out of public conveniences with his bin-freshening granules and his rubber gloves; waiting for Friday, to see if he'd have the courage to go through with it.

It had happened four days earlier, on a bone-chillingly damp morning, when he'd pulled open the door to his thirteenth ladies' toilet on that shift. It was his least favourite of all the pickups – he had to leave the van a good hundred feet away in the car park and, once he'd emptied the bins, carry the full plastic bags back across the muddy parkland.

''Ello?' he'd called out, as he always did when heading into public loos. 'Anyone in here?'

There was no reply, so he stepped inside, his eyes adjusting to the dank gloom. All the green cubicle doors were open, bar one in the middle of the row. He was about

169

to head into the nearest to grab the bin's contents when he heard a hesitant voice:

'John?'

He froze. 'Who's that? How do you know my name?'

There was a pause. 'Well, of course I had to know your name; otherwise how would I know it's you?'

This made no sense. Her voice sounded quite posh, oldish and deep. He was sure it didn't belong to anybody he knew. It sounded a bit like Sandra from Accounts Payable – but what would Sandra be doing calling out to him from a bog cubicle?

He stared at himself in the mirror over the sink, scowling at the large round badge on his chest. It read '*Hi! I'm your Sani-Man. My name is JOHN*', with a yellow cartoon waving hand next to his name. Whose idea had it been to make a man dress up in head-to-toe grey polyester just to empty used tampons out of sanitary bins? As it if wasn't humiliating enough to start with. But he'd needed a job.

'Anyway,' said Not-Sandra. 'Let's make this quick – I don't want anyone else to come in and find you here. Was there anyone around outside?'

'Er … no,' John said.

'And you're definitely up for this? Our go-between said you were the best in the business.'

'Er … yeah?'

'OK. Good. I've got the first three grand in here – I'll leave on top of the bin. It's in a Jiffy bag. I think it's best you don't see my face, so when we're done talking, if you go into the end bog, count to ten to give me time to get out, then nip back into this one and pick up the cash. Oh, and you'll need this. He's a drag queen. This is him dressed as his alter ego, Patty O'Furniture. He hangs out at the Calypso Club every Friday night. You won't even need to go inside, he – she – comes out every fifteen minutes for a fag. Then he walks down to the cab rank about 2 a.m.'

In the mirror, John saw his eyebrows involuntarily shoot up. His forehead stopped itching. Three grand? Patty O'Furniture?

He heard the woman's knees give a sharp crack, and a photo slid out from her side of the toilet door. It was a creased snap that looked, at first glance, like an attractive woman, with a mass of blond curls, a blue sequinned dress and too much make-up. John studied it more closely and noticed the square jaw, the big hands holding a matching blue drink in a cocktail glass.

'I've put my mobile number on the back – you need to text when you've done it, and then I'll get the other seven grand over to you once I've seen it in the papers … He's an evil psychopath, so don't you feel any sympathy for him. He deserves everything he's going to get, after what he did to me. You'll be doing the world a favour.'

The other seven grand?

As the penny finally dropped, John had to lean against one of the sinks to steady himself.

Oh. Oh man. She thought he was … She actually thought he could …

He opened his mouth to say there'd been some misunderstanding, that he *was* John – but not *that* John. It was a coincidence, that was all. He hadn't meant to mislead her. Sorry for wasting her time, but he'd better slide this photo right back under, and –

What? Wait for the right John to show up? If the woman confessed to the real assassin that she'd messed up, then his own life might be in danger. And … ten thousand pounds! Three thousand right there on the other side of that door. Just think what he could buy with ten grand! He could afford to rent a much nicer gaff; get Ashleigh and social services off his back. He wouldn't lose the twins.

He made his decision. Putting on his gruffest voice, he said, 'That's fine. I know what I'm doing. Leave it to me. I'll scoot in this end one, give you time to get out.'

His fingers were trembling as he shot home the bolt on the end cubicle and crouched stupidly behind the door. Seconds later, the woman unlocked her own door and he heard quick footsteps fading to silence.

John headed straight for the cubicle she'd vacated. It smelled of perfume, something heavy and cloying, and when he picked up the swollen Jiffy bag on top of the Sani-bin, he smelled it even more strongly. It clashed with the air-freshener granules, the container of which he still held in his other hand.

He stood for a moment clutching both envelope and air freshener. He could still do the right thing – take the cash back to HQ and say he'd just found it, or hand it in to the police. Perhaps he'd get a reward or something. There was no point in leaving it there for someone else – or the right John – to find.

But where *was* the real John? He could be here at any moment unless the woman had got the wrong time. John zipped up the money inside his grey polyester jacket and methodically emptied and sanitised all the sanitary bins as hastily as he could before exiting with a clutch of bulging plastic liners in one hand and three thousand pounds next to his heart.

John spent that evening in his damp bedsit, staring at the piles of twenty-pound notes that he'd stacked on the kitchen counter and googling different methods of killing a stranger. Given the conditions he'd be working in, it seemed that a careful hit-and-run would be the best way – if caught, he always could claim it was an accident. It was unlikely he'd get more than one shot at it, whatever he did. As a precaution, he saved the number the woman had given him into his phone, under 'Plumber', and then burned in the sink the photo of Patty O'Furniture.

Around dawn, when he finally managed to get to sleep, he had the dream about Patty O'Furniture's blue-sequinned body for the first time, waking with it stuck in his head like the smell of rotting meat.

He couldn't do it. He couldn't actually kill someone!

But then he thought of the twins, their velvety skin and pealing giggles. They were all he had. He gritted his teeth.

He had to do it.

He rang into work that day, claiming he had a migraine. Then he drove to a nearby town, parked in the multi-storey and browsed charity shops until he found a mothball-scented black balaclava, which he purchased with a jigsaw puzzle of some kittens and a chipped vase, to detract attention from it. He got back in the car and cruised slowly around the outskirts of the town until he found a rusty old Honda abandoned near some remote garages, which he swiftly liberated of its number plates. He then drove out to the moors, pulled off the road and screwed the purloined plates on to his own ancient Fiesta before heading back into town via the Calypso Club and the taxi rank, to conduct a recce of the parking and CCTV situations.

No backing out now. It was kind of exciting, if he was honest.

By Friday at 9 p.m. he was as ready as he'd ever be. Adrenaline whooshed through him, from head to toe and back up again, and he felt as high as a kite as he parked up on the main road, at a discreet distance from the club. Every time he felt a pang of guilt or regret, he quashed it with a vague mental notion of *karma*. Patty O'Furniture was getting his comeuppance for his (unspecified) crimes. He, John, would be rewarded with enough money to be able to rent a new flat and not lose his kids.

For the first time since Ashleigh had claimed he was a loser and kicked him out – of the house that he'd bought! How was that fair? – John felt a sense of purpose. As he sat watching a series of gender-fluid people go in and out of the Calypso Club: men in drag teetering proudly in, fluffing their wigs and glossing their pouts; men not in drag scurrying in with their eyes darting from side to side; giggling fag-hags already swigging alcopops – he experienced something akin to happiness. Perhaps it was the party atmosphere he was witnessing – he had to admit, it looked like fun. Ashleigh had often suggested he dressed up in her undercrackers just for a laugh, since they were the same sort of size and build (he was slight) but he'd always felt too shy to do it. Then she accused him of being boring, unadventurous and weedy, and chucked him out of his own house.

Ha, he thought. She wouldn't think him weedy and dull any more, not if she could see what he was about to do. He felt like a real man.

There was no sign of Patty O'Furniture for ages. John was starting to get worried, when suddenly the door swung open and there he was, on the pavement, lighting up, just as the woman in the loos had said he would. He was even wearing the same dress as in the photograph.

John had to admit that Patty made a hot woman. Patty's hips were curvy and his bust looked almost natural, if you didn't already know. For a moment, John's resolve wavered. What if Patty scored tonight and took someone home? Would it be a man or a woman? John wasn't sure how these things worked.

Then he'd just have to do it next week, he thought. The woman in the loos hadn't put a time limit on it. But obviously, the sooner the better. Get it over with.

Patty came out several more times for more cigarettes, mostly alone but once with another drag queen, a much portlier one in a Dolly Parton wig. They were arguing, and at some point Patty slapped his hand against the brick wall in what looked like frustration. The next time he came out, he looked like he was crying. Perhaps feeling guilty about whatever he'd done to upset the woman in the loos, wondered John.

John found that as the night hours crept past, he became ever calmer and more focused. Maybe he'd found his vocation in life. He stopped seeing Patty as a person and instead concentrated on the outcome. Was that what they called mindfulness? He wasn't sure, but whatever it was, it made him feel good.

People began leaving the club at around midnight, swaying and happy, some of them linking arms in pairs and singing. John smiled as he watched them. A deep peace had settled on him, and when Patty finally emerged at two-thirty, heading towards the cab rank, conveniently alone, John's hands weren't even shaking. He drove around the block, pulled on the balaclava and doubled back.

Patty had taken off his stilettos and was weaving gently along the pavement next to the park – the park housing the same toilets John had first met the woman in just five days earlier – trailing a high heel along the railings like a small child with a stick. There wasn't a soul in sight, nor another car on the road. No cameras winked at John from the tops of lamp posts.

This was it.

John took a deep breath, revved the engine and put his foot to the floor.

Obviously, it hadn't been pleasant. But even so, it had gone even better than he'd hoped. After removing the stolen number plates and dumping them, plus the balaclava, into a bin suitably far away from his bedsit and carefully checking the front of his car for damage and/or blue sequins, he went home and got into bed. He even managed a couple of hours' sleep that night, in which he didn't once have the nightmare about the spinning body. Seeing it in real life must have banished it. Perfect.

The only unknown was whether he'd managed to kill Patty or merely injure him. He was fairly sure it was mission accomplished – his last memory of the event had been a blur of sequins and the horrible crunch of bones being crushed between his bumper and the park railings – but he needed to be sure before he could claim the remaining seven grand. It would be most un-ideal if he had to give a repeat performance.

When he awoke, feeling remarkably refreshed, he checked the local news on his mobile. The headline was the first thing he saw – *Fatal Late Night Hit and Run on Park Road* – and he read the article with his heart in his mouth in case the police had any incriminating evidence. But there was nothing: no CCTV footage, no description of a car, no eyewitness accounts. He was clear!

He was about to text the number saved under 'Plumber' on his phone when the last sentence jumped out at him:

'The dead woman has been identified as 47-year-old Julie Sanderson. Her family has been informed.'

What? But Patty O'Furniture was a man! Who the hell was Julie Sanderson? Did Patty have a twin sister?

He hadn't got the wrong person. It was just not possible.

John had memorised every last pixel of that photograph.

With a very bad feeling in the pit of his belly, John texted the number the woman had given him: IT'S DONE. I WILL WAIT TO HEAR FROM YOU RE SETTLING UP. JOHN.

Maybe the woman in the loos had been mistaken. She'd been mistaken about his own identity, for a start, so perhaps she was one sandwich short of a picnic, hiring the wrong hit man for the wrong murder.

Oh shit, please don't let him have murdered the wrong person.

All his newfound positivity and calm evaporated, and the psoriasis on his hairline immediately flared up in a scarlet halo.

John spent the whole weekend staring at his blank phone, but there was no reply to his text, not even after he re-sent it twice. He paced around and scratched, scratched and paced, until his whole body was covered in itchy red welts and he started wishing that Patty O'Furniture had been the one driving at eighty towards him and a set of railings. He was too distraught to wonder, as he usually did, who was babysitting his twins while Ashleigh was out partying.

By Sunday night he was exhausted from waiting for a knock at the door – which thankfully never came – or the bleep of an incoming text.

He managed to go into work the following week, keeping judiciously silent when his colleagues discussed the murdering bastard who'd mown down a woman on her way home from a night out, as they unloaded bin bags from their vans at HQ and hurled them into the skip for incineration. Left behind a distraught husband and two motherless kiddies, the bastard had.

As the days passed, John's shock and horror changed to outrage. He didn't know how or why, but he'd been conned. Yes, he had three grand – but that wasn't enough to afford him a better flat, or any closer to being able to afford the sort of legal fees he'd need to find in order to take Ashleigh to court. He wished it had been *her* he'd run over.

In fact … now there was an idea … but the trouble with that would be that the police would immediately suspect him, and he was pretty sure he'd crack under interrogation.

No, for now he would have to concentrate on trying to track down the woman in the loo and get the rest of the money owed to him. He'd killed the person he'd been asked to kill. If her name (and gender) happened to be different, what of it?

That Friday night, he applied Betnovate in an extra thick layer on his forehead and waited for it to absorb before getting a cab over to the Calypso Club at 11 p.m., by which time he figured it would be busy enough for him to blend in. His nerves jangling, he queued up with the same characters he'd seen going in the previous week. It was weird, seeing them up close. He wondered if, had he seen Patty at close quarters, he would have clocked that she wasn't a man at all? Although in fairness, it was hard to tell which sex some of them were.

He paid his twelve-pound entry fee and found himself

inside a small working men's-type club, with a disco ball over the dance floor and a stage at one end. It was packed full of all sorts of people, a few men like himself in normal gear, but mostly transvestites and women of a certain age in short skirts. They were concentrated in a clump in front of the stage, where a shiny-suited compère was introducing an act.

'… so put your hands together in a warm Calypso Club welcome for my favourite and yours, the utterly divine Amanda Reckonwith! And what a trouper she is – give her a huge hand and let her know how much we support her and love her for being brave enough to come back so soon after last week's tragic events!'

Loud cheers and whoops as a stocky person in a white-blond Dolly Parton wig, a tangerine satin dress and an unmistakable five o'clock shadow waltzed onto the stage. It was the person that Patty had been arguing with outside the club the previous week.

'Good evening, darlings! Thank you all for your support. It means everything to me,' Amanda trilled before launching into some jokes about Botox and the price of Spanx. She sounded like someone John knew, but he couldn't think who. He was just about to go to the bar to order a drink when he remembered: oh yeah, Sandra from Accounts Payable.

Wait …

No, not Sandra from Accounts Payable.

Not-Sandra, from behind a toilet door.

John goggled in horror at the burly figure on the stage.

Surely not … but yes. It was the same voice, he was now certain. For a moment the floor began to spin below his feet as much as the disco ball was doing above his head.

He sat heavily down at the farthest table in the darkest corner to try to marshal his thoughts. This didn't mean he'd been taken for a ride, not necessarily – instead of being hired by a woman to kill a man, he'd been hired by a man to kill a woman – so what? What difference did it make? This revelation was actually a *good* thing, because now he had a fighting chance of getting the additional seven thousand pounds he'd been promised. Now he knew who to demand it from!

Of course, Amanda Reckonwith might turn out to be just that and deny ever having spoken to him before. But in that case, John thought frantically, he'd threaten to go to the police and have him arrested. Amanda and Patty – Julie – obviously had history of some kind.

As Amanda's act continued, to appreciative cheers from the audience, John staggered up to the bar and bought a double Scotch to calm his nerves.

Yes. That's what he'd do. Demand the money he'd been promised or go to the police. After all, Amanda still believed he, John, was a professional hit man. She wouldn't for a minute believe that a real hit man would grass her up.

Well, she – he – was in for a shock.

Amanda announced that she was going to finish with a song and launched enthusiastically into 'Big Spender' – which John thought was not without irony. The crowd joined in, and with every verse and chorus, John's head itched more urgently as the moment grew nearer. Finally, Amanda flounced off the stage to rapturous applause, disappearing out of sight through a door next to it.

John panicked momentarily. What if she got changed out of her costume and came back as a man? He wouldn't recognise him! John squeezed through the crowd and slipped through the same door.

Amanda was standing in a small backstage area made even smaller by a dozen boxes of crisps, ripping off his wig, revealing close-cropped dark hair covered up by a stocking cap. Under all the foundation and false eyelashes, he was a lot younger than he looked on stage. He was talking to another, slimmer man with a beard, in a suit, trilby hat and dark sunglasses, despite the backstage gloom.

'Oi, I want a word with you,' John said, the intolerable itching of his head dialling his righteous anger up to eleven. 'Where's that seven grand you owe me?'

'Dunno what you're on about, sugartits.'

But then Amanda laughed, a deep, guttural, forty-a-day laugh that made John think he knew exactly what he, John, was on about. Amanda plunged a hand into his cleavage and removed a lump of something jellylike from each of his bra cups, which he handed to his bearded companion, who stuffed one in each jacket pocket without comment.

'I'm going to the police if you don't hand it all over in the next twenty-four hours,' John said, trying to sound hard. 'You fucked up big time. You thought I was a hit man when really I was just the guy emptying the bins in those bogs. We just had the same name, that's all. But the job's done, and now I want the rest of the cash. Or I'll give in the first three grand and tell the cops everything – everything apart from the fact that it was me who carried out the hit, of course. They'll believe me and you'll be banged up.'

Neither Amanda nor his bearded friend seemed fazed by this. 'See, that's where you're wrong, *John*,' Amanda said, in that annoyingly husky voice, carefully placing his wig on a featureless bald polystyrene head that had been on the top box of crisps. 'You're the one who's gonna get banged up for murdering my missus, Julie.'

'Your – missus?' John was momentarily thrown by this.

''Cos unless you get your scrawny little arse out of my life and stop buzzing round me like a bluebottle, I'll be the one going to the police.'

'You?' John couldn't stop himself scratching at his hairline until he realised he probably looked like the skinny one out of Laurel and Hardy.

'You killed my missus, thinking it was me,' said Amanda, throwing the back of his hand theatrically to his brow.

John snorted. 'I have absolutely no reason to want to kill you – unless you don't pay up. That's insane. I don't even know you!'

Amanda smirked. 'Yeah, you do. You wanted to kill me 'cos I'm shagging your wife. You heard I was a tranny and you came down here and waited for me – but you got the wrong person and killed my Julie instead.'

'You *what*? Mate, you're off your head. My wife left me, as it goes. She might well be shagging someone, but there's no way it's you.'

'Why'd she leave you, then? For being unobservant?' jeered Amanda, and he and his companion both cracked up laughing.

For the first time, John looked at the companion. There was something familiar about his slight build, and the way he stood on one foot with the toes of the other foot resting on the ground behind him. As John watched, the guy lifted one hand – small, pale – to his face and took off the shades and the trilby before peeling off the beard in one quick rip. Then he slipped his free hand into Amanda's, giving it a tender squeeze before turning to John and speaking for the first time, in a voice that John knew all too well.

'Hello, John.'

At that moment John realised everything. It hadn't been a mistake, his getting approached in those loos. Amanda had known exactly the time he'd be there, exactly how badly he needed money to get Ashleigh off his back, and what lengths he'd go to in order to get it.

In return, they'd got *him* to dispose of the one obstacle in their way, at the cost of just three grand and no provable link to themselves.

'Hello, Ashleigh,' he said miserably, looking his triumphant ex-wife in the face.

How was that fair?

THE RETURN

D.E. MEREDITH

Officer Umwana was stuck in a quagmire, cicadas buzzing close to his eyes, and in the distance somebody was calling his name across the marshes. *Officer, officer …* He was trying to grab a bulrush and pull himself free of the bones, the squelching mud between his toes, straining to hear was it friend or foe coming towards him, an echo across the marshes, black shadows shimmering across the lake, whistles, drums amid a patchwork of moving green. Maybe the hills were coming alive with eyes not stones, mouths not ditches, coming ever nearer. *Officer, Officer Ummmmmwaaannnaaaa* the radio crackled him back into reality, the cold light of day still grey at this hour.

Officer 623 … are you …

He flailed around, dropping the receiver on the floor. He'd been asleep at the wheel, dreaming. But the ignition was off, glory be to God and Jesus loves me, he thought, making the sign of the cross. How many lives did he have left on this job? The car was in the middle of the road, for pity's sake. A truck could have flattened him, one of those juggernauts on its way to Tanzania full of contraband timber, coltan, gold. He was sweating as the radio spattered.

Officer 623, I repeat … Are you reading me?

He put the receiver to his mouth, his breath stale from the night shift and the *urwagwa* swigged from a coconut cup at the joint on the Boulevard Mandela, the last place he remembered.

Ai. Roger that. Yego.

I'm not waking you, am I? From your beauty sleep?

Oya. As if! As if I even need it.

He recognised the voice. It was Valentine, of course, so he gave a quick, sleepy sort of half glance in the wing mirror to check his beret was, although not perfect, miraculously still on his head. He must have nodded off, for what? Five minutes, if that. Wiping the sleep from his eyes, he yawned, stretching in the confines of the car. On the dashboard, the time was barely illuminated in this demi light, but his eyes were sharp, like a leopard's. 5:00 a.m.

Yampaye Inka!

That made him sit up. Five whole hours lost? Unbelievable. He was filled with shame that he should neglect his duty thus, but in his defence, it was his tenth night on the trot out on patrol.

Sorry to wake you, Officer 623. Long shift, oya?

He felt himself weaken, felt a tightness in his loins. They'd had a drink at the local cabaret just over a week ago, *on me* she'd said. He thought it might have been a glimmer of something, in her offering of the word *oya*, that he might have a bit of luck for a change, but then her brisk business voice was back, *Where are you, Officer 623?*

He glanced out of the window, at the river sluggish as ever, the marshes, the sky arching over it the colour of tin. *The bridge on the Nyamata road. Over.*

Bon. We have a major incident at the Hotel Boni Consilii. Over.

Incident? He didn't like that word. It was too vague. Or perhaps it was just the way she said it? A dubious, worrying second of hesitation.

The manager there has reported … another crackle. He pressed the button, the wire like a snake in his hand.

Pardon? Repeat, s'il vous plaît.

Bungalow three. In the grounds of the Boni Consilii. Are you listening, 623? Are you writing this down?

Dead. White. Male. Over.

White? Was it possible? The last dead tourist in Butare was decades ago. There had been trouble over the border in '92, of course, beheadings, terrible, a disaster, seven in all, swinging in the trees like monkeys. But Butare? So few tourists came here, almost none, if truth were known. All they got was NGO do-gooders, UN types, or coltan merchants raping the country of whatever was left. There was nothing for tourists. No gorillas in the mist, no lions, not even savannah. Just a bottomless lake, full of bilharzia and crocodiles. He was really awake now. So he switched the engine on, the car spluttering into life.

Ndaji! I'm on my way. Over.

Before you get there, Officer 623, the manager is very good friends, you know, with the committee, the bwana, the Big Man, ai? Monsieur Ernest ... the crackle came again.

He lost her for a second, foot on the gas, drowning her out, his focus no longer on Valentine nor who was who in this dreary little town, but on a card embossed with a dove, tucked behind his rear-view mirror. Virgin white, arcing its feathers in flight, symbolic of a brighter future, God, and the National Rwanda Police Force. It was a parting gift from his commander, a reminder that these days his duty was to ensure that *all* the people, whoever they were, whatever they'd done, were offered *Service. Protection. Integrity.* Wherever they came from, even if they were a word one didn't say any more, must never say again. *Ancient history, ai* ... He shook the past away, out of his head, like a cockroach in his ear. The clock clicked on. 5:02.

A dead *muzungu* meant one thing – hurry. So Umwana swung the car right, taking a short cut back to town, past a spreading acacia, bumping and juddering down an uneven track, every bone in his body feeling it. Out of the window, the dawn's rainbow light danced on the surface of the paddy fields, the irrigation channels, mercurial lines of silt. The ditches by the track no longer overflowed with broken shards of corrugated metal, discarded jerrycans, dirty ochre rags. Everything was beautiful. As God meant it to be. Squadrons of brightly coloured birds swooped across the water, petrol blue, saffron yellow, flashes of scarlet, bee-eaters nodded overhead on the telegraph wires, and a troop of talapoins stole fruit fallen into the road from the mango trees. Narrowly avoiding them, he swerved sharply, found the centre of the road again, and with just six minutes on the clock, shot out onto the glistening tarmac of Highway 7.

Two minutes later, Officer Umwana was pulling over in front of a sign that announced in foot-high lettering, The Hotel Boni Consilii. And underneath, even larger, STRICTLY FOR HOTEL GUESTS ONLY.

He got out of the car and, quieter than a papyrus breeze, whispered to himself that this place was … *encore plus belle. Paradis*. Nothing to remind him of home. Instead huge tropical gardens stretched before him, hibiscus and silver eucalyptus trees casting long, ponderous shadows across acres of lawn, criss-crossed with neat lines of bushes, gravel pathways bereft of weeds, so many flowers filling the well-tended beds, pyrethrum, spider lilies, lobster claws, the candy pink of lantana. *Ai, delightful*, he thought. To cultivate such beauty here, of all the places in the world? A sprinkler swished its helicopter blades around, thwump, thwump, thwump, and he dipped his head two seconds too late. But it was only soft, cool water that splashed across his face and shirt these days, not hot blood and anguish.

Even at this hour, old men gardeners were dotted about the grounds, bent over, earth coloured and earthbound, sweeping, raking and hoeing. Umwana passed through them and up a short flight of steps into the hotel reception.

Here air con hummed, and everything was strange and breezy, with whitewashed walls, white shades and shining floors. Muslin drapes billowed under the ceiling fans. God's Waiting Room, sparse and empty. And in keeping with its history, for this had been a mission once, a cross hung on the wall, a lurid depiction of Our Lady of Kibeho, her dark Ethiopian eyes following the long, thin shadow of Officer Umwana as he crossed towards a desk at the back of the lobby. Here a young woman sat alone and, seeing him, stood up, extending her hand, enquiring, '*Bonjour, monsieur?*' as though she didn't know who he was or why he was here, which was ridiculous. His policeman's dark blue shirt and slacks, black boots, a baton, the crackle of his two-way? Who the devil else would he be? He read in her face an underlying current of anxiety and flipped open his badge.

'Officer 623. At your service.'

First impressions? A returnee, he thought, from the diaspora, or a sophisticate from Kigali, an intellectual even, she was pale enough. She was about to say something when his radio crackled and a tinny voice filled the air. *Come in, 623. Are you reading me? Over.*

He shrugged an apology at the receptionist, with his schoolboy charm.

I'm here. Yes, already. I took a short cut. Oya. I can handle this. Over. No, Valentine, there's no need for backup. I know what I'm doing. Unlike the rest of those fools, he thought, amateurs. Backup from the traffic cops? Was she kidding him?

He turned his attention back to the young woman dressed not in a *bufu* but Western style. A cream chiffon blouse smothered in ruffles, so many it made her look like a strange bird of paradise, for she was a beauty, wasn't she? Pinned to the ruffles was a name tag, *Francine Mugiraneza, How May I Help You?* By answering my questions, he thought, his eyes running down her neat, well-put-together body to a red patent belt, a tight black skirt, the curve of her buttocks, and then her bare legs, smooth and glossy like the rest of her, very shapely indeed.

Those ruffles, like feathers. And like a bird caught in a trap, her chest was rising and falling rapidly, much too fast. Her pupils were dilated. Huge. He knew when people were under strain, when they were covering something up. It takes a liar to know a liar, his commanding officer said to him once, chucking him under the chin. But to be certain, he needed to touch her skin.

'Thank you for coming. This is a terrible business.' She shook her head. 'But before I take you to see …'

'The body?'

'What's left of him …' She crossed herself, then said quickly, 'Maybe a cha or a Fanta from our fridge, perhaps? It's just you look hot, very hot, if I may say so?'

He wondered if she was paying him a compliment for a moment, but then understood. 'It was the sprinkler, uh? The gardens are beautiful, sister.'

Sister. He'd chanced familiarity, but she wasn't having any of it, correcting him. 'Madam, to you.'

'Madam? Forgive me, you don't look old enough.'

'Old enough for what?' she said. Then, 'I have the master key right here.' It hung around her neck, on a little silver chain. She handed it to him, and just as he suspected, her skin was cold and clammy. This young woman was afraid of something.

'This has never happened before,' she said. 'Some petty

theft one expects, a camera, a phone? But to kill a man? Who could do such a thing?'

'His wallet is gone? Money? Passport?'

'I'm not sure. The maid found the body, and after I checked why she was screaming her head off, I left as quickly as I could.'

'So what do you know of him?'

She shrugged. 'Very little. He's been here before. He likes the gardens. He said he had a memorial he wanted to visit, that he lost a friend.'

'When?'

'I don't know. Maybe during the war. I don't discuss such things. Anyway, he said he was a writer, that he needed peace and quiet, that he was writing a book.'

'A book, I see,' he said.

'The *muzungu* was our only guest.' She couldn't hide the disappointment in her voice, but then brightened. 'We have a delegation coming next week from Kigali, and things are bound to pick up over the next few months … For you, too, I suppose?'

Umwana's heart sank just thinking about the elections. Security. Visiting dignitaries. Drunken brawls and recriminations in the cabarets, fights over who did what to whom back in 1994. 'You'll be rushed off your feet then too, uh?' he said.

'Wall-to-wall bookings, like all the hotels in Butare.' She glanced up at him, an odd look in her eyes. 'There are rumours all over town. People are saying there will be trouble. You think the burgomaster will be elected again?'

Umwana looked at his hands, then rubbed the lower part of his face and took a deep slow breath. 'I think these things are in the hands of God, and people will do the right thing.'

She smiled, but her look was suddenly far away. 'The right thing? You think people will do the right thing?'

Her face was impassive now. Impossible to know what she was thinking. Of course, it was right to remember the million dead, the war, the bodies rotting in the ground wherever one walked in this town. But it was vital too, for the sake of sanity, to keep your eyes straight ahead, your head down, work hard at whatever you were put on this earth to do, and build a brighter future. That was what the president said in his speeches on the radio. The country was new, emerging, born of blood, death, hatred and division. But democracy was still an idea, free speech an ideal. It wasn't wise to be too open with strangers.

Umwana flipped open his notebook. Work was the only thing that made a man feel better.

'He had a hire car? This only guest of yours?'

'Yes, he must have rented it in Kigali. The keys are … I don't know where.' She paused and pursed her lips. 'The fact is, Officer, I didn't look. I didn't stay in his room for longer than was necessary.' Their eyes met, but she quickly clicked the roof of her mouth and pushed herself up from the desk. 'I'll show you.'

As she walked ahead, he couldn't help but notice how her calves were tightly formed, full of muscle like a runner, her tidy little heels and tapering feet encased by high-heeled, open-toed sandals clacking on the marble floor. Not an émigré, but a survivor … yes. Ten or eleven she would have been when she hid under bodies or sold herself.

'The muzungu insisted on a garden bungalow. Number three. Where he'd stayed before. He liked whiskey of an evening. He went to a cabaret last night, I think, on the outskirts of town. He said he was catching up with someone. He liked to sit in the Bamboo Bar during the day, just there through the double doors.'

Umwana glanced towards the bar, trying to make it casual. But it wasn't. Inside, he could feel the sinews in his gut pulling. This feeling was something he hated, resisted as best as he could, but he couldn't help himself. Bars held a special appeal for him, but who the hell could blame him?

I'm nothing special, he reminded himself. *One million dead. One million fled.* Everybody in this country was messed up, traumatised, as the minister said in the Pentecostal church he went to sometimes when his nightmares were bad. So he tried not to blame himself, his weakness and desire for occasional obliteration from the place where he lived, a shitty little hut up near the marshlands, the difficulty he had sleeping most nights, the difficulty he had fitting into a place where he didn't really belong, but had been sent to by some bwana man.

The young woman seemed to read his thoughts, 'Can I offer you a beer?' she asked. He shook his head and tapped the silver badge. She batted him a look, and as they reached a door into the gardens, she paused for a moment, tutting and readjusting her skirt, and spoke quickly in a mixture of French and English, not a Bantu word in sight. Educated, he thought. A survivor, but still out of my class.

'Ask whatever you like, of course, but …' She looked at him. 'We've all seen bodies. But this one has implications. I don't have to spell it out. You strike me as an intelligent sort. And a dead white man killed here under my watch with the elections coming up, well, jobs are hard to come by, and the Ibis in town has a concierge from Paris and Wi-Fi, and whilst it's peaceful here, I will be honest, we struggle to fill the rooms …'

He felt suddenly sorry for her. He wanted to touch her arm and tell her not to worry, that all would be well, the body would be dealt with quickly, the culprit found, that he knew how to track down a killer. That he'd done it before.

The sun was rising now, a copper line, then coral pink into grey low-hanging clouds, the smell of rain like metal in the air among the eucalyptus and chit chat trees. Around these gardens would be walls, a security hut with some dozy drunk swigging banana beer from a jerrycan, wearing fatigues, cursing the day he was born. And beyond that, the ever-encroaching bush and the marshes, still stinking of the dead, full of ghosts. It would be easy for someone to come into these gardens at night, unseen. But also easy to track them, or so he hoped. If he could face the marshes.

As they walked down a dusty path towards the largest of the chit chat trees, the figure of an old woman emerged out of the shadows, crouched on the ground.

'*Muraho,* mama.'

Low on her haunches, her face cupped in her hands, she was rocking on her heels, making a low, visceral, animal

195

moaning, which cut Officer Umwana to the quick. He hated to hear any woman cry like that. There was something unspeakable about it. Auntie, sister, mama.

Thank God, Francine *How May I Help You* went straight to the old woman's side. 'Please, mama. Enough! Did the cha not help? Stop that now.'

'This is the maid who found the body, I presume?'

'Yes. Her name's Bertha. She's worked here a long time, longer than me. Mama! Stop it, please.'

The woman smelt strongly not of cha but *urwagwa*. Toxic stuff if drunk early enough, for long enough. *Takes one to know one*, he thought. She wasn't just crying, she was completely drunk. Clearly embarrassed, the young woman continued, 'Mama, please. I know it's been terrible, evil beyond evil.'

The old woman spoke at last, but Umwana could barely understand what the devil she was saying. 'Don't be silly, mama,' said the girl. 'Nobody's accusing you of anything. Pull yourself together and tell everything to Officer …' She glanced over her shoulder at him in unspoken enquiry. The old woman was clearly terrified of men in uniform, and in Rwanda who could blame her? So he put his hand to his chest in respect and bowed. 'I am honoured to meet you, mama. My name is Officer Umwana.'

'Umwana?' said the old woman.

'Ah, *oui*, mama. It's such a sweet name. *C'est bon*, uh?' said Francine, and then turned to Umwana. 'May we be impolite and ask …'

Umwana was used to this. People always wanted to know

about his name, who he was and where he came from. He'd invented a story, or someone, a priest or an aid worker, had invented it for him, and he'd repeated it so many times he believed it as if it were true.

'I grew up in a place just like this,' he said. 'A mission. Not near Butare, you understand. Far away in the north, towards Uganda. It's nothing special to be called "child" there. It's a northern name.'

'You hear that, mama? This young man is a northerner.' She nudged the old woman. 'You've seen the gorillas, then? There were so many, I'm told, before the genocide, but now with poaching, the new wars, the landmines?'

He shrugged. He had seen the mountain gorillas beating their chests, like warriors, defending their territory. But wasn't he supposed to be asking the questions and not these two women? It was always the same. Talk, talk, and gossip was what they liked to do best. At the markets and cabarets.

'Well, thank you, Officer, for coming to help us. Nobody likes to deal with a dead body, after all that's happened here, you understand?' The young woman had inexplicably extended her hand to him once more, and he took it again. How warm her skin was. No longer afraid. He held her hand for a second too long, and as he did, her fingers left on his skin the oddest impression, the sense that he had just agreed to some sort of bargain. Like the bargains these hotels had with police, or with his commander in Butare?

He wasn't interested in bargains. He wiped his hand without thinking on his thigh. Corruption was everywhere, creeping over the border from Burundi and Tanzania, along with coltan, prostitutes, diamonds, guns, refugees. It would undo his country if they, the police, weren't on constant alert. And it suddenly struck the officer that perhaps this young woman had rehearsed all of this? The tight skirt, the high heels, the lipstick at 6 a.m. in the morning, the offer of a drink, the mix of charm, reticence and vulnerability, the old drunken woman? All of it to disconcert him, to put him off the scent? But he wasn't anybody's fool. He knew robberies in hotels were usually down to the staff. Francine slept here; she had the keys and could slip in and out of the rooms as she pleased. She was the *mwami* queen of all she surveyed. He glanced at her shoes again. They were good Kenyan leather, the best money could buy, but they were also spotted with blood.

His face now set in stone, he asked her why. But she simply shrugged. 'What do you expect?' She looked down at her sandals. 'There was so much blood. That's why mama is hysterical. You're not from Butare; we saw the worst of it back in '94. My people are buried here. That's why I returned. And then to find a body like that. Cut.'

He did a double take. 'Cut?'

The mama started to weep again.

'Can't you understand?' said Francine. 'To see a body like that brings back bad luck, bad memories, bad everything.'

He hadn't even seen the body yet, but he felt unbelievably weary. Maybe it was his hangover creeping up on him from that damned cabaret last night, where the women and elders were talking in whispers, or maybe his malaria starting up again, or perhaps it was the rainy season clouds rushing in over the brows of the hills, bearing down on him. Pressure. Too much pressure.

Umwana suddenly had no desire to speak to these women any more. He looked over to the bungalow, which lay just beyond the chit chat tree. Bungalow three, shrouded in a tumble of bougainvillea.

Cut?

The radio in his belt crackled once again. *Officer 623, come in …* Ignoring it, he told himself to trust his instincts, and digging out his gloves and his courage, he went up to the front door, pushed it ajar and stepped into the shadows.

He could hear nothing but his own breathing, ragged like the light in the room, the bulb flickering on and off, thick with swirling flies. He crouched to look at the body. *Such a savage end, monsieur. Who would want to do this to you, and why? Could it really be just for money?* People were poor, and poverty a yoke that ground a man down, but why not just tie him up, threaten him, take whatever you wanted, and run? It would have been easy enough to climb through the window and silently disappear.

This sort of savagery spoke of something deeper. To take a machete and brutally decapitate a man, to make this violent cut, a professional arc through the arterial veins, fracturing bone, ripping tears of flesh and sinew, to take the head completely off?

He thought about the old gardeners outside. Too old. And as for Francine or the mama, no woman could work this sort of violence. This had been done by a young man, strong and with a farmer's skill, someone used to slashing the thorns and bulrushes of this unforgiving land. He sucked air through his teeth. *Ai! But what does this tell me?* There were a thousand young men just like that, out there in the bush or an adobe hut or a shanty village, within a few kilometres radius, if you took this blood-soaked body as the centre of the world.

And you're the centre of my world, now, monsieur, he thought.

No longer white, in death the man was black like molasses, marbled with blue. The atmosphere in bungalow three was so hot, Umwana was dripping with sweat. He swallowed, wiping his mouth with the back of his hand. The body had sweltered all night, given the smell and the flies. He prodded it with his gloved fingers, gauging the stiffness of the muscles, then turned to the head, which wore an expression neither surprised, afraid, angry or anything else – just blank, giving nothing away.

But a room, like the depths of a forest or the bed of a river, bore patterns, imprints and signs, if you were clever enough to read them, so maybe the bungalow could tell him more? It was the sort of place he'd seen in abandoned game lodges in Uganda. Faux African batik on the walls, bamboo furniture bought on the Rue de Kigali, a lamp in the shape of a giraffe. The interior of an adobe hut to a white man's eyes, but if you looked closer, it was terra cotta paint not mud on the walls, and the bathroom was glossy, tiled, Lux soap smelling of lemon against the cut of the blood. *I should like to live like this,* he thought. *Like a mwami king for a day, ai.*

There were no signs of a struggle. Whoever had killed this man must have hidden in the bathroom or the wardrobe and eased himself out, slowly, quietly, most likely barefooted, then sliced the victim from behind. So much blood, but no footprints leading away from the body. Odd but … *take your time, Officer Umwana. More haste, less speed, didn't the brothers always say?* His eyes re-scanned the room. Empty bottles of beer, an ashtray full of cigarette butts, and by the bed the victim's holdall, neat and tidy. He opened it. A couple of shirts, a pair of jeans, underwear, deodorant, condoms, mints, a brown pill bottle, which Umwana shook. *You won't be needing those any more.* He stuffed them in his pocket. He had trouble sleeping sometimes, and perhaps the dead *muzungu* had the same problem. He opened a Belgian passport.

Monsieur Thierry Duchamp

Occupation: Photographer

Date of birth: 01/10/1955

1955? That made the victim old, but white men didn't age like Rwandans. No toiling in the sun, no malaria, no war, no genocide. With a bite of envy, Umwana flicked through the passport's jewel-like impressions of multicoloured stamps – red, green, blue, topaz yellow – from Egypt, Syria, Sierra Leone, Thailand, Mali, Bosnia, Bhutan, Afghanistan and more, and where all Rwandans yearned to go one day, the USA. Oh, to be so free …

At the bottom of the bag he found a brown leather wallet, and inside it, his eyes grew wide. A whole wad of Rwandan francs, English sterling, American dollars. Money beyond your wildest dreams. Enough for a whole village to survive for a year. Enough to send your child to school. To get out of Rwanda. To travel to Paris, London, even New York.

This crime made even less sense now. He furrowed his brow. Why not take all this money and disappear forever, why not change your name, face, life, destiny, vanish into the great plains of Tanzania or the forests of Burundi?

He'd go out into the grounds and check for footprints, tracks, and tyre marks before he left with the body, but right now? The overhead light was winking, the flies making his head pound. Hard to focus at the best of times. He needed quiet. Peace. He walked over to the switch and turned the flickering off. The blinds were down, but between the cracks leaked molten fissures of zinc and blinding lemon from the sun. 7 a.m. He sat at the bamboo desk, just as the dead man had, and there before him, silver and sleek, was a laptop.

He touched the cold metal, opened the screen, to see his own reflection in the dark glass, a ghostly negative. A small green light winked at him. The laptop was charged – *bon*. A tap and the screen lit up.

Qui est-tu?

Looking back at him was a black and white image of a boy. Good looking, beautiful in fact. His bare arm was outstretched, pointing a gun. There was power in his limbs, a premature manliness in his pumped-out chest and tiny bulging muscles. But there was reluctance and fragility too, cleverly caught, in the attitude, the light, the grain. The boy soldier's chin was lifted against the lens of the camera in a jut of defiance. His eyes were saying, *take my picture, uh, but then there is the matter of payment, ai. I know how to get what I want, what I need. What do you take me for, a little African boy without a thought in my head? Not so stupid when I hold a gun in my hand, not so little when I am doing business like this, saying pay, monsieur, for the privilege of witnessing my suffering and the suffering I bestow on others. I am a businessman as well as a soldier. Five dollars!*

The boy's arms and face were splattered in mud, his neck beaded with sweat, his skin covered in battle scars, but still he was a survivor. Like all poor boys running from something, his clothes were the only clothes he had. Grabbed from a hut in a burning village, as the mamas screamed and the babies howled and the soldiers came with their rat-a-tat-tat and flashing machetes. His T-shirt, old when he first laid hands on it, was now ripped to shreds, like his soul, like his brain, and across his chicken muscle chest, no future ahead except death or prison, brave words, a logo, ridiculous really … MAKE IT HAPPEN.

There were tropical fronds in the foreground, beads of perspiration on the boy's face, dewdrops on the leaves overhanging him and in the air a fine mist. It was the rainy season. Umwana could make out, beyond tyre tracks and huge puddles like lakes on the road, a ditch to either side, running with thick muddy water. A cow farther up the road, and farther on piles of rags, more shadows, undulating hills, smoke plumes rising in the distance, forests shrouded in mist.

And in the bottom of the left-hand corner, the photographer's name: THIERRY DUCHAMP, REX PHOTOGRAPHY, 1994.

1994. The war. I was seven at the time. Seven.

The boy looked straight at the officer, as if they might have something to say to each other, but Umwana had nothing to confess.

For God's sake, he knew he got drunk last night, met a man in a bar who said he was working on a story that was going to be big. A story involving a child who committed a crime, joined the army just to survive, was raped, taken to a church in Uganda where, who can blame him, he'd slashed a Brother's throat. A bad man amongst many bad men. Had gone on the run, a street child, into juvenile prison for a while, turned tricks to survive, and there, thank God, he was spotted by the commander, who remembered him from the war, who put him to use, who gave him a whole new life – a police uniform, a little silver badge. What was that to do with anything?

The child's eyes had a truth in them. *Help me. Save me, Officer Child.*

Umwana put his head in his hands, hearing his own rough breathing. Was it that damn malaria creeping up on him again? Maybe these pills in his pocket would help. The doctors hadn't helped, the aid workers, the priests, the shaman on the edge of his village. *I need to sleep tonight,* he thought, *to try to recall what I did last night. What did I do last night? God help me, forgive me.* His eyes came back to the screen. The boy was a picture. No more. A still life in black and white. Most likely dead already. Mulched into the earth like leaves in the jungle. As good as forgotten.

He's not me. He's just a shadow on the wall.

Click. Delete.

Now, Where Was I?

Alison Joseph

So – do I speak into this thing? It's very small. Do you police do this with everyone? I suppose with us witnesses you have to. At least you have all this technology these days. Now, where was I? My name? I'm called Moira McPherson. Wife of the deceased. Is that OK? Gosh, such a tiny microphone, are you sure you can hear me? OK.

Oh dear, where do I start? With my husband, I suppose. Everyone loved him, you see. Dear Robert. We were married twenty-eight years. Nearly twenty-nine, I know, that was my first thought when I stood there, looking at him, what a shame we never had that anniversary dinner we'd promised ourselves. Shock, they said. It does that to you. It would only have been an ordinary dinner, nothing too special; we're careful with money … I mean, we were. Oh dear, I can't see I'll ever get used to it.

I used to think I wasn't the marrying kind. Mother used to say that too, when I was young, 'You'll be lucky to find anyone prepared to marry you,' she'd say. Funny old thing.

Then, when Robert came along, she changed her tune. 'You could do worse than accept his proposal,' she said. 'For all you know, you'll never get another chance …' She was very keen on him, thought he was charming, and he'd got the huge house, inherited from his parents – it became our marital home, and there was room enough for Mother to move in with us, she liked that. And of course, he was always so sweet with her.

Oh dear, it's so upsetting. I don't know how we're going to manage. His own brother, can you imagine? I don't have brothers and sisters, just me and Mum, but how could you fall out with your own brother like that? Jason determined to do him harm, apparently, and in the end succeeded. Which is why I'm here talking to you.

Did I know Jason was after him? Well, it was a kind of background conversation, that's the problem. I didn't realize I should take it seriously. Until it was too late. 'Brotherly love?' Robert used to say. 'That man doesn't know the meaning of the word.'

It all goes back to the house – Jason was supposed to get half, but it all went wrong for him when the will was finally revealed, and Robert had got it all, something to do with the fact he already lived there and Jason had moved away, and then, of course, Mother and I moved in. Jason had been seeing lawyers about Robert buying him out. He wouldn't give up; it had gone on for years. Robert would always complain that people exploited his good nature. Not just Jason, in fact. There was Amir, his business partner. Claimed that Robert had squirrelled away half their takings from the company; they ran a buildings material wholesale business before Robert retired. Amir reckoned Robert was hiding money in the account in Jersey. It's true, we do have an account there. I'm afraid I don't have much to do with it; Mother always says I'm no good at that sort of thing and she's right, of course. But I can't imagine that Robert would have done such a thing.

Me? Occupation? Oh, I'm just a housewife. I did work, just in a shop, but I gave it up when I married. Perhaps if we'd had children … But I keep busy, and there's Mother to look after; she's become more frail now with her heart condition. I did study chemistry, a long time ago. I was always good at science at school. My father worked as a lab technician at the university. I think he'd have liked me to go there too, but he died when I was fourteen. Anyway, after that Mother said it wasn't suitable for a girl to go to university and study, she needed me at home, so I did a pharmacy training and worked in the chemist's in town.

Then of course I married, and Robert said I should concentrate on the home. He always said I was no good at doing two things at once, and I'm sure he was right. There's no point regretting how things turned out, is there? And I have my hobbies. Tapestry. And a bit of knitting, the nieces, Jason's girls, they're twins, beautiful children, I've done all sorts of pretty things for them over the years, cardies, little jumpers with animals on, that kind of thing, though they're getting a bit old for it now. And I collect art. Not real art, of course, just postcards and prints, reproductions of Old Masters. I buy them online, Mother doesn't need to know.

Oh, I love them, those big dramatic scenes, classical tragedies, or stories from the Bible. There's something so stirring about it. I've even started sewing tapestries based on them. I know it sounds odd, I sketch them out on the canvas and then stitch in the colour, bit by bit, it brings it to life, in a way. It means I really, really get to understand what the painter was doing. I've just finished one, 'The Mocking of Christ' it's called, seventeenth-century Dutch, much more difficult than I realized, so much darkness, and then there's this flame in the middle that the guards are threatening Jesus with, really very frightening when you look at it …

Oh dear, you don't need to know all that, I'm so sorry, I do go on. Robert's eyes always glaze over when I chatter on about small things … I mean, they did.

So where were we? Poor Robert being stabbed to death. Well, the day that Jason came round, he was even more furious than usual. I'd cooked Sunday lunch. I have to be careful what I make these days, Mother does complain with her delicate stomach … So we'd eaten, I did a fish pie, not one of my best, the pastry should be rough puff really, not short-crust, as Mother said, and Robert had barely touched it, sitting there looking at it. I was about to ask him whether he'd like something else instead, when there was a ring at the door. So he got up to answer it.

And after that … oh dear, I do get a bit emotional. I told you people all of this at the time, and now you want it on tape, of course, for the courts. I do understand, it's just … the first thing I said was, that's our carving knife. Strange, isn't it – the details. But it was definitely from my kitchen drawer; I don't know how he'd got hold of it. It was the nice one too, ivory-handled, part of Robert's inheritance; we'd hardly used it, kept it for special occasions, not that there are many of those. I last used it for that cake that I tried to make for our wedding anniversary some years ago, the disastrous one, when Robert said I should have known he didn't like sultanas … now, where was I?

So I heard all this shouting from the hallway, it's a big gloomy space, like the rest of the house, Robert could never see the point of decorating. 'It's been like this all my life, why change it?' he'd say … And there was Jason holding the knife aloft, and there's my husband on the old tiled floor, breathing his last. And the blood – blood everywhere, who'd have thought there'd be so much blood. And my first thoughts were that it was like that painting of Cain and Abel, the famous one, Titian. I tried to stitch it once, I thought it would make a lovely tapestry, but all that male flesh, that creamy waxy colour, it needed loads of that particular shade and I ran out of thread. So I'm doing Judith and Holofernes now instead, the clothes are lovely, and of course she has a maidservant too, it gives me the chance to do two lovely outfits, such fun. There's a lot of blood, but I've got heaps of crimson silk, got a job lot down at the market stall, I might as well use it up. He was Assyrian, Holofernes, an enemy of Judith's people, and she took the opportunity of him getting drunk after trying to seduce her to chop off his head. She was hailed as a heroine after that, quite right too … oh dear, where was I? I do go on, I'm so sorry … I think I'm still in shock, that's what the nice policewoman said when I eventually dialled 999. She said that the effects of shock can be quite unpredictable …

So, yes, there we were, Robert on the floor, and Jason like I've never seen him, ranting and raving. He'd found out that Robert was insisting on showing the courts a later will that gave him the whole share of the house; he was saying it was typical of Robert to lie just to get his own way, how he'd always been selfish, always the bullying big brother …

I keep out of it, of course, it's not my family.

Although, come to think of it, I might have let something slip to Jason. He'd popped round the night before, something about the girls' birthday party next month – Robert was out at his bridge club, his regular Saturday night time off, and Mother was upstairs asleep, and I offered Jason a cup of tea. We sat in the kitchen, perhaps I was a bit indiscreet about Robert's plan to put an end to the probate dispute once and for all, as he said, but of course I had no idea about the details.

Jason was absolutely furious. He jumped to his feet, started opening cupboards, drawers, pointing at silverware, glassware, going on about his inheritance. It was very disturbing. And it's true, he did pick up the carving knife then, went on about how valuable it was, waving it around. I was rather worried.

I tried to be sympathetic, to calm him down. Anyway, finally he went off home, muttering about how that was it, there were limits, he wasn't going to put up with it any more.

To be honest, I felt rather sorry for Jason. He's a nice man at heart, and he's got a lovely wife, and the girls are very sweet too. I once said to Robert, surely there's a way of resolving this dispute about the inheritance amicably, but all Robert said was, with me not having any brothers or sisters, how could he expect me to understand? And Mother repeated it, how can your poor husband expect you to understand? Even though it was her decision to make me an only child, funny really.

Anyway, Jason must have made a decision that evening, after our chat. So awful. Coming back the next day with the knife, doing such a terrible, terrible thing …

I'd run out into the hallway, and now I was faced with the whole scene. Robert had been making a strange uneven breathing noise, but that had stopped. His eyes were fixed, open, empty. Jason was still holding the knife aloft, just standing there. There was this long, long silence. They say that, don't they, 'as if time stood still'. And as I said, I thought about Cain and Abel, although come to think of it perhaps it was more like that very beautiful David and Goliath. I've got it on a postcard, Caravaggio, wonderful man. I think it was the way the light coming through the door reflected on the blade of the knife, just like a painting. Funny how one's mind works, isn't it?

And then everything started up again. Jason dropped the knife and just ran, ran out the door. I heard his car screeching out of the drive.

And I was left there, just standing there. I thought, no more. I called to Mother, but she didn't answer me, poor thing, hearing's going. I stood in the hall, thinking I'll have to go in and tell her my husband's dead.

I pulled up my jumper and looked at the scars. Burn marks. He'd use cigarettes. He'd tell me to stand still, and I was so scared of him, I did as I was told. I've got lines across my ribs where the skin's all flayed. Like the Dutch painting, now I come to think of it, the Honthorst, with Jesus in the middle and the guards holding the flame to his body. Funny I should have chosen that painting. As if it was a cry for help, the way I sat there, sewing away at it for all those weeks. Well, I don't need to cry for help any more.

I stood in the hallway, looking at the body. I took a deep breath and thought, now I can breathe. From now on, I'll be able to breathe.

I went back into the dining room. I must have told Mother, blurted it out. She sat there, not reacting. I called you people then, dialled 999, said my husband's been murdered by his brother. I hung up and looked across at Mother again. It was only then that I realized that she wasn't moving. Not breathing.

The shock must have killed her. That's what all the ambulance men said when they came. So kind to me, after all the events of the afternoon. One of them made some joke about either that or my cooking, and we had a bit of a laugh, strange in the circumstances.

They took her away, then. I was left in an empty house. For the first time in my life. It was a very strange feeling. Rather enjoyable, in fact, though I'm sure that's just the shock too. The odd thing was that Mother's pill dispenser was all wrong, as if she'd taken far more of her heart medication than usual. I always made sure I'd put out the right dosages, and she'd always query it. 'Are you sure that's right?' she'd say, and I'd try to tease her and say, but Mother, I'm a pharmacist, I know about these things, and she'd say, only a shop chemist and that was years ago, don't you go getting ideas …

Anyway, something had made her change all the doses around. It must have been the shock.

So, now, here I am. I've packed a small bag and locked up the house. A bit of a holiday, I thought, now no one needs me any more. Italy, yes, my flight leaves later on this afternoon. I'm going to look at all the paintings. The Judith and Holofernes I've been sewing, the original is in Florence. I've always wanted to see the real thing. Just stand in front of it and breathe. There's nothing to stop me now.

I gather Jason's owned up and is pleading guilty. It's a shame, really. I know I'm an only child and I don't understand these things. I suppose it's true they never got on, even as small boys. But brothers … you'd think there'd be some kind of bond. That's what's so wonderful about the paintings, like that Cain and Abel, they touch on such big truths, don't they? People always say that my Judith and Holofernes painting is an angry work, full of rage. It was painted by a woman, Artemisia Gentileschi, and reflected events from her own life – not that she killed anyone of course. But I don't think of it as angry. It's just so beautiful, the colours, the heavy folds on the dresses, and her maidservant, so loyal and supportive. Tomorrow I shall stand in front of it and really, really see it, really look at it, at their faces, their lovely clothes. Who'd have thought …

Is that it now? I'm very happy to help you, of course. A terrible business, I know. You've been most kind, all of you.

I'll just switch this off, then, shall I? Goodbye, Officer. Thank you for everything. Yes, this afternoon – I thought I'd better leave lots of time to get to the airport. The switch – ah, I see. Just here. Goodbye.

JUMPING AT SHADOWS

EMMA KAVANAGH

Grace snapped awake. Her heart thumped, loud in the cavernous darkness. She didn't know what had awoken her. Her fingers quested, reaching out for James the way she always had, for the curve of his shoulder, the soft down of his back. But her fingers scrabbled, farther and farther, finding only cool sheets. Of course. She had forgotten. She was alone now.

She twisted onto her other side, fighting back the nausea that always came upon first waking, upon remembering the way that life had twisted itself out of her control, flinging her into night after night punctured with nightmares.

What had woken her?

She tried to still her breathing, finding in the darkness the burr of the freezer, the clunk of old and yet new-to-her plumbing.

Her fingers found her phone, a quick tilt lighting up the screen.

And there it was, the cause of her wakefulness – Alert on camera 1.

'Bloody things,' she muttered. CCTV had seemed such a good idea at the time. What with the weight of starting a brand new life in a brand new house, it had seemed like a balm to soothe her fears. Yet each time her phone buzzed, the cameras springing to life to record the postman, an errant cat, a car driving too fast, those eternally present fears of hers would reawaken anew. She should take them down. Disrupting her sleep as they were, they were doing more harm than good.

She jabbed her thumb at the still image. The garden beyond her back door alien in the dull grey of night.

Then a movement caught her eye. A flicker of something in the bottom right of the frame. Grace sat up. It was sleep, still clawing at her senses, creating the illusion of something that was not there. Then another flicker, a shape emerging in the darkness.

A figure stood at her back door.

Grace let out a small 'oh'.

She could make out little, only the merest outline of a head pressed up close to the glass of her back door. Looking in.

Grace put her hand to her mouth, her breaths coming short, sharp.

Then the figure at her door drew backwards, disappearing into the shadow. Then another movement, lower down, a hand placing itself onto the handle of her door.

He was trying to get in.

What came next was the result of the channelling of pure

terror. Grace threw back the covers and, phone clutched in her hand, dived towards the light switch, flooding the room with a searing white. She yanked open the door, grabbing hold of the baseball bat, the one that her father had given her – you know, love, just in case – running towards the stairs, flicking on the stair light as she went.

She shoved open the kitchen door, a bang as it bounced off the worktop behind it, and hit the kitchen light switch, the bat held out in front of her.

The glass back door stood directly across from her, reflecting back an image of a wild-haired woman dressed in penguin pyjamas. Grace stood, bare feet on cold tile, her heart thundering in her ears.

Beyond, the garden lay in darkness.

Backing away, tucking herself into a nook that could not be seen from the back door, she checked the camera, pulling up the live feed of it on her phone.

Nothing.

She tried to calm her breathing, staring at the image of the now empty garden. You could see where the workmen had marked out the dig, the lines of it shaped into her scrubby grass. The extension work would begin tomorrow and the garden seemed to wait for it, biding its time.

Had it been a nightmare, a hard-edged dream spilling over into sleep-stained reality? Grace pulled up the camera's log, clicking on the most recent alert. No. There was the figure. There the hand.

She risked another look towards the back door. Whoever had been there, they were gone now.

It was nothing, she told herself. Some drunk meandering his way up from the Padstow harbour pubs, a wrong turn, mistaking one house for another.

She felt fear roar in her and pushed it back down, hard. She must not let it take over. She must not let it win.

It was nothing.

She was fine.

Grace stood there for long moments, her cheeks and fingers tingling.

The surgery's waiting room was full. A toddler ran in dizzying circles, bumping into the knees of increasingly irritated patients, his younger sibling wailing in its mother's lap. The GPs were running late, a couple of overly chatty patients pushing the whole day into chaos, and tempers had begun to rise, along with the heat on the unnaturally warm spring day.

Grace took a deep swallow of coffee, wincing at the chill. She had slept little last night and had spent the remainder of the darkness lying on her bed, her eyes wide open, simply waiting. Had checked the camera, once, twice, enough times that the word 'obsession' could be applied. Had finally fallen into a doze at a little after five, so that the alarm came crashing through her consciousness, sending her adrenaline spiking anew.

She glanced at the waiting throng, then quickly down at her mobile cradled in her lap. She brought camera 1 into view, and a movement made her breath catch. Then she breathed out, telling herself she was being ridiculous. The builders had let themselves into the garden and were laying the groundwork to begin digging. The extension had seemed like a good idea at the time, the chance to turn a narrow galley kitchen into somewhere spacious that led out onto the garden. And of course, the builder, Elijah, was local enough – four doors away – that, should anything go wrong, he would be unlikely to slip out on her. Or if he did, he couldn't slip far. She watched Elijah saying something to one of his lads, well-muscled arms waving in emphasis, and felt something in her loosen.

It was okay. Last night was far away now. It was her location, that was the thing, just a couple of streets back from the harbour and its drinking holes.

Grace watched the builders, Elijah saying something, the others laughing, and she smiled, sheepish. She had overreacted. Didn't her family always tell her as much. That she was too emotional, too quick to think the worst.

It had been a misplaced drunk.

It was all okay.

Afternoon surgery, Mr Feely standing before the desk, rolling like he was on the deck of a ship, the sweet stench of alcohol flowing over her in waves.

'The thing is, Mr Feely,' said Grace, 'your appointment was this morning. The GP is out on house calls now.'

'I … now, see here, I'm telling you, an' I know, 'cos I wrote it down, where is that … anyway, i's this afternoon.'

'Mr Feely …'

Her phone pinged. An alert on camera 1.

It would be the builders, she told herself.

'There is no afternoon surgery today, Mr Feely …' She

pushed the view button, her finger moving without her consent. 'Now, if you want to discuss making another appointment ...' Her rear garden filled the screen, the scrubby grass still untouched. Then a figure stepped into camera view. Hooded and tall.

She felt her heartbeat quicken.

'Not even bloody listening to me now,' muttered the elderly man.

Grace ignored him, picking up the surgery phone, and dialled the number quickly, still watching the figure on the screen. 'Elijah?'

'Yeah, sorry, Grace. Bloody digger's broken down ...'

'Elijah, your guys are still in the garden, yeah?'

A silence. 'No. Thing is, there's nothing we can do there now, so we've gone ...'

'So none of your guys are there?'

Another silence. 'No ...'

Grace's stomach plummeted. She hung up the phone, cutting Elijah off mid-apology, and watched the figure as it walked the length of the marked-out ground, pulling the screen closer to her, looking for features, anything that would identify him. But his head remained turned away. Then, a startled movement, like he had heard something that worried him, and the figure moved quickly out of camera view.

'So can I see the doctor or no?'

Grace stood on her lawn, where the figure had stood, and stared at the markings left by the builders. What had he been looking for? What the hell would anyone find so interesting about building work? She shivered, wrapping herself tighter in the thick cardigan. Perhaps it was one of the neighbours, someone nosing about, wanting to see what work she was having done but not mouthy enough to ask. That would be it. Simple. Perhaps, she thought, it was her own fault. Keeping herself to herself the way she had. There had been overtures back when she first moved in. The elderly woman across the way had brought her banana bread. Elijah and his wife had invited her for drinks. She had been polite but distant, had told herself that it was okay, that she was still grieving all that she had lost, that she had to deal with things in her own way, in her own time. But that was the problem, wasn't it? When your life is flipped upside down and all that you thought you knew turns out to be wrong, you stop trusting your instincts, start questioning your every move. Maybe she should have been friendlier, embedded herself within the community more. Maybe then this would be … what, less terrifying? Or was 'terrifying' the word? After all, to her family, she was the drama queen, the one for whom there were no molehills, only mountains. And she had trusted James to be there forever so implicitly and had been so very, very wrong about that …

Grace shook herself, turning towards the house, the setting sun warm against her face. She could call someone, her parents perhaps. Could tell them what she had seen. But she would hear it there, in the warmth of their voice, the unsurprisedness of their tone, that for them it had been but a matter of time before this call had come. That Grace had a crisis again.

And she couldn't do that. Couldn't be that. After all, wasn't that what this new start was all about? Beginning again. Being someone new. An adult, but an adult without James. She had been seventeen when they met, twenty-one when they married, thirty when they divorced. All of her adult life had been marked by her plus him. She watched as the glow of the sun sank towards the Cornish sea. She had to be different now. Had to figure out a way of being that did not involve another person.

And could not involve jumping at shadows.

Grace let herself in through the back door, quickly locking it behind her. She moved from window to window, pulling the dense curtains shut, closing out the remaining sunlight and plunging the house into a premature night.

And she told herself not to be silly.

That everything was fine.

It had seemed so unlikely she should sleep. Yet Grace had forced herself to lie down, had told herself that sometimes going through the motions was simply what adults had to do. So she had got undressed, had clambered under the covers, her heart beating like a tin drum, had let her gaze linger for long moments on the empty pillow beside her. And somehow, somewhere along the way had slipped beneath the surface into sleep. It was not a restful sleep, but rather one crowded with dreams in which she was running, yet never really sure just what she was running away from.

Then a beep.

Grace's eyes snapped open, her hand grabbing for the

phone. Knowing what she would see before she saw it.

Alert on camera 1.

She sat up quickly, pulling the baseball bat that she had left propped beside the bed quickly to her, her finger on the screen.

She had expected to see a figure, a shadowed face peering into her home.

Instead there was only emptiness, the garden alien in grey.

Then something else, a noise that sat just on the edge of silence. Grace felt the hairs on her arms stand proud, stilled her breathing, listening. What …

Then it came again, and again. Soft, rhythmic. Footsteps on the tiled kitchen floor.

Her fingers moved without her now, taking charge. Dialling 999. Her other hand snapped on the light. Moving with quick, scrambled movements, so that her back was against her bedroom door, the weight of her pushing against it. It wouldn't be enough. If someone pushed against it, if someone wanted to come in, she wouldn't be able to stop them.

'Emergency, can I help you?'

'Police. Someone's in my house.'

'Are you absolutely sure there was someone here?' The officer looked tired, a day's worth of stubble growth across his jowls. He pushed down one more time against the handle of the door, as if this time it would magically have unlocked itself. Then he sighed and peered about the kitchen with the weary air of one who has done this too many times before.

'I … yes …' Grace had pulled the sleeves of her pyjamas down over her fingers and was stroking one of them across her lip the way she used to as a child. Fitting then, that she wanted to cry like one. 'I think so.'

The officer turned, giving her a look that told her 'I think so' wasn't the right answer. 'No sign of forced entry. All the doors and windows are locked up tight.' Then he sighed heavily, forcing his mouth into a smile. 'You lived here long?'

'No. A couple of months.'

'By yourself?'

'Yes. Divorced,' she added needlessly.

'Aye. Get this a lot. It takes some time to get used to living on your own. In the beginning, every sound seems to be an intruder.' He gave her a sympathetic look. 'You'll settle down.'

'But …' She moved her hand, a thought of showing him the camera, its footage. Then she remembered there had been nothing, had there? Not this time. An alert, footage showing an empty garden. And, after all, he was right, the doors were locked. 'I'm sorry I wasted your time.'

It was a little after six. Grace stood in front of her living room window, a mug of coffee clenched tight in her fingers, and watched as the sun crept above the horizon. Seagulls wheeled above her, their caws grating, sounding like so many screams. She had not slept. Instead had sat in the living room, her legs pulled up beneath her, a pillow cradled on her lap. She had cried, the kind of cry that starts out wrenching but lasts so long that in the end it sputters out, the merest shadow of its former self. She wanted James. He made her feel safe. Wasn't that what she had always said? It had somehow never occurred to her to question why she would feel unsafe to begin with, what there was boiling away inside her that made the world feel treacherous and unsteady. She had never pulled back the curtain, ventured into the gloom back there to see what skeletons might be lying about. Instead she had clung to James, her saviour, her rock. She had clung and clung until in the end it seemed that he started to chafe beneath the grip of her. You need some hobbies. You need some friends. She had taken his suggestions for concern. Rather, they had been warnings. You can't keep hanging onto me like this. I can't breathe. Had she known he was moving away from her? Not consciously perhaps, but deep down she had got it. She had understood. Had recognised that togetherness had morphed somewhere along the way into pursuit, her prey becoming ever more elusive until one day he had stopped running, had turned to her and said this isn't working out.

The early morning sun puddled the Padstow street. The sky was clear. Grace sipped her coffee and told herself to breathe. She could not go on like this. She needed help, some positive action to stop this constant turbulence of fear. She'd found the number of a counsellor somewhere around 4 a.m. Once it was a sensible time, she would call. Would take control of this thing that hung over her.

Then a movement caught her eye, a figure standing beneath a dipping oak tree, and her heart froze in her chest, her hand shaking sufficiently that hot coffee slopped across her fingers.

But something had shifted last night, a material change, and Grace spun on her heels, dumping the coffee on the windowsill, and ran from the house. She would take charge of this, would not live in fear any more. She yanked open her front door, the chill sea air lapping at her face, and ran down her garden path. She thought he would have fled, but as she rounded the low hedge, she could see him again, a tall figure simply standing beneath the shadow of the tree, staring.

'Hey!' Her voice came out strangled. 'Hey, you! What do you want?'

The figure twisted towards her, his head tilted to one side. And Grace took in the extent of him and began to slow, the scene shifting to a new angle. He was old, must have been approaching eighty, and his gaze seemed unfocused somehow, as if he was staring right at her yet still not seeing. One corner of his mouth hung lower than the other, and enmeshed in amongst the cries of the seagulls, she could hear a low sound coming from him, a low-throated groan.

Grace stopped in front of him. A sudden thought, that she was hallucinating him, that he was not there at all, made her want to reach out and touch the brushed cotton of his dressing gown.

'Albert! Albert! What are you doing out here and in your pyjamas as well, good lord almighty. I told you to stay put, didn't I tell you?' The woman seemed to come from nowhere, clutching her crimson dressing gown tight around herself, her cropped steel hair standing up on end. 'I get up and you're gone. Now what am I supposed to think.' She bustled past Grace, gripping the man by the elbow. 'You, Albert Edwards, will be the death of me. The death, I'm telling you.' Then, tirade running out of steam, she noticed Grace. 'Oh … oh, love, I'm sorry. You're the new one. In number twelve? Elijah told us all about you. I'm sorry, love, you must think we're loons. Albert, see, he's not well. Tends to wander off. I found him down in the harbour just last week. Goodness knows where he'd have ended up if I hadn't gotten to him.'

Grace stood, her mouth open, and felt everything shift. 'He … he wanders?' A sliding sensation of relief. 'Is it possible he's been into my garden? Only …'

'Oh, love, has he? Oh, I'm ever so sorry. He used to do some work there, you know, gardening and suchlike, for the couple as was there before you. This was back before the stroke, obviously. He must have found his way back, thinking he was still helping out. Oh, I'm ever so sorry if he scared you.'

Grace looked from the woman to Albert, his gaze fixed on her balefully, and she let out a sound, a cry perhaps, or, no, a laugh. Told herself that the tears in her eyes, they were there from relief only. That she had not been insane.

'I … it's okay. I'm glad I know.'

The woman was watching her. 'Name's Ethel. We should have come over and introduced ourselves, but, you understand …' She shook her head. 'And things aren't the same these days, are they? Neighbours, they don't know one another like they used to. Used to be that in this street that everyone knew everyone else. The couple who were there before you – Caleb and Lorraine – they liked to socialise, like, always throwing barbecues and such for the neighbours. Lovely people. Lovely people. But then, you know, life moves on, and things change.' She leaned in confidentially. 'Truth be told, she left him. Awful thing. Just up and left one day, met some new man up Barnstable way, so he told us after. He was crushed, poor thing. And then, things never were the same after that. He stopped working, and, well, you can't live on fresh air, can you? Bank took the house, poor pet. Still –' she looked Grace up and down '– no excuse, I should have come over, said hello, explained about Albert and his wandering ways.'

'It's okay,' said Grace. 'Really. Can I help you get him home?'

'Oh no, love, I'm an old hand at this. You pop off and get yourself sorted.' Ethel gave her a long look. 'Mind, looks like you could do with going back to bed.'

Grace survived that day on the adrenaline brought about by relief, yet, by 6 p.m., her vision was beginning to swim with exhaustion. She stood in the garden and surveyed the site. The digger had turned up, eventually, the topsoil being pulled away, so that now her garden had become a building site proper. They were under way. She had spoken to the counsellor, a lovely woman by the name of Mary, who had listened to her story, of the fears that created monsters in the dark, had told her, in soothing tones, that such things were extremely common, that she was sure she would be able to help, and had made an appointment for her for the following Monday. Grace ran her fingers through her hair and felt, for the first time in an extremely long time, light. She had endured an end, that was undeniable. But somewhere in amongst that ending perhaps she could find for herself a new beginning.

Grace turned, looking out into the street towards the house of Albert and Ethel, and she smiled. Hopefully Albert would stay put tonight.

She turned to go into the house, her gaze falling on the discreet little camera hidden high above the door. It had been meant to make her feel safe. Instead it had created a shadow play, where finger shapes become monsters.

Almost without thought, Grace pulled her phone from her pocket, pulled up the app, entered settings, and slid the button for camera alerts to the off position. It did no good to look for horrors.

Then she let herself into the house, making sure to lock the door firmly behind her.

As the early morning sun spilled across the horizon, Elijah pulled his van up in front of Grace's house and suppressed a sigh. He was starting to hate this job. The digger breaking down, problems with the suppliers. It was starting to seem to him that this job was jinxed. He peered up at Grace's bedroom window, the curtains still drawn tight across it, and allowed himself a sniff of surprise. Late for the girl to be sleeping in. She was an early riser normally. But then, he allowed, she had been looking drawn lately, painfully thin, rich black circles beneath her eyes. Perhaps she had finally managed to get some good sleep in. Would do her good, if that was true.

He sighed and pushed open the van door. The boys would be here any minute. They would have to get down to it today, no time to waste, get the footings dug.

Elijah rounded the corner and stopped. The site was not how he had left it.

He frowned heavily, ducking down to inspect the disturbed earth. A hole had appeared overnight, in the shadow of the bulbous bay tree. Now just who in the hell had dug that? A prickle of something crept across his shoulder blades. The hole was large, going down to a good depth, tall enough almost that a man could stand up in it, the edges of it reaching perhaps to his shoulders. Long too, perhaps five foot?

'Bloody onions! Who the hell's done that?'

Elijah's head snapped around, his heartbeat loud in his chest. 'Sean … mate, don't sneak up on a man like that!'

'Sorry, boss.' Sean crouched down beside him and peered down into the dark earth. 'What's going on?'

'I don't know. This appeared overnight.'

They crouched there, side by side, and then Sean let out a sharp, uneasy laugh. 'You know, almost looks like someone had buried a body in there.'

Elijah glanced up at the house. 'I'd better talk to Grace, see what the hell is going on.'

He knocked smartly on the back door. One tap, two. On

the third, he felt a shift, the door moving under the pressure of his hand, swinging open wide onto an empty kitchen.

'Hello? Grace? It's Elijah.'

He stood on the threshold for long moments, uneasiness twisting in his intestines. Then, with a glance back at Sean, he stepped inside. All was quiet. A plate had been left in the kitchen sink, remnants of rice still caked to the bottom of it. An empty wine glass stood beside it, the faintest rim of red visible in the bottom.

'Grace?'

Elijah walked deeper into the house, his boots loud on the tiled floor. A clank sent his heart rate skyrocketing. Pipes, he thought. Nothing but pipes. He was getting jumpy. He peered into the living room, empty, the curtains still closed. Television dark.

Then he stood for a moment, deliberating.

'Grace?'

Finally, Elijah began to climb the stairs, each groaning under the weight of him, an uneven symphony. He paused on the landing, something cutting into his line of vision, making him stop. The loft hatch hung open, the metal ladder standing propped on the landing.

'Grace?'

He climbed up the first three rungs of the ladder, peering into the dimly lit loft. The air smelled different here, unused. It was largely empty. Just a couple of boxes stacked neatly in a corner, the words *Xmas decorations* written across them in black felt tip. Elijah let his gaze roam across it until it came to a stop on a patch of insulation no longer tucked beneath the eaves. It had to all appearances been torn out, discarded in the middle of the loft floor.

'What the hell?' he muttered.

Elijah eased his way down the ladder, coming to a stop before the bedroom door. He didn't want to go in. Could not have told you why, just that the hairs on his arms were standing on end, that every instinct in him was screaming for him to run.

He didn't.

He pushed open the bedroom door.

In the gloom, it seemed that all was as it should be, that Grace had just this moment flung back the duvet and slipped out of bed for a glass of water.

Where in the hell was she?

Elijah bit his lip, his gaze landing on the bedside table caught in a shaft of sunlight from the open door, the mobile phone that lay there. He picked it up, unsure, and slid it to open.

He studied the apps until he found the one he was looking for. He had laughed at her for that camera. Had called her paranoid. Maybe she was. And maybe he was a snoop. He opened the camera footage, to see a list of unacknowledged alerts.

He pushed the first one.

It showed a man, hood pulled up, sliding a key into the lock of the back door. Elijah felt something shift. Who was that? Did Grace have a boyfriend? She'd never mentioned one, but then …

Elijah pressed on the second alert, ten minutes later. The

same figure slipping out the back door, carrying something. What the hell was that? It was swathed in shadow, but, where the night vision caught it just right, Elijah could see a flash. Was it … was that a knife?

The man vanished again, reappearing quickly this time, moving with confident steps to the garden. Then, with a quick look over his shoulder, he began to dig.

'Holy shit,' muttered Elijah. He pulled the phone closer to him. 'That's Caleb.' He watched the man, looking older now than he had when he had lived here, in this house, just a year before. An uneasy feeling settled over the builder as he watched Caleb True burrow into the soil. His wife, Lorraine, had left him two years ago now, had slipped out under cover of darkness, never to be seen again. She was supposed to have gone to Devon.

Elijah watched Caleb dig, and suddenly, he knew why the man was here. The disturbance in the loft, almost as if someone had hidden a weapon there and had returned to retrieve it. The digging in the soon-to-be-taken-away earth. Something was down there Caleb did not want them to find. A cold hard certainty settled over Elijah – Lorraine True had never gone to Devon.

Elijah watched as Caleb dug and dug, never once looking to the camera. He didn't know, hadn't seen it.

A strange ringing had begun in Elijah's ears.

And that one question remaining – where in the hell was Grace?

Elijah watched as Caleb moved out of shot, the footage ending.

He drew in a deep breath and pressed his thumb against the final alert.

Caleb coming out the back door, something slung across his shoulder, heavy enough that his legs bowed, something wrapped in a bedsheet.

With a sinking sense of inevitability, Elijah looked up from the phone and pushed the bedroom door open wide, allowing sunlight to spill into the darkened room, puddling on the unmade bed.

There, on the bare mattress, in the shadow of the pillow, lay a burnished pool of blood.

FERTILE GROUND
KATE RHODES

My boss summons me to her office during the graveyard shift. No one enjoys being at the beck and call of every prison in London at midnight, in case a lifer has a psychotic episode, but a senior consultant has to be on duty each evening, and tonight I drew the short straw. The Forensic Psychology Unit has been my workplace for so long, I know the creak of every floorboard as I climb to the executive suite. Jean Maynard's shrewd gaze lingers on my face when she opens her door. She offers me coffee and makes small talk before inviting me to sit down; it's obvious she's playing for time. My boss must be close to retirement, but her exact age is anyone's guess. Her hair is cut into a timeless black bob, a pearl necklace resting on her collarbone, crystal blue eyes that never miss a trick. Her smile evaporates when her gaze finally connects with mine.

'Do you remember interviewing William Jago, Gemma?' she asks.

'How could I forget? He was one of my first cases. I

assessed him for the Home Office after his killing spree.'

'The children's bodies have all been recovered except for Sharon Roberts. He's promised to share the location of her grave if you see him again.'

'I worked with him twenty years ago. Why me in particular?'

'He wants someone with local knowledge. Apparently he thinks you know Cambridgeshire well.'

'That's not true, I lived there a lifetime ago.' It requires effort to suppress the memories that rush at me, of weeping when I packed the removals van, vowing never to go back.

'Jago's been studying environmental science in Broadmoor; he's made himself an expert on the area.' Maynard shakes her head in disbelief. 'He's being held at a safe house in Wicken Fen. Do you know the village?'

'Pretty well. I lived a mile away, in a place called Fordham.'

'Do you feel strong enough to interview him?'

'What do you mean?'

'Another consultant could go in your place. I need to be sure you're fully recovered. We've hardly spoken since your illness.'

'That was months ago. I'm fine now.'

'Stress can worsen depression. You don't have to do this if it feels burdensome.'

The sympathy in her voice sets my teeth on edge. 'It might help my research on psychopathic behaviour traits.'

'Look at the case file before you decide.'

The photos make my vision blur. Jago buried his victims

close to my former home, in the wide-open landscape where everything fell apart. A police photographer has recorded each shallow grave, showing the victims' remains in various stages of decomposition. I can feel Maynard assessing my body language, determining whether to send me on such a challenging assignment. After five minutes I shut the folder, but one of the images has lodged in my mind: a skeletal hand rising from peat-blackened soil, finger bones beckoning the sunlight, like a winter plant returning to life.

'I'm prepared to see him again.'

'You're sure?'

'Why would I agree otherwise?'

She gives a rapid nod. 'Broadmoor have released Jago into police custody for the whole week; he's saying it could take that long to locate the child's grave. You've got clearance to interview him daily, starting tomorrow.'

'I'll go home and pack.'

'Keep me informed, won't you, Gemma?' She presses the case file into my hands, ending our conversation with a distracted wave.

The sky is patchy with clouds when my car edges north through London's traffic the next morning. It's a typical February day, frost lingering on the pavements, pedestrians swaddled in thick winter coats. The drive gives me time to recall facts about the case. Jago worked as a primary school head teacher, a pillar of the local community. He selected his victims with care, too smart to abduct pupils from his own school. He slaughtered nine children before a neighbour grew suspicious and alerted the police. By now my Ford

Fiesta is racing over the Fens, where tilled fields stretch to the horizon, the earth more black than brown. My ex-husband told me once that it was the richest loam in Britain, ideal for growing nutrient-hungry crops, like asparagus and strawberries. I banish Simon and his passion for geology from my mind, but the scale of the landscape still feels daunting. The farmland is so low and featureless I can see church spires piercing the horizon five miles away, houses pressed flat by the weight of the sky.

I resist the urge to make a detour to my old village, arriving at Wicken Fen early for the appointment. When I park by the side of the road, a nervous-looking fifty-year-old peers back from the driver's mirror, my face shrouded by a frizz of mousy hair. The prospect of seeing Jago calls for an extra layer of war paint, so I blot my cheeks with powder and draw on some dark pink lipstick, hoping no one will notice the panic in my eyes. All I remember from my diagnostic interview is the scale of the man's delusions. His psychosis manifested as a sublime certainty that his deeds held moral authority, no matter how evil. I give myself a pep talk as the minutes tick by: I'm fully qualified to complete the task, with all the appropriate letters after my name, and my professionalism is still intact, despite my illness. It's tempting to take a nip from the vodka bottle concealed in my glove compartment, but drinking before lunchtime would be an admission of weakness. I wait until midday then grab my briefcase and launch myself from the car.

The safe house is a solitary Victorian building at the end of a rutted lane, with three unmarked cars on the driveway.

The uniform who greets me is in his thirties, a frown settling on his face when I explain the purpose of my visit.

'Good luck getting anything out of him. We took him over the fields this morning, but he just banged on about local tree species.'

My heart thuds against my ribs, even though I've spent plenty of time with mass murderers, including an eventful afternoon assessing the Wyedale Ripper's state of mind. Child killers are always the worst, the atmosphere inside the safe house adding to my unease; the hallway is painted dark green, the colour so oppressive it feels like every breath of oxygen has been squeezed from the air.

'Ready to see him now?' the cop asks.

'As I'll ever be.'

He ushers me into a room that smells of dust and stale food. The bay window ahead reveals acres of empty fields, the territory so flat it looks like it's been steamrollered. When I turn round, Jago is on the far side of the room, hair styled in the same Eton crop he wore as a young man, faded now to a dry pepper and salt. He looks like an elderly librarian as he inspects me through horn-rimmed spectacles, but the intensity of his stare is unchanged. His hands are padlocked to the arms of his chair, two uniforms seated behind him. Jago's consultant at Broadmoor insists on round-the-clock security, his severe personality disorder putting him in the highest risk category.

'A pleasure to see you again, Dr Ash,' Jago says. 'I'm afraid these barbarians won't allow me to shake your hand.' His voice is genteel, with the assurance that comes from public school, followed by Oxbridge.

'No need to apologise.'

'We were on the same wavelength last time we met. I've been looking forward to speaking with someone who shares my passion for the Fens.'

'It's a long time since I visited the area, Mr Jago.'

'Will, please. And may I call you Gemma?'

'If you prefer.' I flip open his file. 'I hear you're ready to share the location of Sharon Roberts's grave. Is that correct?'

'All in good time.' His smile widens. 'I've never understood why people say the area is dull and featureless. Tell me, have you ever visited Swaffham Prior?'

'Once or twice, to go walking.'

'The romance of the place is extraordinary, isn't it? It was a favourite birdwatching haunt of mine, for the swifts and fieldfares. You went there with your husband, I imagine?' His gaze skims the bare fingers of my left hand.

'It was a long time ago.'

His eyes brighten. 'But you must remember the beech woods. Why don't we compare notes?'

Our first session is a masterclass in time wasting. Jago asks if I ever walked through the fields at Chippenham in high summer, to admire the meadowsweet, vervain and wild poppies? The truth is I can remember little about my last visit to the beauty spot, except a brutal spell of morning sickness that cut our walk short, Simon insisting on driving me home before we'd covered a hundred metres.

It's a relief to breathe clean air after the meeting finishes, but Maynard's PA calls to say that I'll be lodging at the pub in Fordham for the entire week. My discomfort grows as I drive back to my old village, but the place has prospered since my divorce, an artisan deli replacing the Spar where we bought nappies and formula, neat terraces of houses stretching from the main road to the recreation grounds. The landlord at the Fleece provides me with a spacious room, but when I sit on the edge of the bed, the jangle of slot machines drifts through the floorboards, the sound tinny and hard to ignore. It takes effort to make myself open the case file again; Jago has attacked a fellow prisoner since his incarceration, leaving the man blind in one eye. In the meantime Sharon Roberts's parents have been campaigning for more searches to find her body. I'm about to return the documents to the box file, when a photo flutters onto my lap. It shows Sharon Roberts giving the camera an optimistic smile, freckles strewn across her cheeks, black hair tied in uneven pigtails. The image has appeared on the news often enough to become an icon of lost innocence. Her gaze holds mine as I return the photo to its plastic wallet, aware that tomorrow I must find a way to end Jago's distraction techniques. Sharon's parents know he's agreed to cooperate; if I fail, their hopes will be dashed again.

Sounds from the road outside grow louder as darkness thickens. So few cars pass by at night that each one proclaims itself like a fanfare, headlights piercing the thin curtains of my room. I'm still awake at 2 a.m., peering out at the crescent moon, a glitter of stars overhead. The skies here are less polluted than almost anywhere in the UK, but my direct view of the constellations brings little comfort.

Jago starts our second meeting with an announcement. 'I had a dreadful night's sleep, Gemma. I can't face questions today.' His thin hands twitch in his lap. 'Why don't we discuss the local flora and fauna instead?'

He launches into a lesson on biodiversity before I can stop him, stating that the rare swallowtail butterfly can only be found in the Fens, alluvial soil providing the perfect habitat for marsh orchids and fen violets. The cops stationed in corners of the room give me pitying smiles, and the third visit brings more humiliation. Jago recalls watching bitterns, teal and marsh harriers at dusk. We both know he's goading me, so I hold my tongue. It's only on my fourth visit that his behaviour changes. Jago's manner is calmer than before, his voice less strident.

'Let's go for a drive, Gemma. I'm ready to help you now.'

Jago is flanked by guards on the back seat, while I perch beside the driver. He calls a halt by the road sign for Swaffham. I don't need a map to recall that this is the centre of his terrain. During a five-year period, he planted boys' and girls' bodies over a radius extending from this point for several miles. Jago gazes at a line of poplars marking the boundary with the next field, standing motionless as he sniffs the air.

'Such a rich aroma, isn't it, Gemma? The ground reeks of volcanic lava in winter, salt and decaying leaves.'

'Shall we cross the field to look for the grave?'

His eyes darken until they match the rain-sodden earth. 'Not today. The wind's biting, I'd hate for you to catch cold.'

My fifth meeting with Jago is so fruitless, it drives me into the bar at the Fleece early in the evening, to knock back whisky. The booze should put me to sleep, but rest seems impossible, so I slip out through the fire escape. It doesn't take long to walk back to my old house. I sit on the wall opposite, half-hidden by overgrown bushes. Through the front window I can see a young couple. The woman is walking up and down, with a baby draped across her shoulder. When her partner lifts the infant into the crook of his arm, I have to turn away. A replacement family has flourished here in my absence. Despite spending a fortune on counselling to forget this place, Jago has catapulted me back into the past.

I'm hungover when the sixth interview begins, in no mood for games.

'Tomorrow morning you'll go back to Broadmoor. This is your last chance to say where the girl's buried.'

'I thought we were friends, Gemma. Why spoil things by nagging about petty details?'

'Sharon Roberts's parents need to give her a proper funeral.'

'She had one.' He gives a brilliant smile. 'Reassure them that I said a prayer before burying her. I'm not a complete philistine.'

I push the map in front of him, pockmarked with crosses, showing the name of each child. 'Show me where she's buried, or was this trip just another publicity stunt?'

'You're so angry, Gemma. I can hear it in your voice.'

'Her parents deserve closure.'

'It sounds more personal. Did you lose a baby too?'

'You promised to lead us to her grave.'

'Was it a boy or a girl?' He leans forwards, his thin face looming closer. 'I knew you were grieving the first time we met. Tell me what happened; then you can have your wretched cross on the map.'

'How do I know you'll tell the truth?'

'Be honest with me and I'll return the favour.'

I swallow a deep breath. 'His name was Ben. He was six when he died from an asthma attack.'

'How long ago?'

'Twenty-one years.'

'It happened before you interviewed me?'

'A few months earlier. He was my only child.'

'I thought so. Did you bury him in the local cemetery?'

I give a single nod, my hands shaking when I offer the map again. 'Now it's your turn.'

Excitement glitters in Jago's eyes, as if he's claiming my child's death for his tally, but there's regret in his expression as well. By revealing the location of his last victim, he's handing over his final bargaining chip.

'Sharon Roberts was a crybaby. She screamed so loudly, it almost put me off, but luckily my appetite rallied.' He inspects the map carefully, then places a precise cross on a boundary line. 'Remember the poplars we saw near the crossroads? She's buried below the first one on the left, closest to the road.'

'Thank you.' The word escapes from my mouth on a gush of relief.

'An eye for an eye, as they say. My condolences on losing your son, Gemma. He would have been a man by now if he'd survived.'

Jago's tone is a clever piece of mimicry; it could be mistaken for genuine sympathy, with a little more warmth behind it. His gaze crawls across my face before I hurry away to show the police team where to find Sharon Roberts.

The digging begins immediately. I stand by the edge of the field while half a dozen men remove frozen earth with spades and pickaxes, a trench slowly forming around the base of the tree. The peat releases its odd smell as they work: yeast, excrement and decaying fruit. After half an hour a shout goes up. A white shard of bone stands out against the mud. The men abandon their shovels and gather round, but nothing more is uncovered; the six-inch fragment probably comes from an animal, but it's placed in a sterile bag for the lab to analyse. Stars emerge slowly as the work continues, riming the fields with silver, lights from the next village marking the join between sky and land. By the time arc lamps are carried across the field, the men look exhausted. The outcome is obvious from the police inspector's body language as he trudges across the field, with hands buried in his pockets. It's 10 p.m. when the site clears, the excavation team finally downing tools.

When I return to my car, I'm too cold and angry to put up a fight. I grab the bottle of vodka and tip it back, the liquid searing the back of my throat. How could I have been stupid enough to believe the word of a confirmed psychopath? Desperation made me reveal Ben's name, my child's death adding spice to his day. I carry on drinking, then collapse into a drunken sleep, oblivious to the cold, my face pillowed against the steering wheel. When the dawn light wakes me, the internal voice that keeps a check on my behaviour is silent for once. My head pounds as I walk across the Fens, the sky's huge grey dome hanging over me. I trudge back to the row of poplars, daylight revealing how hard the diggers worked, cutting an ugly scar across the land.

It's 10 a.m. when I return to the safe house, clothes creased from a night hunched in the driver's seat, my face pale as candle wax. Even in this state I know that personal anger is unjustified. I've been a forensic shrink long enough to understand that psychopaths' worlds run parallel with ours, never overlapping. But I can't forget that Jago knew exactly what he was doing by stealing those children's lives. Guards are already leading him to the car outside. Soon Jago will be bundled into the vehicle, so I stop him in his tracks by throwing out a question.

'Why did you send me in the wrong direction?'

'That's my greatest skill, Gemma.' He gives a vicious smirk. 'I gave you a lie because you were so desperate for the truth.'

'Don't you have any regrets?'

'Of course not. For a brief period I could take lives or preserve them; it made me feel like a god.'

'Why did you say we were on the same wavelength?'

'I cause pain, while you prefer to suffer. We're opposite sides of the same coin.'

A switch flicks in my mind, the sensation finally

liberating me. I reach into my shoulder bag before Jago can tell another lie, then smash last night's empty bottle against the side of the car. It takes a split second to swipe the jagged glass across his throat. Things go into slow motion after that; blood gushes from the arterial wound, police guards panicking as they fail to staunch the flow. One of them pushes me to the ground. My eyes are level with Jago's as his lifeblood enriches the soil. I can see terror on his face, and it's a pleasure to witness real emotions there for once. My name will be printed beside his in the history books, but that doesn't matter. A sense of triumph is building inside my chest. I lied to him about my son, keeping Ben's memory out of his reach. We opted for cremation, not burial, Ben's ashes safe on my mantelpiece at home. The police officer is gentle as he applies handcuffs to my wrists, his voice comforting as he reads me my rights. When I look up again, the clouds are parting, and the light flooding down is purer than before.

THE HOUSE BEHIND

JANE CASEY

She should have left the keys where they were, sticking out of the slush at the side of the road. Elaine recognised them immediately: the big pink Perspex V on the key ring was the one she'd seen dangling from her neighbour's fingers a hundred times.

Her neighbour. The woman who lived in the house behind. The woman Elaine had been watching ever since she moved into her shabby, poky but affordable one-bedroom flat. The mews house was an award-winning architectural marvel of black slate and huge windows that was just *perfect* for a perfect person like Vix Graham. Vix was a nickname, of course – she was Victoria, really, born and raised in a dull little suburb of a boring town. But she'd left that identity behind to become an exercise and healthy-eating guru, a girl about town, an Instagram favourite with extravagant taste in shoes. She was Vix the Body, a miracle of honey-coloured muscle and enviable curves.

Elaine seemed to have spent most of the last four months

in the dark, in her bedroom, staring across the small back garden. Vix moved around her two-bedroom house as if on a stage, sublimely unaware of Elaine, the audience. And what Elaine saw was the house and the garden – not a garden at all, really, all stone slabs and spiky plants and a streak of glistening black that was a water feature. A table and benches stood on a patio sunk below ground level, with an outdoor fireplace at one end. On the first floor, there was a small terrace outside a bedroom, where the bed never seemed to be made. The kitchen and living space were on the lower ground floor, open plan, white, flawless. As flawless as tall, elegant Vix and her boyfriend, a personal trainer named JP who was corrugated with muscle. They were almost too perfect, the pair of them. And their relationship, as viewed through Instagram and Facebook, was everything Elaine had ever wanted – weekends away, bike rides in the sunshine, wetsuits and surfboards on empty beaches, sunsets and flowers and romance.

Elaine knew everything about them, but she had never spoken to them. Actually, it was more that they had never spoken to her. She had tried, twice. The first time she gave JP some small change in the local shop when he was short of cash. He took it as his protein-shake-drinking, body-beautiful due, and Elaine burned with shame all the way home. She would have done the same for any of her neighbours, she would have liked to explain, but the words hadn't come to her. For a day or two she left the lights on in her bedroom, defiant of their presence as she hung up clothes and got ready for bed.

They hadn't seen her.

She started to think they *couldn't* see her.

The second time she almost spoke to them was a month later, outside the house. Elaine was carrying a load of shopping in from the car. Vix and JP – together! – came haring around the corner at top speed, Vix laughing as she ran. Afterwards, Elaine wasn't sure if she had deliberately moved into the other woman's path or if Vix had changed course at the last second. Either way, Vix collided with her, hitting her in the stomach with a flailing arm. Elaine slumped against her garden wall, clutching her stomach but dredging up a rueful smile.

What she'd intended to say was: 'No, no. My fault. No need to worry – I'm fine. I'm Elaine, by the way. Why don't you come in for coffee after your run?'

What she actually said was: 'No.' It came out as a wheeze. If Vix heard it, she didn't acknowledge it. JP didn't break his stride. It was as if Elaine were invisible. As if she didn't even exist.

The pair of them had tormented her with Christmas parties, with late-night drinking sessions, with a New Year's Eve party that had gone on until four in the morning and had left seven champagne corks in Elaine's garden, JP firing them off like mortars while their friends laughed and sang and generally behaved as if they were the only people in the world. Elaine had stayed in bed despite the noise until she couldn't bear it any longer. Getting up, she'd peered across at them, bleary-eyed. Most of the guests were slumped on the long, low sectional sofa. Vix was dancing alone, swaying in a tiny strapless black dress, slopping champagne from the vintage saucer glass she'd photographed for Instagram a few hours earlier.

But JP was upstairs on the terrace, in the dark. And he was following someone into the bedroom – someone Elaine couldn't quite see, but someone who was definitely not Vix, since she was downstairs. Elaine caught her breath. In the living room, Vix drained her glass and went looking for another bottle of champagne, oblivious. Elaine watched for a while before climbing back into bed. She cuddled her pillow, feeling betrayed. It was *awful* to suspect that JP was cheating on Vix. *Horrible*. It made her cry before she went to sleep, just thinking about it and the way he was abusing her trust. Using her.

Men were evil. It made Elaine glad she was single.

Should she tell Vix? Maybe it was none of her business. Elaine tried and failed to imagine what she would want in Vix's situation. She sat on her unwanted knowledge like a hen trying to hatch a stone, and in the end she said nothing.

In the cold light of January, Elaine looked at herself – grey, lumpy, unloved – and decided to change her life. It was Vix that inspired her, that and a flurry of motivational posts that caught Elaine at a weak moment. *Summer bodies are made in winter. Nothing tastes as good as thin feels. When it hurts, it works.* She spent a fortune on manuka honey and coconut oil and chia seeds to make startlingly small and gritty meals. She started swimming in the local pool, scuttling from the changing rooms to the safety of the water, where she puffed and panted up and down like an elephant seal. She knew she had a long way to go, but as Vix said, a journey of a thousand miles starts with a single step. That made Elaine cry a little as the chlorinated water slapped her face. But it was an *empowered* kind of crying, she told herself. She was taking ownership of her own body. She was *loving* herself.

That worked for a week and a half, until the terrible day when she arrived at the pool to find a caramel-coloured body ploughing noisily up and down the lap lane, doing showy tumble turns at either end. It was JP, whose gym, he explained to the admiring lifeguard, was closed. He couldn't do without his swim, he said, laughing, all white teeth and eyelashes like stars. Elaine hated him for flirting with the pretty lifeguard. She submerged herself and began her slow, torturous progress through the water. At the other end, JP slid back into the water and embarked on yet another length of front crawl. As he went past Elaine, splashing mightily, she caught a wave straight in the face and inhaled at just the wrong moment. She stopped swimming, coughing and spluttering as the water burned her nose and throat.

'Are you okay?'

It was the lifeguard who asked. Elaine floundered to the edge of the pool, too weak to lever herself out straightway. She coughed and coughed again, nodding until the lifeguard padded away. A little bit of water came up mixed with sick. Elaine swept it off the side of the pool and into the water, hoping JP would swim through it.

Selfish, evil, horrible man. He'd nearly killed her and he hadn't even noticed.

That was the last time Elaine attempted swimming. She went home via the shops and bought pizza, cream buns, cheese, ice cream, sweets – everything she had denied herself. Because what was the point?

Now it was a cold February day, the slush in the gutters solid after a hard frost, the pink V half-hidden in the snow. Elaine bent down and hooked the keys into her hand, shoving them into her pocket before she walked away. It was the work of seconds. No one would have noticed, she assured herself, her breath clouding around her, her heart pounding so hard she couldn't even hear the traffic. She walked home, forgetting the milk that had been her reason for going out in the first place. In her mind a little scene played on a loop:

Vix, hassled and beautifully distraught, knocking on her door. 'Sorry, have you seen a set of keys anywhere? With a pink V on the key ring?'

And Elaine smiling. 'That's an amazing coincidence – I actually found them.'

Or, icy cool: 'No, sorry.'

Or, vague: 'I really couldn't say.'

Or: 'I did, but I can't tell you what I did with them. Come in and have a cup of tea and I'll have a look for them.'

In the fantasy, Elaine looked great, with her eyeliner flicked the way she couldn't ever quite manage to do it and her hair freshly blow-dried. A glance in a car window told her the truth: she looked like an overheated hedgehog in her woolly hat and scarf. Anyway, why would Vix come and knock on her door when she had no reason to know Elaine had found the keys? She'd have to put a note on the door of the mews to say she had them.

Elaine wrestled her hair into submission, just in case. She wasn't planning to use the keys. She'd run around to the mews, leave the casual little note that she'd rewritten four times now, come home and await developments.

But when she had slipped and slithered around the corner, into the narrow little road where Vix's house was the only residential property, Elaine hesitated. There was no one else around, the businesses all shuttered and quiet. She knew there was no one home at Vix's house – she had spent ten breathless minutes staring out of her window for signs of life before she left. And the keys were still in her pocket.

It couldn't hurt to go in, just for a quick look around. The whole house appeared on Vix's Instagram account daily; it wasn't really private in the way that an ordinary person's house was private. No, this was more like visiting a gallery or a museum.

Elaine chewed the inside of her cheek. She shouldn't go in.

She'd never have a better chance to see if she was right about JP cheating on Vix.

She'd never have a better chance to find out what they were really like.

It would take five minutes to walk around the house, if that. To see what she couldn't see from her window. To imagine she was part of their lives. Just to breathe the same air as them felt as if it would answer a question she couldn't put into words.

Elaine unlocked the heavy front door, the keys turning

easily in the locks as if the house was welcoming her. And there was the hallway. It had been the backdrop for hundreds of pictures of Vix, going out for a run or to a film premiere or just back from Pilates. It was narrower than Elaine had expected, and dark. She walked down to the kitchen door, smelling bleach and something that was a lot like stale cigarette smoke. The sink was piled with plates and a dismantled blender that had seeped juice onto the marble worktop. It would stain, Elaine thought. She flipped open the bin and gasped. Not only was there a pile of cigarette butts but handfuls of chocolate bar wrappers, sweet wrappers, plastic trays that had once held donuts – donuts! – and the bag for a loaf of the whitest, most mass-produced bread you ever saw. Elaine snapped a picture of it, self-righteousness surging through her. Vix didn't deserve her privacy any more than she deserved her 150,000 Instagram followers or her sponsorship deals. Vix was a lie. A hypocrite.

A fake.

It should have cheered Elaine up that Vix wasn't as perfect as she pretended to be. Elaine, after all, was single and dumpy, and cellulite puckered her skin, and her hair was baby-fine. She had a boring job as an administrator. She was the opposite of Vix in every way. But what she felt, mainly, was betrayed. She had almost believed that if she went to the gym every day and switched to almond milk and porridge with fresh berries and generally put in some effort, she might tap into whatever it was that made Vix so glowing, so glossy, so utterly enviable. She had *wanted* to believe it.

Truthfully, she still wanted to believe that Vix didn't

know the truth about JP – that she was, in her way, just as much a victim as Elaine herself. But upstairs it was clear immediately that they weren't really a couple. JP slept in the small bedroom at the front of the house, the one Elaine couldn't see from her flat. The bedside drawer contained some very advanced sex toys, lube, condoms and a card from a gay sauna in Berlin.

'You dirty git,' Elaine breathed, staring at it before she snapped another picture. Brazen, it was. He was as gay as Christmas. His relationship with Vix was just for show, to hide the truth. And Vix had to be in on it. Liars, the pair of them.

Vix's room was untidy, the bed unmade as usual. Behind the bed there was another pile of sweet wrappers and the en suite bathroom smelled of vomit. The bowl of the toilet was flecked with it. Elaine pulled a face, revolted. She hurried over to the door that led onto the terrace and propped it open. Even though the air was cold, it was at least fresh.

She had intended to go in, look around and leave again, but now that she was in the house, the sense of urgency faded. She had spent so long imagining what it would be like to be Vix – the things she, Elaine, would do if her appearance and her weight weren't holding her back. Here was an opportunity to live the life she'd imagined, even for a half-hour. It was irresistible.

Elaine sat down at the dressing table, noticing the mirror with a residue of white powder on it – drugs! Well, that explained a lot. There were the drawers of make-up, the cosmetics, the perfume bottles, the tools that went to making Vix look like something you'd want to be. Slowly, dreamily, forgetting to hurry, Elaine selected make-up from the drawers at random. With false eyelashes and a lot of contouring, she didn't look so much like herself. She painted her mouth scarlet and liked it, surprised at herself.

The walk-in wardrobe was a disappointment because everything was a size six. But the shoes were better. She was able to force her feet into Vix's heels, even if they were too narrow for comfort and an inch too long for her. She must have tried on eight or nine different pairs of shoes, all designer brands, all impossible to walk in. But Elaine could pose. She took picture after picture, getting careless about putting the shoes back where they had been. The heels piled up in confusion around the base of the three-way mirror. It was a kind of madness, a recklessness. Elaine felt untouchable for the first time in her life. She felt superior.

It was a feeling that lasted right up to the moment where she looked at herself in the mirror and made eye contact with the slender figure standing in the doorway.

'What the hell do you think you're doing?' Vix let her gym bag slip off her shoulder and fall to the ground. 'Who are you? What are you doing in my house?'

'I-I can explain.' Elaine faltered. 'I found your keys. In the street.'

'How did you know they were mine?'

'The key ring. The big V. I've seen it on the Internet.'

'But how did you know where I live?'

'I live behind you, in that house over there. I've been watching you.'

'Watching me? *Stalking* me?' Vix whipped out her phone. 'I'm calling the cops.'

'No, don't.' Elaine began to waddle towards her, the heels making it impossible to move normally.

'Stay back.' Vix held out a long finger in warning. 'You fucking *freak*.' In a different voice, she said, 'Yes, police, please.'

In the nick of time, Elaine found something to say. 'At least I don't have an eating disorder. At least my pretend boyfriend isn't *gay*. At least I don't *smoke*.'

Vix stared at Elaine for a few seconds. Then she ended the call and lowered her phone. 'What are you talking about?'

'Everything you pretend to be is a lie.'

'That's not true.'

'You're not fit. You're not healthy. You're sick and your perfect relationship is an invention. There's nothing real about you. You're a fraud.' Wobbling, Elaine pulled the shoes off her feet and threw them at Vix. 'You're a joke.'

'Don't say that.' Vix backed away, into the bedroom.

'I know what goes on behind the cameras. Little Miss Perfect. But you're pretending, all the time.' Elaine held up her own phone. 'And I've got the proof. Do you think people will still want you to promote their products when everyone knows the truth?'

'You can't tell anyone.'

'You can't stop me.'

Vix's lovely mouth fell open. 'That's blackmail.'

'Better than fraud.'

The two women stared at one another for a moment. Then Vix made a grab for the phone.

'Give me that!'

'It's mine!'

'Give it to me, you little bitch.' With longer arms, Vix had the advantage. She slapped Elaine's face, then grabbed her hair and pulled it, hard. Elaine howled.

'Get off me.' She managed to get hold of Vix's ponytail and half of it came away in her hand.

'My extensions! They cost a fortune.'

'They're just another lie!' For some reason it was the hair that made Elaine really furious. All that time she'd spent buying volumising shampoo and coaxing her hair to look fuller and really she should have bought someone else's hair and had done with it. She dropped the handful of hair and punched Vix in the face as hard as she could. 'And your nose is fake too. I've seen the before and after pictures.'

Vix reeled backwards, blood pouring from her nostrils. 'I had a deviated septum.'

'A likely story.' Elaine shoved her. 'What about JP?'

'What about him?'

'He's gay. You're not a couple at all.'

'You can't tell anyone. He's not out. His parents –'

'Don't pretend that you're doing this for his parents. Hashtag relationship goals – that's what you say, isn't it? All those cute little videos and selfies and it's bullshit. It's just another way of making yourself look good.'

'Stop it.' Vix smeared the blood from her nose on her sleeve. She had stepped back farther, onto the terrace.

'How can you justify it?' Elaine's voice cracked. She was almost crying. 'I believed in you.'

Vix narrowed her eyes. 'Then you're an idiot. No one is perfect. And if someone tells you they are, they're lying. They're selling you something. It's up to you if you buy it. No one made you. You fooled yourself into thinking you could be something you're not. But none of it is real.'

'I wanted to be you.' It was the first time Elaine had admitted it, even to herself.

'You all do.' Vix tilted her head back, looking more beautiful than ever despite the smudge of blood under her nose. 'Don't tell me you wouldn't do exactly what I've done if you could.'

'I wouldn't lie to people.'

'You would.' An unpleasant smile spread across Vix's face. 'But we'll never know, will we? Let's face it, you could go to the best plastic surgeon and the best beautician and you'd still never be a supermodel. You'll always be a fat little loser.' She leaned forward. 'And that lipstick makes your teeth look yellow.'

It was as if the surge of anger short-circuited Elaine's brain. For a moment everything went white. When she blinked and came back to herself, her hands were stretched out in front of her. Where Vix had been standing, there was nothing but thin air. Three footprints in the snow showed where she had stepped back, off balance, and collided with the balcony. The snow was scuffed away along the railing.

Elaine stood absolutely still, afraid to move – afraid to look over the edge of the terrace to the paving slabs below.

There wasn't a sound. The daylight was fading fast, the short winter day drawing to a close. There were no lights on yet in the houses that overlooked the garden. No one had seen anything. After what seemed like a long time, she looked down at the trampled snow, at her stubby bare feet. They were blue with cold.

She needed to move.

Carefully, Elaine stepped back through the door. She found her socks and pulled them on. Then, carrying her trainers, she hurried through the gloomy house. What had she touched? She couldn't remember. She had been everywhere. She grabbed a tea towel from the kitchen and ran around the house, wiping surfaces. It was better than nothing.

She was standing at the door, ready to leave, when she stopped. She couldn't just go. Not without checking.

Vix lay just outside the living room window, her long limbs twisted awkwardly. Her eyes were open, staring up at the sky. The snow around her head was dyed red, spattered with pinkish material from the impact that had crushed the back of her skull. The Body was nothing but a body now.

Elaine ran down the hall and slipped through the front door, pulling it closed behind her. Then, blinded with tears, shivering as if she had a fever, she pulled on her trainers and ran home.

In her bedroom, in the dark, she watched it all play out as if it were on a giant television screen. JP came home, flicking on all the lights as he moved from room to room, eating an apple, checking his phone. He stopped in the doorway of Vix's bedroom, then strode across to close the balcony door. And stopped. And walked forward to look over the railing.

The police came quickly, and the ambulance crew, and more police, and a forensic team in white boiler suits. Elaine sat and sobbed, blowing her nose loudly. How could she have done it? Even if Vix had been a liar and a cheat and really a bit of a bitch? How could it have happened? She was a murderer and she was going to spend the rest of her life in prison. She had always thought Vix was better than her, but now, when it was too late, Elaine was discovering she really cared about herself. Vix was dead, but Elaine had a life to lead. She was a good person who deserved a second chance.

JP sat on the sofa in the living room, his head in his hands, as the detectives came and went. Elaine watched them showing him evidence bags. The contents of the drawer in his bedside table, she guessed.

JP was going to have a lot of explaining to do.

And JP couldn't. Elaine watched him pacing back and forth, shouting at the police until the tendons stood out in his neck. Losing the plot. It couldn't happen to a nicer person, she thought.

An hour later someone knocked on her door. She ran down and opened it to see a policewoman holding up her ID.

'Just routine door-to-door enquiries. Did you see anything that happened in the house behind you earlier today?' She held her pen over her clipboard, evidently ready to tick 'no'. Elaine peered over her shoulder at the police car that was sliding past, its wheels hissing in the slush. JP sat in the back seat. His face was pale, strained. He stared at Elaine intently, his eyes fixed on hers. He looked desperate.

It seemed to Elaine, looking at him, that the entire situation was his fault. She would never have gone into the house if she hadn't been looking for evidence he was cheating on Vix. And maybe Vix would have been happier without him, without the strain of living a lie. So she hadn't been what she pretended to be. So what?

Elaine wished she could speak to JP. She knew exactly what she would say.

Can you see me? Can you see me now?

'Did you notice anything out of the ordinary?' the police officer asked again.

'Yes,' Elaine said. 'Yes, I saw everything.' She looked the officer right in the eye. 'I saw what he did. I saw the whole thing.'

THE CORPSE IN THE COPSE

SHARON BOLTON

1.

Lacey Flint, a woman with more secrets than Victoria's flagship lingerie store, walked the long, high, carpeted corridor and paused at the door of apartment 5b. In the last couple of years she'd swum through the sewers of London, tackled terrorists on the Thames, hunted down a Jack the Ripper copycat, and slit her own wrists.

Today would be something else.

'Do I curtsey, sir?' she'd asked, back at Wapping Police Station an hour earlier.

'Do you know how?'

'Not really.' She'd pushed one foot back and bent at both knees. Wobbled a bit.

'I wouldn't,' said Superintendent David Cook, head of the Metropolitan Police's Marine Unit. 'Call her ma'am, be polite, don't commit us to anything daft. Word has it she'd be called a brick short of a load, only that would be disrespectful.'

Lacey pressed the buzzer with one hand and, with the other, pulled down the jacket of the dress uniform she rarely wore. After thirty seconds, she heard the sound of high heels making their way, with neither rhythm nor pace, across a hardwood floor. She took a step back as the door opened.

The elderly woman looking out was small and slight. Her hair had been backcombed to disguise its sparseness and there were elongated holes in the lobes of her ears where, over the decades, heavy jewels had nearly ripped the flesh in two. Her face was visibly powdered and rouged whilst her pale blue cashmere sweater had tiny holes on the arms where moths had found it, and a dribble of yellow where her breakfast egg had.

'I was expecting a man.' Her voice whispered of expensive gin and menthol cigarettes.

Lacey held up her warrant card. 'I'm Constable Lacey Flint, ma'am. Are you Princess Tabitha?'

'Who else would I be? This way.'

The old lady turned and clicked her unsteady way back across the hardwood floor.

Princess Tabitha Iris Elizabeth, the widow of Prince Edward, Duke of Shropshire and daughter-in-law to the late King George V, was one hundred and three years old. She lived alone, visited by daily carers, in a grace and favour apartment on the top floor of London's Kensington Palace. She had been complaining for several months – first to her family, then to the palace groundsmen, the royal protection unit, and finally the commissioner of the Metropolitan Police – about a corpse in a tree in Kensington Gardens.

'Your lot pull bodies out of trees, don't they?' the commissioner had apparently said to Superintendent Cook.

Whilst the Marine Unit's prime responsibility was safeguarding the River Thames, it also contained the Line Access Team, the specialist climbers who conducted searches at height. After the 7/7 bombings in London, it had been the Line Access Team that had combed the treetops around Tavistock Square for evidence. Not an occasion any of them remembered fondly.

'Send someone over, Dave,' the commissioner had said. 'The old love has important relatives.'

Lacey followed Princess Tabitha to the end of the corridor, where a door opened upon an old lady's bedroom. The bed was trimmed in lots of pink nylon. The curtains almost matched. The cluttered, untidy room smelled of TCP, lavender and urine.

'Lovely room,' said Lacey, because the old lady's silence was becoming unnerving.

Princess Tabitha snorted. 'Don't lie, woman, it's hideous. I'd replace the lot at Ikea tomorrow, but do you know what my annual furniture budget is?'

'I don't, I'm afraid.'

'Have a guess.'

Lacey risked another glance around. Dressers, mirrors, chests of drawers, at least seven tables of assorted sizes, each laden with photographs and ornaments. 'Um, a thousand pounds?'

'Nothing. This load of junk is intended to outlive me. Well, I suppose it will.'

'Ma'am, could you show me the tree you're concerned about?'

'I'm not concerned about the tree, woman. I'm concerned about the dead body in the tree.'

Princess Tabitha walked to the window and picked up a pair of opera glasses from the ledge. 'There.' She pointed out over the park. 'That one. Tall horse chestnut. Plain as day.' She raised the opera glasses to her eyes and nodded slowly. 'Still there.' She held them out to Lacey.

Lacey dug into her bag. 'Actually, ma'am, I brought my own.' She focused her binoculars on the copse of trees the princess had indicated.

'Are you a bird watcher, ma'am?' she asked as she moved the sight slowly over the crests of the trees.

'No, I watch people,' the old lady replied. 'I've seen infants grow and fade, alliances formed and broken. I've seen more than one soul die in the gardens, but I've never seen a dead body in a tree before. Have you found it yet?'

Leaves, more leaves. Some of them bright green still, others bronzing as the air turned colder, clusters of conkers, some bursting open, others tight in spiny buds. And something else too. Something that, with poor eyesight and a strong imagination, might possibly be mistaken for a torso and extended arm.

'Ma'am, I can make out something that doesn't seem to be part of the tree, but it's hard to be sure. It's very high off the ground.'

'That's it. That's the body. How will you get it down?'

Lacey lowered her binoculars. 'When did you first spot it, ma'am?'

'Spring. Early May, it would be, because the tree was in bloom. The Duke spoke to the head groundsman about it.'

'Ma'am, I think I need to look at the tree from the ground now and speak to the park keeper.'

'Groundsman, dear. His name isn't Percy.'

2.

Lacey stood at the base of the tree, looking up. 'Sir, it's massive,' she said into her phone. 'It must be thirty-five metres high and wide too. If it is a body, it's right at the top. You can't see it from the ground.'

'Lacey, please explain to me how a body ended up at the top of a thirty-five-metre horse chestnut tree in Kensington Gardens?'

'Princess Tabitha thought it might have fallen out of a helicopter, sir,' said Lacey.

An exaggerated sigh down the phone line. 'The only helicopters to fly over Kensington Palace have members of the royal family on board. I think we'd have noticed if one of them had gone missing.'

'Thrown out of a plane was another theory of the princess's, but she feels that working out how it got there is our job, not hers.'

'Lacey, I'm glad you're having fun, and I hope you enjoyed tea and biscuits at the palace, but there's a launch going out in an hour and I'd like you on board.'

'Actually, sir, I've got a meeting with the head groundsman before I can come back. I think this is him now. Toodle-pip.'

'Good morning!'

The man approaching was in his early thirties, a little below six feet tall, and broad at the shoulder. His hair was dark brown, close cropped, his skin tanned, his eyes a soft hazel brown. 'Hudson Jones.' He held out a scarred hand that wasn't clean.

'Constable Flint.' Lacey felt the rough skin scratching against her palm. 'You're the head groundsman?' She'd expected someone older, a little stooped, wind beaten, deep wrinkles around his eyes.

'Duty head groundsman.' He was still holding her hand. 'The actual head doesn't get into the park much. What can I do for you?'

'Have you noticed anything unusual about this tree?'

Lacey pulled her hand back and together they looked up.

'Pretty healthy specimen of a horse chestnut,' Jones said. 'Mature tree, up to its full height and spread, about to drop a whole load of conkers.'

'So what do you make of Princess Tabitha's theory that there's a body at the top?'

Jones puffed out a long, slow breath. 'Still on about that, is she? There's no way someone could get a body up there. And why would they try? This is the busiest park in London. And given that half the royal family live in the palace, the best guarded.'

'It's closed at night, isn't it?'

Jones inclined his head.

'Have you noticed any unusual activity around the tree? Anyone trying to climb it?'

He gave her an almost apologetic look. 'Dead bodies can't climb.'

'No, of course not. I appreciate your time, Mr Jones.'

'Hudson. I'll walk you out.'

They set off towards the administration buildings at the back of the palace. As they reached a line of red brick huts, Jones pulled a door open.

'Have you got a minute?' he said. 'You might find this interesting.'

The room Jones showed Lacey into was large and rectangular, with a concrete floor and a central table. A counter ran around the outside, shelves above it, cupboards below. The shelves were packed, the counter and table likewise, with musical instruments, carved and plaster figurines, lanterns, clocks, vintage toys, picnic baskets, a stuffed badger, a pair of embroidered, satin high-heeled shoes.

It was like Dickens's Old Curiosity Shop.

'Stuff we've found in the park over the years,' Jones said. 'We record everything in lost property, and most gets disposed of after three months, but if it's quirky enough, it ends up here.'

'Is this an urn?' Lacey stopped in front of a black marble, lidded vase.

'Complete with ashes,' Jones told her. 'We think someone sneaked in one night to scatter their loved one, only to be frightened off. Been here for five years, not claimed.'

'False teeth?' Lacey said, moving on. 'Who takes their teeth out in a park?'

Jones pointed to the top shelf. 'There's a prosthetic leg up there.'

'You're kidding me.'

Lacey turned the corner and stopped. 'OK, these are a bit sinister.'

She was looking at guys, inanimate stuffed figures, sitting on shelves and leaning against walls. She counted six.

'We usually get at least one each bonfire night,' Jones told her. 'Kids bring them in, get bored, leave them behind.'

'Could it be a guy, the thing in the tree?' she asked. 'One of these figures, or a shop-window dummy, put up there as a joke?'

'It's supposed to be right at the crown of the tree?' Jones said.

'That's right.'

'How would they get it up there without a system of ropes and pulleys? We'd spot them in daylight. Even at night, the gardens are patrolled.'

She gave him a quick smile. 'Good point.'

'And pranksters want their efforts recognized. There'd be pictures on Facebook. I promise you, no one's shown any real interest in that tree. On the subject of creepy though, you need to look at these.' They'd reached a cupboard. He pulled open the double doors.

Lacey said, 'Oh, good God.'

Thirteen carved wooden dolls sat in the cupboard, all obviously made by the same hand. Each was something short of a foot high, each had a large white-painted face. The limbs were made from stuffed cotton, darkened to a greyish yellow. Each was dressed in regency costume, one male figure was a mini Napoleon. Most disturbing, though, were their expressions. Wide eyed and snarling.

'Exactly.' Jones was visibly pleased at her reaction. 'We can't keep them out. Some of the kids we get in here are quite young. We've even had twelve-year-olds running out in tears.'

'I'm not surprised.' Lacey leaned closer. 'That hair looks real.'

Each doll had long, straggly hair hanging down from a central parting.

'We think it is. And not from the same person.'

She stepped back, resisting the temptation to close the cupboard doors. The dolls didn't smell too good. 'Where did you find them?'

'We've collected them over the last couple of years. They're found tied to tree trunks, about five feet off the ground.'

'Different trees?'

He nodded.

'The horse chestnut we were looking at?'

He thought for a second. 'I don't think so. If you give me a number, I can check.'

Lacey gave him the number of Wapping Police Station and pretended not to notice that he looked disappointed.

3.

'Sir, I've just heard back from Kensington Palace. A wallet was found beneath that tree on the eighth of March. Credit cards, library card, no cash, but that shouldn't surprise anyone.'

Cook didn't look up from his desk. Outside the first-floor window Lacey could see a Marine Unit launch pulling up at the police jetty.

'So our body in the tree has been identified?' Cook never bothered to hide his sarcasm.

'It's not impossible, sir, because Mr David Sivers, who owned the wallet, was reported missing by his neighbour on March twenty-second. She hadn't seen him for some time and thought he might be dead. She let officers into his flat, with her own key, but the search showed nothing out of order.'

Finally Cook looked up. 'Any reason to suspect foul play?'

'Not at that time, sir.'

'Vulnerable person?'

'In his forties, believed to be in good health. And with no worried relatives hassling us, the case went no further.'

Cook sighed. 'Why do I have a feeling that's about to change?'

'Also, sir, a car registered to Mr Sivers was towed from a residents-only parking zone in Pembridge Crescent on the eighth of March. As the traffic authorities are very strict in that area of Notting Hill, it seems safe to assume he parked overnight on March the seventh and his car was ticketed and then towed the following day. It's never been claimed.'

'Does he live in Notting Hill?'

'No, he lives in Kennington. The Victoria Estate.'

Cook frowned. 'That place where –'

Lacey spoke quickly. 'A couple of blocks away but close enough. It's just under a mile from Pembridge Crescent to

Kensington Park Gardens, about a fifteen-minute walk.'

'So he parks in Pembridge Crescent, some distance from the park, goes to meet persons unknown, who bump him off and hoist his body to the top of a thirty-metre-high horse chestnut tree?'

'I know it doesn't sound likely, sir, but we know he was in the park that night, because his wallet was handed in the next day.'

'What is it you want me to do, Lacey?'

She smiled. 'I'd like to have a look around his flat, sir.'

The woman with scarlet hair – in black leggings and an oversized black tunic top that clung to, rather than hid, her enormous hips, her sagging belly and her surprisingly small breasts – clutched the bannister rail. 'Don't suppose you could have a word with them about fixing the lift?' she managed, when she could speak again.

Lacey had been waiting for several minutes on the fourth floor. She didn't like the Victoria Estate in Kennington. Not since a woman had bled to death in her arms here a couple of years ago. 'I doubt the council would listen to me,' she said. 'Can I just check when you last saw Mr Sivers?'

The woman needed a few more seconds of heavy breathing before she could reply. 'Hard to know for sure. He keeps himself to himself.'

'How long did you wait between seeing him last and reporting him missing?'

They'd reached Sivers's flat. 'Dunno. A week. Maybe a month.'

'Was he a friend of yours?'

'Hardly knew him.'

'Yet he gave you a key to his flat?'

'No, he didn't give it to me. I had it left over from the last owner. I used to clean for her.'

The door was open. The smell that hit Lacey was musty, stale, and had the unpleasant odour of rubbish, but didn't strike any alarm bells.

'Thank you.' She smiled at Sivers's neighbour. 'I'll take it from here. Would you like to leave the key with me, and I'll bring it back down? Or you can wait outside.'

'I'll show you where everything is.'

Lacey stood her ground. 'That won't be possible, I'm afraid. If this is potentially a crime scene, I can't allow it to be contaminated.'

Muttering, the woman waddled off along the corridor. Lacey pocketed the keys and closed the door. The lights didn't work. She took a torch from her pocket and switched it on.

A decent size, 1980s furniture, a little cluttered, very untidy. A plate, knife and fork on the floor by an armchair showed the remains of the last meal Sivers had eaten here. A copy of the *Evening Standard* was open on a side table. It was the room of a man who lived alone and who had probably expected to return home after his last trip out.

One wall was lined with cupboards that seemed out of place somehow. They were made from hardwood, old and scuffed, dull from years without polish, but had once been good quality. There were four of them, each standing over five feet high, with multiple drawers, each with dull brass handles. The sort of cupboards you might see in a museum basement.

One of the drawers, third cupboard along, fifth drawer from the top, was open. Lacey stepped towards it and saw eggs. At least two dozen, ranging in size from tiny ones that might sit on a teaspoon to those that measured five inches from top to bottom. All shades of white and cream, some pale brown, blue, even soft pink. Sivers had been an egg collector.

Unless the collection was antique, that wasn't legal.

'Nobody put his body in that tree, sir, he climbed up by himself.'

'Lacey, I'm not paying overtime for this.' Down the phone line, Cook sounded as though he were eating.

'He was stealing eggs. Probably selling them on the black market. I found a lot of cash in his bedside table. And the groundsman I've been dealing with tells me that long-eared owls have been seen in the gardens. They're very shy, so no one's sure where they were nesting, but they think it was somewhere in that copse.'

'So he climbed up to nick a couple of eggs and what? Decided he liked the view? Fancied playing at Tarzan for a bit?'

'We won't know unless we take a look, sir.'

'Lacey, any time you fancy a transfer to bomb disposal, just say the word.'

4.

'She's the only one light enough, Sarge.' Constable Finn Turner was known to his fellow members of the Line Access Team as Spiderman because he could climb anything.

Anything except this tree.

'I can get up to twenty metres, no sweat,' he went on, 'but the top branches won't hold me.'

Already kitted up – rumour at Wapping had it that Spiderman slept in his harness and helmet – he was making a monkey's fist, a heavy and complicated knot that he would throw over the lower branch to get the climb started.

The rest of the team weren't happy, but then neither was Lacey. When she'd gone all out to persuade the boss to authorize a search of the tree, it hadn't occurred to her that she might be the one to do it. She'd only ever taken part in training climbs.

'Finn, how about we send you up as high as you can go, then you talk her up?' suggested the team sergeant.

Spiderman shook his head. 'Nah. Double the number of lines makes it more likely she'll get caught up. She's a good climber. She should go first; I'll follow.'

With grudging permission from the sergeant, Spiderman threw the monkey's fist over the second-lowest branch and caught it. That was the main line that would take Lacey up the tree. Use of a lanyard, a shorter length of rope, would anchor her to the branches.

The first part of the climb would be the most physically demanding; and watched by everyone: the Line Access unit, the park staff, even a small crowd of early dog walkers. Lacey let the line take her weight and began to pull herself up using a technique known as body thrusting. After just six repetitions, her breathing had spiralled. It's not about strength, Finn had told her in training. It's about power-to-weight ratio. You're strong and light, you'll be fine.

She wasn't even at the first branch and she was feeling anything but fine. Finn, she knew, would be ten feet up by now.

'Slow it down, Lace,' he said from directly below. 'You'll be knackered before you start.'

Drawing level with the first branch, she pulled herself up until she was standing on it. It would be easier from here – for a while. She looked down. Finn, only a couple of feet below because at six foot five, he was exceptionally tall, gave her a thumbs-up.

'Can you see anything?' he asked.

She looked up. 'Leaves. Conkers.'

'Lanyard as high as you can get it. Throw, attach, release, climb.'

Turning back to the tree, she spotted her next branch and threw. Catching the lanyard, she secured herself, released the main climbing line, and went up another four feet. She threw again, attached the line, released the first and climbed. Did it again. And again. She'd barely begun, and already her muscles were feeling the strain. It was a cool morning, but sweat was breaking out on her neck and temples.

'You're doing well.' Finn's voice came over the radio now. 'Don't rush it. Keep throwing high.'

The line got stuck. She pulled it back, attached the throwball and tried again. The weight of the heavy leather ball did the trick, taking the line up, around the branch and back down to her. She climbed again.

She was breathing too fast.

The radio crackled. 'You're about halfway, Lacey, which means the branches are getting thinner. Test them out. Use the trunk if you have to. I'm following you up.'

Lacey's limbs were shaking with the effort of pulling up and holding her body weight, and an illogical fear had sneaked up on her. She wasn't afraid of heights, but being so far from the ground was unnerving. The rough shell of a horse chestnut scratched against her face. A couple of seconds later, she misjudged what was above her and her helmet crashed hard into a branch.

'You alright, Lacey?'

She'd sworn out loud. 'Fine. Banged my head.'

'You're out of breath. Slow it down.'

Wise words, but she didn't want to slow it down. She wanted to get it over with. Throw, attach, release, climb. It was getting windier and the tree felt less solid. The branches were thinner and moving with the wind. Several had broken away. How high up was she? She looked down, the tree seemed to tip, and a wave of nausea washed over her. She looked up and saw an impossible task.

'Finn, I'm stuck.' There was nowhere else to go. None of the branches she could reach looked solid enough.

'Wrap the rope around the trunk. Check it before you use it.'

Gritting her teeth, she did what she was told. The rough bark held the line in place. She advanced a little farther and reached a branch that looked reliable. She transferred her weight carefully. It held.

'I can see you. You look great.'

She glanced down and caught a glimpse of Spiderman's red helmet fifteen metres beneath her.

'Take a breather,' he told her. 'Can you see anything?'

'Not yet.'

Ignoring his advice to rest, she looked up for another branch and saw one that was a possibility. She threw the rope, secured the line and climbed another four feet. On the last pull she spotted something. Sizeable, a few feet to her left. A piece of climbing equipment attached to a short line.

'Sarge, is Hudson Jones with you?'

The radio crackled and then: 'Right next to me, Lacey, what's up?'

'Can you ask him when this tree was last professionally climbed?'

A brief pause and then: 'Not for years. Why? What's up there?'

'A lanyard, about eight feet long. It doesn't look that old. I think someone climbed up here in the last few months.'

Checking she was secure, Lacey pulled out her phone and took pictures of the lanyard. Looking up, she saw the broken remains of a branch, about twelve or so feet above her, that it might once have hung around. Had the branch broken, the climber would have fallen. If he'd relied only on a lanyard, and the chances were he had, because a main line would be visible and obvious from the ground, he could have tumbled until something broke his fall.

'There's something else.' Lacey was looking up again. 'About six feet above my head.'

'What?'

'Stand by, Sarge, I'm going up.'

Throw, attach, release, climb. And again. Until the thing she'd spotted was hanging only a foot or so above her.

'A shoe,' she said. 'It's a shoe.'

Not just any shoe but a specialist climbing shoe. Black with green laces, minimum sole, designed to grip and bend. Size seven. The shoe of a small person, probably not much bigger than she was.

'Is there a foot inside?'

Impossible to tell from this angle. She threw the lanyard and climbed again. Another couple of feet and she was level with the shoe.

'Yes, Sarge,' she said, in a voice she wasn't sure the radio would pick up.

Not only was there a foot inside the shoe, but a leg too. A leg that was a seething mass of maggots. This close, she could smell it.

The climber had been wearing jeans, but much of the fabric had been ripped away. It had been torn in tiny shreds, as though by the pulling of small knives.

Or beaks.

Moss had claimed the shoe, covering its once glossy black in a green velvet sheen. At some point seeds, blown on the wind, had become trapped around its rim and in the lace holes. Tiny, cotton-thin stalks had sprouted up around the foot. Stuck to the leaves surrounding it were hundreds of husks of insect cocoons. Several generations of larvae had fed on the body.

She couldn't see anything beyond the knee.

Without refastening the lanyard, relying only on the main rope, conscious that she was making exactly the same mistake that the climber had made, Lacey went up a little higher. There was a thick canopy of leaves above her, and a network of small thin branches. They seemed to be weighted down though, and some of them had broken. She climbed up. She would have to push through the foliage now. There was a reason tree surgeons usually worked in the autumn and winter.

She pushed her head through a barrier of green as a bird flew away in alarm.

The corpse lay face up, as though he'd fallen from a height and the tree had caught him. Which it had, she saw. It had caught him with a broken, spiked branch that had impaled him through the stomach, pinning him in place, injuring him badly, preventing him from climbing down. He'd bled to death.

It could be David Sivers. It was hard to tell. Birds had eaten much of his face away. Insect larvae had taken the rest.

The smaller branches, the spring and summer growth of the tree, hadn't let the presence of a foreign body hold them back. The tree had absorbed Sivers, wrapping itself around him, growing into his softening, decaying flesh, pushing into his clothes.

Sudden movement startled her and Lacey almost slipped. Four feet to her left, bright orange eyes met hers. The owl was a little over twelve inches high, speckled brown, cream and black. Its ears – not really ears at all, but tufted head feathers, stuck upright like question marks on the top of its head. It didn't seem afraid of her at all. In fact, it was looking at her almost greedily.

It wouldn't want to share, or lose, the good thing that had been left in its tree all summer.

A bird – not an owl, but a different species because the nest was small – had nested in the pocket of Sivers's jacket. The fledglings had long since left, but Lacey could see traces of eggshell. There was another nest in the hollow of his right armpit, a third in a rent of his sleeve. The larvae that had fed on his body would have provided an endless supply of food for the young birds.

Lacey aimed her camera and then looked closer at the nearest nest. It had been made from twigs, in the usual way, but lined with something that looked like human hair. Sickened, she looked up. The corpse's hair had all gone. As his scalp had rotted, it would have been easy to dislodge. Birds from all over the park had eaten Sivers's body, had torn his clothes and hair to build their nests.

Sivers had climbed up here to plunder the tree. The tree had returned the favour.

ABOUT THE AUTHORS

RACHEL ABBOTT

What kind of books do you write? Thrillers based on the relationship between the victims and perpetrators of crime – the *why* rather than the *who*.

Inspiration for 'An Uninvited Guest'? Where I live, nobody ever locks their doors. My sister said, 'I'm not worried about someone breaking in. I'm worried about you coming home and finding there's someone in your house.'

What keeps you awake? My characters, talking to me and telling me what they're going to do next. They won't shut up.

Favourite part of the body? The face – especially as people grow older. Have they laughed a lot or frowned? Each individual face tells a story of its own.

SHARON BOLTON

What kind of books do you write? Contemporary (occasionally twentieth-century) thrillers with a dark and sinister Gothic twist.

Inspiration for 'The Corpse in the Copse'? It gave me a chance to explore the formidable, maybe even vengeful, power of nature.

What keeps you awake? On nights when the moon is entirely absent from the sky, I'm kept awake by the fear of a certain recurring nightmare and a dread that it might, one day, come true.

Favourite part of the body? I find the human body endlessly beautiful, even in age, but blood (the bit we don't usually see) has always held a special fascination for me.

JANE CASEY

What kind of books do you write? A series of police procedural novels featuring a London-Irish detective sergeant in a Metropolitan Police murder investigation team, Maeve Kerrigan. I've also written psychological thrillers and a crime series for teenagers.

Inspiration for 'The House Behind'? I'm mildly obsessed with the clean-eating phenomenon and especially with Internet-famous bloggers who make a fortune from selling diet and fitness advice. I think there's always a gap between how people present themselves on social media and in reality, so I wanted to see what would happen when someone from the other side of the screen broke into the fantasy world.

Favourite part of the body? The nape of the neck, a tender spot. It's as distinctive as a fingerprint and hidden from its owner, so it feels both vulnerable and quietly revealing.

TAMMY COHEN

What kind of books do you write? Psychological thrillers, plus historical mysteries as Rachel Rhys.

Inspiration for 'The Study'? Like millions, I was hooked on the Rob and Helen storyline in *The Archers*, and wanted to explore an abusive relationship based not on violence but on the absolute conviction of one partner that they know what's best for the other.

What is your superpower? I'm currently on my first ever yoga holiday and have just discovered that I can put my big toe in my mouth, which has got to come in useful some time, surely?

Favourite part of the body? Definitely NOT the big toe.

JULIA CROUCH

What kind of books do you write? Domestic noir. It is essentially about the terrible things we do to each other in the name of love; about how the home, the place we should normally see as sanctuary, can become anything but.

Inspiration for 'Beach Ready Body'? I am a bootcamp fanatic. I have been on Hove seafront at 6 a.m., shivering in the pre-dawn drizzle, on many occasions. Neither my body nor my life have noticeably changed, but I keep trying.

What keeps you awake? Plot points.

Favourite part of the body? The rotator cuff – a tiny muscle in the shoulder that looks really boss when you are holding a plank.

ELLY GRIFFITHS

What kind of books do you write? Two crime series: the Ruth Galloway mysteries about a forensic archaeologist, and the Stephens and Mephisto books, set in the theatrical world of the 1950s.

Inspiration for 'Articulation'? A remark from an archaeologist: 'If you've got nettles in your garden, you've probably got a body there too.'

What is your superpower? The ability to diagnose illness in medical soap operas.

What is your guilty secret? Watching medical soap operas.

SARAH HILARY

What kind of books do you write? Police procedurals with a side order of psychological thriller.

Inspiration for 'Ten Things You'll Miss About Me'? I have always wanted to tell a crime story in reverse. It was the perfect story for this.

What keeps you awake? Titles, always titles. I have a mantra that is meant to summon the right story titles from my subconscious as I fall asleep. Sometimes it even works …

What is your superpower? I can sense the best coffee and gin bars in any city, no matter how well hidden they may be. With great power comes great imbibability.

AMANDA JENNINGS

What kind of books do you write? I write about ordinary people coping with trauma. There's always a dark vein running through my books. I'm drawn to exploring the darker side of human nature.

Inspiration for 'Etta and the Body'? The buzz that comes with a lot of retweets!

What keeps you awake? My husband. He suffers from insomnia and night terrors. I've lost count of the times I've been woken by an urgent instruction to 'grab the children and RUN!'

Favourite part of the body? There's something magical about the smell and velveteen feel of a newborn head. Vulnerable yet encasing all that new potential.

ALISON JOSEPH

What kind of books do you write? I write the Sister Agnes series, about a contemporary detective nun. I'm also writing about Malone, a London-based Irishman. And I'm following in the footsteps of Agatha Christie.

Inspiration for 'Now, Where Was I?' I'm obsessed with what makes an ordinary person do something really unordinary. We could all find ourselves there.

What is your superpower? Guessing people's star signs, while claiming not to believe in it.

What is your guilty secret? Needing to know people's star signs.

EMMA KAVANAGH

What kind of books do you write? Psychological crime with a major focus on character.

Inspiration for 'Jumping At Shadows'? Getting a CCTV camera and instantly beginning to imagine what I might see on it.

What is your superpower? I am really good at reading the emotions of others. I was always called 'sensitive' as a child, as I was very reactive to the behaviour of others. I hated that term! But I have come to see such extreme empathy as a gift that too few people are given.

Favourite part of the body? The brain. Everything we do and all that we are stems from its operations, and there are few things that can fascinate me as much.

ERIN KELLY

What kind of books do you write? Psychological thrillers that verge on the Gothic. I'm interested in the way none of us can escape our pasts.

Inspiration for 'Smoking Kills'? Married friends of mine are trying really hard to give up smoking, but they keep 'cheating' on each other and blaming each other for their own relapses. I took that little domestic conflict a few steps further.

What keeps you awake? Paranoia, existential angst, Brexit, the usual.

What is your superpower? Facial recognition of minor character actors. If you were, for example, a guest star in *Casualty* in 1987, I will remember you forever.

COLETTE MCBETH

What kind of books do you write? Psychological thrillers, I suppose, but I think that's quite a wide church.

Inspiration for 'Happy Anniversary'? I was interested in how looks deceive and how we might fall for someone because of their body rather than see the person underneath.

What keeps you awake? Insomnia and thinking too much. My husband falls asleep the moment his head hits the pillow and I find this incredibly annoying because often I can be awake for hours. That said, I have some great ideas at night and can often be found scribbling in the dark.

Favourite body part? Arms.

MEL MCGRATH

What kind of books do you write? Books with strong stories, in several genres. Story is the thing for me.

Inspiration for 'Eye on the Prize'? I've always been fascinated by the idea of eyes as the windows to the soul. I'm also squeamish about them, and the tension between intrigue and repulsion really spoke to me. I once went to a party at a house overlooking the Thames. It was owned by surgeons who collected antique surgical equipment. There was something captivating but creepy about the place. Eyes, windows and souls. What are we seeing when we look into someone else's eyes?

What keeps you up at night? I'm an insomniac, so pretty much everything.

What is your superpower? Not sleeping.

KATE MEDINA

What kind of books do you write? Thrillers and crime novels with a strong psychological element.

Inspiration for 'Baby Killer'? The narrator is a young girl trapped in a dysfunctional family. As a psychologist and mother of young children, the fear and helplessness experienced by a child in that position was, for me, a very powerful emotion to explore.

What keeps you awake? I have only ever spent one night alone in my house. I didn't sleep, as my imagination went wild at every creak. Now, whenever my husband goes away, I ask a friend to stay.

D.E. MEREDITH

What kind of books do you write? Historical forensic crime series set in the 1850–60s, and now a contemporary crime series set in a mythical city.

Inspiration for 'The Return'? My return visit to Rwanda twenty years after the genocide.

What is your superpower? Time travel.

What is your favourite part of the body? The brain – I got to semi-dissect one once.

LOUISE MILLAR

What kind of books do you write? Psychological thrillers.

Inspiration for 'Tick List'? Overhearing a woman judging physical features of men on a dating website, in minute detail, which made me wonder about all the nice men she was never going to meet.

What keeps you awake? A cat who announces his latest frog/vole catch in the tone of someone being strangled.

What is your superpower? Spotting fibs. Unfortunately for my teenagers.

KATE RHODES

What kind of books do you write? Contemporary detective fiction. My Hell Bay series features DI Ben Kitto and is set in the Isles of Scilly.

Inspiration for 'Fertile Ground'? Hearing about the death of Ian Brady. It made me wonder how mental health professionals dealt with such a monstrous and unrepentant killer, without becoming traumatized.

What keeps you up at night? Everything: the wind, loud noises, vivid dreams. I'm the world's worst sleeper.

Favourite part of the body? My brain. Without its quirks and eccentricities, I could never spin another story.

HELEN SMITH

What kind of books do you write? Mysteries and thrillers.

Inspiration for 'Nana'? I sometimes wonder if we're living in a dystopian nightmare.

What keeps you awake? Wild parties.

What is your superpower? I can change the way you feel. If you're feeling sad, I can make you happy. And if you're feeling happy …

LOUISE VOSS

What kind of books do you write? I write 'domestic noir' as a solo author and a police procedural series (DI Lennon) with Mark Edwards, with whom I've co-written six thrillers. I also have four contemporary women's fiction titles available on Amazon.

Inspiration for 'How Was That Fair'? It came out of a discussion with an author friend who once worked as the guy who emptied the sanitary bins in ladies' loos. What a job.

What keeps you awake? Pretty much everything, at the moment. It's me 'ormones.

What is your superpower? Um … I can write backwards and stand on my head, although not at the same time. And neither attribute will help me save the world.

LAURA WILSON

What kind of books do you write? Psychological stand-alones, mainly contemporary, and a series featuring DI Ted Stratton, set in the 1940s and '50s.

Inspiration for 'Sex Crime'? One came from a chance remark, the other from listening to a hammer-and-tongs argument about objective reality. I was trying to imagine circumstances in which knowledge that objective reality does (or doesn't) exist would be vitally important when I remembered the remark and realised that combining these two things could result in a story about a *really* disturbing way of messing with someone's head.

What is your superpower? I can twitch my nose like Elizabeth Montgomery in *Bewitched*, but I've never managed to cast a spell.

What is your guilty secret? If I told you, I'd have to kill you.

SUSAN OPIE

Susan has been an editor for many years, including a long period at HarperCollins and at Macmillan. She has worked with crime authors such as Lynda La Plante and Peter James.

If you've enjoyed this collection and would like to be kept in touch with future Killer Women events and publications, please sign up for our newsletter here:

http://www.killerwomen.org

Made in the USA
San Bernardino, CA
01 July 2019